In the Orchard

In the Orchard

ELIZA MINOT

ALFRED A. KNOPF

NEW YORK

2023

THIS IS A BORZOI BOOK PUBLISHED BY ALFRED A. KNOPF

www.aaknopf.com

Knopf, Borzoi Books, and the colophon are registered trademarks
of Penguin Random House LLC.

LIBRARY OF CONGRESS CATALOGING-IN-PUBLICATION DATA
Names: Minot, Eliza, author.
Title: In the orchard / Eliza Minot.
Description: First edition. | New York : Alfred A. Knopf, 2023. |
"This is a Borzoi book"—Title page verso.
Identifiers: LCCN 2022005158 (print) | LCCN 2022005159 (ebook) |
ISBN 9780307593474 (hardcover) | ISBN 9780593535929 (ebook)
Subjects: LCGFT: Novels.
Classification: LCC PS3563.I4745 I52 2023 (print) |
LCC PS3563.I4745 (ebook) | DDC 813/.54—dc23/eng/20220207
LC record available at https://lccn.loc.gov/2022005158
LC ebook record available at https://lccn.loc.gov/2022005159

Jacket images: bluecinema/E+; birdigol/iStock;
Mint Images; all Getty Images
Jacket design by Jenny Carrow

Manufactured in the United States of America
1st Printing
First Edition

For my family,

Eric, Roan, Lila, Tess, and Finn,

and to all the mother creatures

paying special close attention

to the minutes as they pass

What is life?
It is the flash of the firefly in the night.
It is the breath of a buffalo in the wintertime.
It is the little shadow which runs across the grass and
    loses itself in the sunset.

—CROWFOOT'S LAST WORDS

In the Orchard

1

A fluffed-up, blown-out wave of positive feeling is welling up inside of the young mother Maisie Moore, ballooning, perhaps too quickly for comfort, but expanding in a good and promising feeling nonetheless. She is teetering with hopefulness. She is tensely optimistic. It is glee. It is thrilling. She lets out a wiggled scream in a spasm of relief.

Oh, what luxury! What absolute bliss and heavenly release to live freely and without a mortgage! No credit card debt! No student loans or used-up equity lines! No faceless, hulking banks lurking around every turn of thought, methodically withdrawing from her accounts so stealthily, so regularly! Was it really possible? Was it really happening? No more uneasy insomniac nights when her nervous stomach felt as though her guts had been scrambled frothy like eggs! No more wondering if she was possibly causing a disease in herself, always returning, in lulled moments, to the same raw cavernous worry corner of her mind, of her abdomen! Alas, who in the world ever wants to talk about money unless there is plenty of money to talk about in the first place?

Oh, debt was so unsexy! Debt was such a *drag*!

A banker man with a fresh crew cut sits before Maisie and her husband, Neil. The banker is like a mortgage broker in a 1950s Hollywood movie, as clean and as smiling as a toothpaste ad. The walls of his office are white. His desk is entirely orderly. He brandishes a silver pen that twinkles in the sunlight. He smiles at Maisie and Neil, then neatly gathers the crisp papers that they've just signed and consolidates them into a compact white pile that resembles a gift box that might contain a folded men's dress shirt. The man nods to them reassuringly. He gestures with his arm as though he's waving a magic wand, motioning that they are free to go. Their debt—credit cards, student loans, mortgage, overdrafts, home equity lines—is as vanished as though it never was. Overbearing and invincible yesterday, it is miraculously invisible today!

Outside, Maisie and Neil stand holding hands on the sidewalk under a blue sky. Small green-and-white-striped awnings gleam over the windows of the tidy house across the street. The green grass is mowed in a plaid diamond pattern. The trees are healthy, tall, and idyllic, and their leaves flip flap playfully in the wind. The air is soft—neither hot, nor cold. The space is tranquil and vacant. A woman wearing a yellow poodle skirt is walking a standard white poodle down the sidewalk.

"*Wait* a second," Maisie says to herself.

The woman with the poodle clicks smartly toward them. Maisie senses her own extraordinary focus on the *poodle;* everything else has fallen away except for this white dog with its perverse pink bow in its cloud of silvery hair. It is close enough that Maisie pats it. Goopy discharge from the dog's wet raisin eyes is purpling its face. As it pants, Maisie can see that its pale upper gums are speckled with brown spots, like a ripe banana.

It clamps onto her calf. Quickly, it tugs and snarls. A portion of Maisie's calf pulls away and scatters as though it's made of stuffing that pulls apart like cotton candy.

"What the . . . ," Maisie says, puzzled, detached, imagining it's all some joke since she's not as frightened as she should be.

"Whoa whoa whoa . . . ," she says in the same tone she uses to calm her kids when one of their arguments turns shrill. The stuffing from her leg is strewn all over the sidewalk. *Here's some,* she says to herself, carefully gathering it. It is light pink and fluffy like insulation. *Here's some more. . . .*

She looks around for Neil. She is in a different place entirely. The bank is no longer there. There is a barn with stables? Mammalian nostrils appear at the stables' edges, sniffing through cracks. Are they horses? Maybe pigs?

The dog is back, tugging at her shirt, growling a little more wildly when, with the adrenaline-fueled style of a penalty kick from the soccer days of her girlhood, Maisie hops forward on her left foot, winds up with her right, and boots the dog into a large and elegant arc that sends it sailing skyward. The poodle's whinnies swirl away as it soars, a kaleidoscope of snarls and whimpers in Maisie's ears that mewl into the guttural cat cries of her newborn in the flouncy bassinet next to her bed.

Maisie rises robotically in the dark of her bedroom to lift the baby. Buzzing cries and silent screams vibrate the small body as though it is motorized. Even in the dark, Maisie can sense and feel with her hands that the receiving blanket's swaddle has come undone. Baby Esme's scrawny, primate arms flail about in spasmic jerks. One of her tiny hands abruptly knots onto Maisie's hair and yanks it.

"Oh my goodness," Maisie finds herself saying gently, patting her baby's back.

"Goodness me," she says softly at the ruckus.

"Goodness gracious," she says, all words that Maisie probably never uttered until she had her first baby, Xavier, nearly nine years ago. Other such words included *potty*, *sippy*, *playdate*, *binky*, *cross* (as in angry), *Pull-Up* (as in diaper), and, altogether: *Use your words*.

Maisie sniffs Esme's tiny rear end to check her diaper—it is still weightless and clean!—then tightly reswaddles her charge with the efficiency of an experienced mother, unfazed by the escalating screams. She tucks the swaddled football of baby into the crook of her neck, like an old-fashioned phone receiver, as she sits back down in bed and arranges, with her free hands, the pillows in their usual configuration for plugging the infant onto her nipple. When all is tucked and flattened, smoothed and forcefully secure, she places the screamer on her shoulder to gently calm her so that she doesn't nurse while hysterical and swallow air to make gas bubbles and misery.

"Shhh," says Maisie, patting the diminutive taut torso in rhythmic thumps, "shhh shhh shhh." Gradually, Esme's tight muscled body grows more lumpish and relaxed, and Maisie can feel, in miniature, on her shoulder, against her ear, against her collarbone, a new life go from high alert to quiet exhale.

Maisie's own body feels like it's exhaling as she, with her own cheek, smooths the cashmere-soft newborn hair that smells like beach stones that have baked in the sun. The heavenly weight of the baby, the living warm loaf of her with her green hay-bale smell, is almost too much for Maisie to bear. She breathes in a deep gulp of baby-green straw, sunlight, the faint sweetness and prick of lilies of the valley, of cucumbers. She inhales it all in a gulp of air as though she's about to go underwater. She restrains herself from snorting in hungrily the sweetness of her infant's not-yet-there neck, like a pig looking for truffles in damp brown leaves.

Esme's warm skull is as delicate as an ostrich egg, as perfectly and magnificently shaped. With her ear cupped up against Esme's shoulder, Esme's neck, Maisie can hear her baby's breathing magnified, like breath close to a microphone. The same breathing machination—so small now!—that will carry Esme through her entire life! *This tiny body,* thinks Maisie. As she listens, Maisie imagines that her baby's insides resemble the inside of the bedroom that they're in: contained and calm, dark blue because of the night, with indistinguishable corners but somehow spacious. The room, and maybe the space inside Esme, possesses the diorama stillness of a woodland night scene, or maybe a meadow with winking fireflies. Maisie considers for a moment what doctors must imagine when they listen to breathing and heartbeats through a stethoscope. Wild sounds? Textbook murmurs? Do they see the guts all crammed in there, dark and oily, winding around like a tangle of snakes? Or do they imagine it like a poem, vital and strange?

At the doctor, when she heard the baby's heartbeat for the first time, it galloped like a quiet siren: *Wow Wow Wow Wow Wow.*

→>−‹‹

These bodies, thinks Maisie, these *lives.* Her life, her husband's life, and the making of these other lives that have cropped up behind them like stepping-stones on a path that have somehow transformed from flat things into plants that keep growing, vessels of pure amplitude, trumpet flowers, these other lives sleeping on in the house, in this home that Maisie and Neil have somehow (well, with much effort, every single day) managed to create. There are three other children out there beyond the bedroom door: three-year-old Romeo, most likely sleeping in child's pose in his twin bed, the orb of him resembling a watermelon, rounded and slightly oblong with his butt up in the air, face squashed to the side, under his fleece blanket in the dark; eight-year-old Xavier sleeping up on his top bunk, his well-chosen posters looking down on him from the ceiling; six-year-old Harriet, bottom bunk, probably sleeping with one leg flung out over the covers, her arms over her head like a vanquished ballerina, her Hello Kitty night-light partly obstructed by her bedside table, her collection of stuffed animals sleeping in a crowd at the foot of her bed with their litters of "babies" (corks, barrettes, bottle caps, seashells, ribbons) nestled in the crescent of their forms.

In fact, *everything* in the house was having babies. Harriet was keeping track with her wildly scrawled drawings in her amassed notebooks. The sofa delivered the child-sized rocking chair. The TV gave birth to a slew of gray pebbles from the neighbor's gravel driveway. The front door made way for a new-born "room" that Maisie couldn't see, but she nodded quietly at Harriet's declaration, at the way she put her small arms out toward the floor to identify it. The water in the bathtub bubbled up washcloth after washcloth, another bar of soap. A rock and an acorn cap welcomed a crab apple. The salt and pepper shakers turned out the coarse brown sugar held in a mussel shell. Xavier's laugh and Romeo's sniffling his nose, according to Harriet, together made the sound of a bike ticking by.

→≻◄←

The hullabaloo of infant cries is soon replaced by a frenzy of suction sounds, murmurs and grunts, when baby Esme starts nursing. Maisie doesn't remember her other babies making such a racket when they nursed. In fact, she can remember the others allowing the milk to spray past them when they couldn't swallow it quickly enough, unclasping from her nipple, their brand-new lips glazed in milkwash, turning their small heads reasonably aside until the overwhelming spray subsided. Small plumes of breast milk would mist their tiny cheeks and leave miniature white caviar pearls along their hairlines and their barely-there eyebrows. They'd squint, their head still but slightly removed, through the misting milk with the expression of a patient person getting sprayed by a sprinkler while adjusting its setting. This baby, thinks Maisie, can keep up with the supply that she demands.

Maisie glances around the room. Everything is a shade of indigo, violet, or black as though it's been dipped in dye, a deep end drained of water and light. For a moment she is underwater but breathing, and her baby, her children in the other rooms, are moon jellies, drifting luminescent, moonlit and translucent, *pulse pulse pulse* as they climb toward the water's surface through the silent underwater. . . .

Maisie's husband, Neil, makes a quick snore in his sleep, so she looks at him. She can barely make out the blot outline of Neil's face, though she can sense that he's facing her. Does he know, after all these babies, that nursing, when the baby's new, hurts her? Not just pricks and irritation or the blistery raw nipples, but rather a full-bodied sting as if two or three wires are needling through her breast, then reaching down into her abdomen, where they pull tight to bite her womb back to shape. She nudges Neil slightly with her knee. He stirs and looks up at them in the dark. She can't make out his face, but she imagines he's raising an eyebrow at Esme's noisy smacking. Instead, he rises a little higher, cobra pose, and blurts out at her, full voiced, like a horn in the fog, "Diana! Why aren't more people interested in this position?"

Esme stops suckling for a second, pops off the nipple as if to listen, blinks her tiny eye, and looks sidelong into the dark—*Who was that?*—then resumes.

Maisie would have dubious thoughts if she didn't know that Diana was an elderly lesbian, also Neil's boss, and that "this position" was far from untoward. It was a job at the company where Neil worked, an organization that recruited doctors to areas of the world where they were sorely needed.

Neil plunges back into his pillow and sighs sleepily. He takes a firm hold of Maisie's ankle, as if his hand is an anklet cuff, then lets go, a shiny touch like a tossed coin in deep water.

When she and Neil met for the first time, she was in college leaving the hockey rink and he was leaving the basketball court. It was misty out, spring, and their sweaty heads were both steaming. They emerged from the athletic complex simultaneously and started walking out of it together as though they had planned to meet each other. Maisie felt his attractiveness dive into her body, a zing throughout her that made her want to look at him but also look away.

They walked near each other, almost as though a giant child were playing with them like dolls and decided to walk them side by side. They smiled next to each other as they walked. The lilac bushes were huge on either side of them, half-covered in mist that disappeared into white gray fog. Maisie grabbed one and tore it off its bendy branch, then felt a little violent for doing so. She shoved it under her nose, its transporting scent and the cool mist trapped in each of its blossoms feeling like a kind of food nourishing her. She asked Neil where he was going, and he answered with a question, "Should I take a shower? Before I have to teach some second graders?"

"Yes," answered Maisie, imagining him in a shower.

When she asked about the teaching, he explained that it was for an early-childhood-education class, and three times a week he helped in a second grade at a nearby school. He had a puzzled look on his face, and Maisie thought he was about to start complaining about something—the second graders, the teacher—as people tend to do. Instead, he took the lilac from her hand as if he knew her already and said, "There are three kids who are *really* waiting for a cherry tomato to appear on the plants. I think today might be the day." His head was wet and sweaty, steamy in the drizzle. The dewy lilac in his hand near his head made her want to push it all over his face.

"A tiny baby tomato," he said. "Really exciting."

She imagined it: a little green pearl appearing in the folds of the stem, growing to a little red-green marble. She thought of her clitoris—and it trembled! He had no idea. The body! What a riot!

Later on in life, lilacs would smell like the way love feels sometimes, and, just like the cherry tree, which would grow larger than a normal cherry tree and bloom like crazy every spring in front of their house, would look like how love feels sometimes when its bloom-filled branches tossed in the wind; lilacs, too, would look like love.

⌁

Esme suckles. Maisie drops her head back onto the pillow and the back of her head clonks against the wall: *bonk*. She tries to shed her bedroom and everything in it, for a couple more hours at least, wanting very much to get back to sleep, please; she doesn't want to get *worn out*, and then sick, though she wants *very* much to avoid another anxiety dream about money. The brief thought of the poodle causes her to feel something light-hearted, followed by an attached dread, money—*money*. Debts, large and small, grow on their house like moles or tumors, like rot. Their mortgage is as big as the house itself; their equity line is used up. Whatever they'd dutifully started to save has been shaved into almost nothing with the market's plunge.

They had come to an end. Through the years of small babies, of pregnancies and Maisie not working, and Neil's switching jobs, and their living off the value of their house, of convenient and opportunistic refinancing to pay off those credit card debts or to buy that car they could all fit into, they entertained the assumption they'd be making more money *later on*. Of course! They were resourceful and clever people! Educated and capable people! Were they not? They were, but now they were at the end. Maxed out here, second mortgage there, the equity line shot up to its limit like a meat thermometer stabbed into a slab of well-done roast. How many credit cards could she rack up to the max? Even she, in all of her financial desperation and ineptitude, knew that two (or three) were far too many cards to max out. At least one ad that she'd see on TV made three seem like a cakewalk: "Do you have *six* or *seven* credit cards with balances that need squaring away? Shoring up? Credit consolidators! We're here for *you*!"

Shoring up, squaring away. The terms always puzzled her when that ad came on, conjuring images of cubed boxes and the Giant's Causeway in Ireland with its leprechaun mists and lyrical foam-trimmed waves spanning wide, wild beaches. The beach made her think of *spiriting away*. The term was more appropriate, was it not? *Do you have debt that needs* spiriting away? *Yes! Yes, I do!*

In the dark of one wakeful and restless night, head mashed into her pillow, hiding under her covers as numerals floated left and right in her head like primary-colored clouds, even Maisie knew that on that ad, that dopey ad that she liked to think made her feel better, that the credit cards that needed "squaring away" were probably maxed out at a pittance compared to the wall of money that Maisie would somehow, eventually (really? was she? were they?) going to have to pay off.

Numbers floated ominously through her head like ribbon banners behind propeller airplanes at the beach, crowding one another in the sky, large numbers, long numbers in black print that began to merge into one black ribboned thing, like a serpent's tongue, licking. Her stomach began to sour again, pricking up from the inside out. Maisie thought of Harriet once waking up from a dream.

"A really, really bad dream, Mama," Harriet had said. A polar bear was seated at the foot of her bed, wearing dark sunglasses, "with black *numbers*, Mommy, *numbers*," and at this Harriet's face issued an expression of complete and utter terror. "Numbers!" She grimaced. "All, all *over* it!"

The truth of the matter was that the Moore family couldn't keep on living the way they were living, overextended and beyond their means. They weren't doing anything fancy at all, *really*, but were simply figuring out ways to make ends meet, which meant using their credit cards for most everything, usually, and usually overdrawing their checking account. All across the country, savings had been wiped out, and the worth of homes had dwindled. If their house kept depreciating as it had since the whole decline began, what little value their house still held would no longer belong to them. They'd be in the red and then some. They were underwater already! Maisie heard this downer voice every day, every hour, nagging at her like a woman with terrible breath, a woman who doesn't feed herself enough, so her breath is sour. Maisie was used to her.

It was in the blank hours of the night, when the windows of Maisie's bedroom were squares of navy blue behind their wooden blinds, that she and Neil slept clutching each other as if expecting a grenade to explode nearby. It was when she woke on her side of the bed, her body long and flat as though hiding in deep grass, that she was occasionally terrified. She'd peer out of the covers, quickly adjust herself, looking for comfort, looking for . . . what? She'd see, in the early dawn, color beginning to seep into various objects in the room: the rug on the floor faintly turning green, the books in the bookshelf gaining outlines rather than hulking in a mass of darkness. She would lie still, very still, having dreamed of doors left ajar and doors with faulty locks, of living in places where the actual house was just fine but all the doors were problematic: broken, falling apart or too flimsy, unable to close properly, impossible to lock, while something was clearly *out there*, prowling, determined to get in.

There was a letter, unopened, its envelope slightly blue pink like the super white ice of a skating rink, from the mortgage company that was shoved into her underwear drawer amid her intimates and hair elastics and quick go-to standbys for the kids (Aquaphor, A&D ointment, miniature scissors, thermometer, loose Band-Aids, Vicks VapoRub). The letter proclaimed, she was quite sure, that they now owed more money than their house was worth. At least it wasn't a default letter. At least it wasn't foreclosure. But did it make sense to use credit cards for groceries, for gas, to reserve cash to pay the monthly mortgage? No, she knew. No, she knew it made no sense.

But wasn't the entire country dealing with the same problem? Wasn't *that* what was happening with the bailouts and bank foldings, the bank takeovers and mergers, the bankruptcies? Wasn't Maisie, like the rest of the country, for that matter, simply looking optimistically toward the future, when more money would somehow appear? Hadn't they all simply had faith that things would work out in their favor? Wasn't the country joining them, the Moore family, in their plight, or weren't the Moores just joining the plight that had been happening all around them, all along, and now was really starting to matter *across the board*? Maisie tried to find comfort in the fact that she and her family were not alone in their ineptitude. That, in fact, most of America seemed to have behaved likewise. In fact, many families were in the same boat. In fact, her household was simply a microcosm of the national situation, a global situation. Really, she would sometimes tell herself, weren't the Moores representative of the many? Needless to say, this idea was not comforting.

Maisie liked to tell herself how lucky she actually was. She was! She reminded herself repeatedly, almost as a mantra, that to have the chance to own a home in the first place, to have a healthy marriage and healthy kids—these were the important things! How lucky she was to live in a developed country with health care and schools! Overstuffed bounty seemed to thrust its full cleavage at her at every turn: the dizzyingly large new supermarket that specialized in the organic and gourmet foods, the confusingly huge assortment of channels that zipped by on the television set. Any small green lawn in her fairly modest neighborhood probably had more money put into it in the month of August than a family in some parts of the world ever saw in a lifetime.

Oh my, thinks Maisie.

Esme keeps at it, busily feeding, as if to say, *Money? What's money?*—as a flood of raptured relief comes over Maisie, the endorphins, the oxytocin, glazing over her like the baby's milk-glazed lips. It is as though the back of Maisie's skull has been lopped off by a pull of white light, as though she is feeding Esme star powder from her breast and the stars in the sky are inside of Esme's mouth, and throughout the feeding the small stars are like little button snaps, and her mind is snapping the stars together into a satisfying snap-up of the sky.

Women everywhere are possessed! It is one thing, she thinks, to feel your baby inside of you kicking your cervix: *Ping!* Or elbowing your bladder—*Zoop!*—as it moves. But to wake in the night with swelling breasts that feel as though they are packed with grainy glitter, filled with sparkling sore sand, and wonder, *Why is my milk dropping?* as they begin to leak, and then pressing those breasts tightly so that they won't spray all over the bed, and then, five seconds later, the baby starts to stir, routing its little mouth sideways like an old man mouthing an invisible cigar, looking for a light, looking for that full breast to suckle. Who was calling who? Was the baby reading her mind? Was the baby smelling her milk release? Or was she telepathically waking the baby like an automaton: *Time to eat, infant being. Time to eat.* There was nothing robotic about it. It was all fluids and warm mouths, tightening muscles and then softening skin, and bittersweet smells. The animal reflex of it all encouraged Maisie. Nature *knows.*

Nature knows more than I know, Maisie would think. *Or, my body knows more than I think that it knows. Deep down, the animal part of me knows.* What does it know? It knows how to listen to the thing it is caring for, to release, and to provide. It knows how to keep something alive through connection. It knows how to connect.

It was true that as she got older, and as she cycled through pregnancies and deliveries, her body felt more fine-tuned. The mechanisms inside of her had become more clear and more sensitive. There were the almost out-of-body maternal experiences of pregnancy and mothering with the milk-drops and the uterine contractions, the hormonal surges to fold, to organize, to stock up, to argue, and to weep. Once, when she was pregnant with Xavier, she came across three or four tiny mouse turds near the sink in their small apartment in the city. In ordinary life, she would have wiped up the area and called it a day. While she was pregnant, however, the level of disgust at the rice-sized turds made her feel like throwing up, as though they were twenty times their actual size; she ended up scouring the counter, cleaning every pot and pan in the cabinet next to the stove, reorganizing them neatly to fit one inside the other after bleaching multiple surfaces along with meticulously undoing, cleaning, and neatly putting the spartan flatware back in the utensil drawer. All of these uncontrollable impulses and reflexes, she wondered, how did they translate into mothering older children? Teenagers? Young adults? One of the wise, older preschool teachers, Ms. B, told Maisie that when her own daughter was a teenager and would try to sit on her lap, Ms. B would sometimes have a reactive impulse to practically shove her daughter off away from her. It was a new sort of impatience, unexpected, when the large baby-woman body would seek her out for baby comfort. She attributed it to instinct. "Mother Nature," laughed Ms. B, "tells us what to do!"

When she got her period for the first time, Maisie was completely astonished that her body worked. She was even more astonished that her body worked like all the other females in the world. She wondered where her own mother had been, how old her mother was when she had gotten her period for the first time, but there was no way to know because her mother was dead. The one thing Maisie did know, because her mother had died when Maisie was five years old, was that anything can happen, to anyone, at anytime, anywhere.

Maisie was also astonished that the discomfort, the cramping and irritation of character, the inconvenience of blood and bleeding, was shared with more than half the world, and there hadn't seemed to be much discussion about that. At the same time, in the warm pain of the cramps, there was something that wasn't painful at all but instead something that was like Time and Fate, kneading around in her lower abdomen, her lower back, pressing and pulling. She wondered about other women. At school, she wondered which teachers were having their period. At the grocery store, women she hadn't even paid any attention to had her wondering whether they used pads or tampons. Riding her bike home from school, trailing her older brother, Miles, on his blue bike, her semi-blooded maxi pad stuck to her striped underwear and getting crushed against her bike seat, she'd think of how Miles only had a bum hole and here she was with another opening that bleeds, with organs that flex and flush and receive implantation and react to the *moon phases—what?!*

She and her friend Gina had read about the moon-cycle stuff in a book of Gina's mother's about the female body. The moon was on a twenty-eight-day cycle, or roughly thereabouts, from one new moon to the next, waxing and waning and pulling the tides of the oceans to bulge to one side of the earth, then the other, all as the world turned, putting pressure on the brain, pressure on the ovaries. The female body was generally on a twenty-eight-day cycle as well—What were the odds?!—as though all females were moon witches, children of the moon, relatives of the moon, nocturnal creatures whose bodies morphed with phases of the moon and whose eyeballs and teeth shone moon-colored, moon-matching on blue nights, with full moons.

She and Gina had laughed at the moon stuff for reasons they couldn't identify, since they were twelve and thirteen years old, but it was because of their own astonishment, and their own delight, at the mystery of both their own bodies and their own universe, and the two aligning beyond their control, and maybe they laughed, too, because they were confused by such an alignment of something so large with something so small, but then again their own selves were in fact not so small after all, they felt in fact bigger than the actual universe because they *were* their own universes, and the ends of themselves seemed to never reach an end but stretched out and out and out to landscapes, terrain, space, skies, and horizons that were all never-ending. The largesse of their tiny private parts, the little bead of clitoris and its expanse of physical feeling and transport, all of this was puzzling and funny, which made them laugh, along with their pleasant astonishment, and along with their delight.

They also laughed at the plain old pencil drawing illustration of the vagina because it looked like—"she" looked like, they decided—a little hooded face, silly and cockamamie with one eye and her mouth open, oblong, in a wobbled song or a scream. Later on in her life, when Maisie first saw Edvard Munch's painting *The Scream*, she would think of the female genitalia illustration in Gina's mom's body book because the screamer's oblong mouth looked so similar, and the screamer's hands clasping the sides of the screamer's head looked like the parenthetical folds of the labia. Also, when Maisie read Sylvia Plath's poem "The Rival," the moon's "her O-mouth grieves at the world" also was an image that took on the illustration's oblong opening, in her mind. It was Georgia O'Keeffe's sumptuous paintings of irises and lilies that erased the oblong cartoony silliness and instead brought the succulence and bright strength of a flower to the shape between her legs, as something she could walk into. Later on, Louise Bourgeois's watercolor paintings—red babies upside down in utero, or nipples like little mountain crests waiting for a baby's mouth to suck onto them, or blue watercolor splotches inside of a belly's outline—were what seemed to capture what was going on, what seemed to be taking her over.

Maisie thinks of when she had first gotten her period, trailing her brother on his bike on their way home from school on that warm spring day, the dampness of the crushed, bloodied pad curling up in her underwear inside of her shorts. She rode single file behind him along the side of the road in their seaside town—careful to avoid puddles of sand that might cause her to wipe out, as had happened in the past, careful to remain on the inside of the white line on the busy road to avoid being honked at and startled—as they coasted past the street with the public access to the beach. Day-trippers from the city, all girls, were emerging from the beach in their brightly colored beachwear, their bodies spilling out of string bikinis and towel wraps the same way the group of them were spilling onto the street, the same way their hair was spilling around their shoulders, around their faces.

These young women day-trippers had Maisie wondering about new, period-related things. She used to wonder, Where are these young women from? From what outside world did they come? Are their mothers dead? Have they always lived in the city, or did they once live in a small town where they sunbathed in their own miniature backyards with the crabgrass prickly under their towel? But with her period now and with no older girls or women—no sisters, no mother, no aunts—to tell her that a tampon shouldn't plug her like a cork but should be unnoticeable in her female cavity, and with the wad of a maxi pad in her shorts as she pedaled past the throng of femaleness, Maisie instead wondered: Does a tampon string dangle out of bathing suit bottoms? Does the string stay in place if it is tucked in carefully? Pads are obviously bulky for skimpy beach attire. . . . And if a girl bleeds into the ocean while they swim, will a shark come? As far as she knew, no menstruating girl had ever attracted a shark, especially in New England, but how would she ever know such a thing? Who would have told her? She had her brother and her father. They wouldn't know. She had her friends. But they were about the same as her, pretty clueless. Gina's mom's book on the woman's body didn't get into the details of living daily life while menstruating. Nana would know, but a conversation about menstruating with her grandmother would maybe feel like they'd have to have bigger conversations about her mother, and her mother dying, and death.

It *was* her nana, though, who had put pads and tampons in the bathroom for Maisie, under the sink, "just in case." Alone, Maisie carefully inspected the stuff. She unwrapped a couple of pads of varying thickness and peeled off the adhesive to sample stick them to her pant leg, her sleeve. She undid two tampons. One had a pearlescent purple plastic applicator, like a long bullet, and smelled like cheap perfume. Another one had a cardboard tube. She pulled out the cotton wad by its string and dangled it, like a tea bag. Later on in her life, one of Maisie's small children would report nonchalantly, "Mom just pulled a dead mouse out of her butt!" at the passing sight of Maisie removing a tampon and wadding it up in toilet paper for the trash.

In the kitchen, her nana was over to make their dinner. Maisie said, "I got my period."

Nana stopped chopping and looked at her. She smiled at Maisie without opening her mouth. Her eyes softened and filled with tears, and Maisie knew it was because Maisie's mother was dead and here was a granddaughter who would never have a mother back, and here was also a mother—Nana—whose son would never again see his wife. But Maisie could feel something else, something new, of sadness, of heaviness, that came through her nana's arms when they came over and squeezed her.

"It's not easy being a girl," said Nana, and Maisie could hear in her grandmother's voice the menacing glances from men in cars as they passed her.

"It's okay," Maisie told her. "I'm excited to grow up," to which Nana sighed and squeezed her a little harder.

"Nature," Nana said into the top of Maisie's head. Maisie could feel Nana's lips, like a caterpillar, move across her scalp. "Nature will always send you messages."

→►◄←

In college all the girls on the hallway in her dorm got their periods at the same time because, underneath everything, unconsciously, they could smell one another's pheromones, the ovulating, the menstruating, and would sync their cycles together. What other things were happening inside of her, outside of her, that she couldn't ever see? There was so much mystery in every nook and cranny and curve of life. How would so much mystery ever be uncovered? Before she ever became pregnant, she had no idea how it might have felt to be pregnant and to bear a child. She was like a man in that way, in her imaginings, though the difference was that she could imagine it based on menstrual cramps, which, of course, a man doesn't experience. She had read that it was the same cramping in menstrual cramps that a woman felt when she was in labor, albeit far stronger, and larger, since the womb was not the size of a pear anymore but a basketball, a watermelon, a medicine ball, taking up the abdomen's entirety, and the thing that was coming out of it was not a minuscule unfertilized dot of an egg but rather a thickened body full of body matter and organs, the placenta like a giant serving platter matted alongside the hunched-up body, its heft of an entire lifetime within it. Once she was pregnant, she thought, *Could I have imagined this?* She couldn't remember what she could have imagined, and what she *did* imagine, other than the trace ideas about menstrual cramps. Once the real thing came, she couldn't remember what she'd thought it would be like, and then after the baby was out, things about the whole experience were hard to remember.

It was so strange, Maisie would think, how hard it was to remember sensations, like all the different categories of pain, and of emptiness, and of joy. It was so hard to remember how, while breastfeeding, alone with a baby, she might feel home-sick, suddenly, but for no home, like her body was opening, as though the baby was sucking her open, a deep dark hole. But there was also the feeling of caring for a newborn that was like being in a massive back garden that no one knows is there, secret and disorienting, like those bonus areas in dreams that are add-ons to familiar territory—*This apartment had a ball-room! Or Instead of our tiny backyard, we had a pool and a park out there!*

How could she remember these feelings? It was like trying to remember anything—does one do it as a picture? Or does it come in wafts, like a smell, that fill out the shapes of phantom feelings that wander in and out of the scaffolds of one's self? She remembered her mother's face from looking at pictures, but she couldn't remember it moving close to her, or herself moving close to it. She couldn't imagine smells of her mother, but smells of her mother would find her nose sometimes in daily life—honeysuckle, or a certain kind of lily inside of a cedar box—to tweeze out little slivers of the past that lived in her brain. All the things in life that were passing past her . . . how could she trap them, like wild stray kittens? And if she possibly could, what in the world would she do with them all?

When she and Neil had first gotten together, Neil had said to her, "You're so lucky that you get to be a mom one day if you want." Her brother, Miles, had said the same thing when they were little, tightening their skates.

It was so hard, thinks Maisie, to imagine what other people might imagine. It was hard enough to remember one's own thoughts and feelings.

Once, on the train back from the city, Maisie overheard two women seated in front of her slightly arguing. Romeo was asleep on her chest in the baby carrier. Over the top of the seat, Maisie could see the tops of their hair—like spun sugar, on one woman, bleached and fine and somewhat flyaway, and a tight high bun on the other that looked like a fist. The tops of their heads, their hair, bobbed about like puppets in front of Maisie, animated and jittering with their conversation as though it was the hair fluff and bun that were talking to each other in a puppet show of hair.

"You're telling me—I *think* what you're saying is"—the blond hair quivered subtly, but dramatically—"that it's impossible for me to imagine what being a mother is like? Because I have no children?"

The other voice, the tight bun on the right, was firm and completely still. It said patiently, after a pause, "Imagining something isn't the same as experiencing it."

The blond hair quivered. A hand quickly swept over it. "You think that I can't *imagine* something just because I haven't experienced it?"

The firm bun, looking glossy and confident, like the proud nose of a horse, spoke gently. "I *am* a mother," it said, "and Jackson's five years old, and I *still* can't understand what happened or what's happening. I'd say it's surreal, but, as we can see by all the people in the world, it's certainly very ordinary."

The blond fuzz and the shiny bun looked at each other, thinking.

"Just because I've never had a baby . . . ," said the blond fuzz.

Maisie could see that a woman across the aisle from them, her seat facing in Maisie's direction, was listening as well. She was older than Maisie and had been reading an article in a magazine. She had since stopped reading. She looked like Oprah. She looked at Maisie over her reading glasses, raised her eyebrows, and then winked at her.

The woman's wink startled the milk in Maisie's breasts, and then her milk, stirred, seemed to wake Romeo up telepathically as he began to squirm and make squeaky noises like a puppy. Maisie pressed the insides of her wrists against her nipples as her milk began to crinkle them up, as it surged forward, a sensation and action she never before could have imagined.

She couldn't have possibly imagined any of it . . . each of her children, the way they behaved, the things that they'd see and do. A month earlier Maisie had brought Xavier and Harriet to one of Romeo's newborn checkups. It was with a new doctor because their pediatrician was on vacation. Xavier's and Harriet's whining stopped abruptly when the doctor entered the room.

"I'm Dr. Noyes," she said. "This must be Romeo." The doctor's face softened as she looked at Romeo's face. "A very cute baby." She smiled. She looked at Xavier and Harriet, standing close by at the examining table and raised her eyebrows at them. "You have a cute little brother."

Xavier's chin barely reached the examining table. Harriet, holding Doll in a swaddle, stood next to him on a rubbery stepstool. The two of them were serious, their faces discerning and suspicious as they watched Dr. Noyes gently unwrap Romeo's swaddle. As she put the stethoscope in her ears, the doctor nodded her head toward Harriet and winked at her.

"I can look at your baby, too, if you like."

Harriet frowned at her and clutched Doll more tightly.

Dr. Noyes slid the silver disc of the stethoscope onto Romeo's chest. He squirmed and sputtered for a moment. Harriet frowned impatiently.

Xavier said, "He—he doesn't like that."

"The metal is too cold," the doctor said gently. She rubbed it back and forth on her lapel, like shining an apple, to warm it up. She was impressive. Her face was bright, her presence commanding. She had a beauty mark like a lentil on her cheekbone.

Xavier and Harriet continued to watch her quietly with the same silenced aspect that they might have looking at a large beautiful bug.

When they returned home from the doctor, Romeo was asleep in his carrier and Maisie went to the kitchen to get some food. When she brought a snack out to Xavier and Harriet, they were milling around near the toy basket, seemingly playing doctor. Harriet had a large black dot, larger than a lentil, on her cheek.

"Like the doctor's," said Xavier, the marker still in his hand. "See, Mom?"

—>—<—

Maisie was five. She and her older brother, Miles, were sitting on the wobbly bench near the front door, a place where they never sat down except for when they were dealing with the on and off of boots and shoes. Dr. McDonald squatted down to their eye level. "Your mother is dying," he said.

"We know," said Miles.

"Well," said Dr. McDonald, "she is going to die soon."

They were quiet. Maisie's father cracked the front door open to let the dog, Major, out. In the cracking of the door, a waft of spring air was let in. The birds chirped; a car revved past.

Maisie's dad sat down on the bench, too. He picked up Maisie and put her on his lap.

"Think about if you have any questions," Dr. McDonald said to them. "Ask me or your dad any time."

"I have a question," said Miles.

"Yes?"

"Is she in pain?"

Maisie doesn't remember Dr. McDonald's answer, but she does remember that she didn't understand the question: What did Miles mean by *pain*? Maisie could think of the pain of stubbing her toe, or skinning her knee, but her mother was just lying there in her bed, sometimes sitting up, no cuts or bruises, only looking pale and smaller but otherwise looking the same.

When her mother was in bed, never even looking very sick, Maisie would spend a lot of time playing next to her on her bed. The quilt had different squares, and sometimes Maisie would spread out on her father's side of the bed and treat the quilt squares like rooms in a dollhouse. Maisie had little shiny plastic people and plastic dollhouse furniture that were mostly in pastels—light pink, light blue, and light yellow—that she could assemble throughout the quilt squares. There was a pink baby fused into a pink high chair. There was no possibility of removing the baby. The baby's head had broken off—perhaps because Maisie had tried too forcefully to remove it from its immovable position, or perhaps because the dog had taken a crack at her—so that its small neck looked like a dangerously jagged crown, which made Maisie think of the neck of Christmas ornaments when they break, and Maisie was able to look inside the tiny plastic baby to see something that resembled the inside of a cleaned-out nose.

Sometimes Maisie would give each of her stuffed animals their own square on the quilt. Sometimes, the light blue square would be the kitchen and her stuffed seal, Andre, would make breakfast in it, while Footsie the rabbit waited in the living room. Usually, what she liked best to do, after all the little animals had eaten and washed, was to tuck them in along the fold next to her mother, who was usually sitting up but sometimes was sleeping. Maisie had the seal, the wood duck, the plush stingray, the miniature but alpaca-soft bear, the velveteen red lobster, and whoever else was around, all in on the action, but most important there was beloved Ella, her rag doll, whose black yarn hair had all fallen out but whose orange cotton dress brought a shot of joy to Maisie's chest whenever she caught sight of it. Ella would get tucked into the most coveted spot on the bed, snuggled next to Maisie's mom, sometimes using part of her mother's body—her arm or the back of her neck if she was sleeping—as a pillow.

Their old dog, Major, a real dog, who was black, brown, and white, hardly ever moved from her mother's legs. Major would watch Maisie closely with both suspicion and care, particularly when Maisie got too close or rambunctious near her mother. Sometimes, playfully channeling his inner puppy, Major would get involved. Maisie can remember looking around for Andre, wondering where he could have gone, only to find Major watching her as he usually did, a couple of feet away, lying dutifully alongside her mother's legs, but with plush gray Andre the seal tucked under his chin like a chin rest.

Other times, Maisie can remember Major's expression as one of kind sternness, as though he were an older gentleman with reading glasses on who had seen a great deal in his life. Lying close to her mother, he would look sidelong at Maisie as though to say, *You must try to understand that she is leaving us.*

Then, the day came that her mother did leave them. It was maybe sooner than they had thought, or maybe just to Maisie's five-year-old self it was sooner. It was a morning, a plain old morning in the ordinary world where it wasn't raining, and it wasn't sunny; it wasn't hot, and it wasn't cold; it was late spring but not yet summer. A plain, nondescript day seemed to be the only sort of backdrop that her mother's dying could withstand, as if the natural world had retreated in order to let the event take place. The story went that her mother had said, simply, "I'm going to close my eyes now, guys," and then she closed her eyes. A couple of hours later, she was as still as glass, her head sunken just so on the white pillow as though she were a princess and someone had gently placed her there, her smooth cheeks as cool as an autumn apple plucked from a tree, her cheeks as cool as a young mother's who has just come in from outside.

Maisie had thought that when her mother died her mother would look shriveled up and ancient, like a shrunken monkey's hand that she saw on TV once. Instead, there was her lovely mom, her smooth skin and her kind, full mouth, all intact like it had always been except the things that made her talk and move, and the things that made her lips the reddish color of an earthworm, had all been turned off. Forever. Where did it go? Where did *she* go?

"That's it?" Maisie supposedly asked, immediately after her mom died. It wasn't as though she was unimpressed, but Maisie does remember feeling relieved that her mother wasn't so different dead than she was when she was alive, except that she was *dead*. She hadn't melted like the Wicked Witch, or morphed into a weird different creature, or shrunken into a withered and wrinkled skeletal woman.

There was a bright red cardinal that bonked into the window, sounding like a padded knuckle. When they went outside, it was tipped on its side. Miles picked it up off the ground and held it in his palm, upright. Maisie can still remember the orange-red lusciousness of the miniature fuzzy feathers around its head. Major was interested in it, too, wagging and sniffing, and when Miles placed the bird on its own twiggy feet on the ground, it stood there for a few moments, stunned, long enough that it looked like it was maybe not going to go anywhere, like maybe it was going to die, too. Instead, it looked at each of them, back and forth, even at Major, and then flew away, first to the pretty fir tree where it looked like a Christmas ornament, and then to the birches, those spectral trees that had always frightened Maisie with their white, ghostly limbs and slender trunks that had dizzying numbers of eyes that stared out from their bark. What soul lives inside those trees, she would think, and which eye, of all those nightmarish eyes, is the one that's really watching? Horizontally, the eye shapes looked like eyes. But some of them were vertical and looked instead like female genitalia.

Did the cardinal happen? She is not certain. Maybe it was a scarlet tanager, bright red with black wings, and smaller like a toy. Was there sunlight coming through the window onto her mother's bed, just like on other days, and was there a pale yellow pillowcase that carried on in its own daily duty of pillowcasing pillows for years to come until it wore through and ripped, and went to the rag bin?

Did her father rock back and forth, hugging himself, and did the hugging-himself habit become general for him in the years that followed? Yes. He would hug himself a lot in the years that followed. He would also hug the steering wheel as he drove.

Was it true that her mother, one winter afternoon in the living room as a low sunset simmered orange on both her mother's face and the white wall behind her mother's head, said to Maisie, "The luckiest thing in my life is being your mom. You'll see." Maisie returned to the image of her mother's sunset-lit face, the sunset on the wall behind her, and usually saw the whole thing in every sunset, anywhere, thereafter, always. It was one of the only memories where her mother's actual face came into focus. Whether it happened or not, the moment happened over and over, every time she thought of it, and it gave her a tiny bit of comfort each time she visited it.

→>-<←

Maisie had been kind of at loose ends a few days before she delivered Esme. Largely pregnant, feeling impatient and weepy, hormonal and impractical, she stood like a swollen tick on the sidelines of Harriet's soccer practice watching the kids run around.

Her friend Carol tried to convince her to go home. "Let Harriet come home with me to play with Maddie," Carol told her. "You go home and nest or whatever it is you need to do."

"I'm all nested out," said Maisie flatly.

"Then go home and take a nap," said Carol.

"I can't sleep," Maisie sighed, feeling puffy, feeling large.

"Oh, Maisie." Carol smiled, touching her back. "Maisie, Maisie, Maisie."

Only recently did Maisie realize that most people didn't regularly hear their name repeated in triplet. *Maisie Maisie Maisie.* She'd been hearing it all her life.

Carol looked out over the soccer field. "Did you see that picture," she asked, "of the uncontacted tribe in the Amazon?"

"No."

"They apparently haven't had contact with, like, the world. An anthropologist took pictures of them from a plane."

Maisie was transported. When she was little, she always thought she'd be a traveler. So far, she'd left the country only once, for her honeymoon to Cancún. She didn't ever want to, like, walk out on her family, of course, but always, underneath everything, she had the mild and consistent urge to flee. But to where? Sometimes the hills, literally, to forested land and open space, somewhere cheap, with a beach.

"Can you see them in the photos?" asked Maisie.

"They're right there looking up at the plane, pointing arrows at it." Carol plucked an invisible arrow that went sailing toward the miniature soccer players. "They're in full body paint."

Maisie watched Harriet kick the soccer ball. Her daughter's little body could run so efficiently and nimbly! For a moment she imagined walking through dense jungle, bending tall stalks to step on them to flatten them as she moved. "How many are there?" Maisie asked Carol.

"In the picture? Like, three. Maybe five. Kick the *ball*, Maddie!"

Maisie looked around the quaint town green. She wondered what the playground, with its netting of climbing walls and mounds of black wood chips, or the towering town hall with its pricking white steeple, would look like to someone who had never been here before. The October trees were psychedelic. The bright red leaves on the maple trees were the vivid rich color of tomato soup. Other trees were chartreuse green, tangerine orange, and saffron gold.

Carol yelled to her daughter, sounding exasperated. "Oh, *now* what happened?" Maddie was walking sulkily away from the players.

"Were they all men?" asked Maisie.

"I think so." Carol cupped her hands around her mouth to form a megaphone. "Go get the ball, Maddie! Don't look at *me*!"

The kids were all running around in a collected group with green or red pinnies on their heads like wigs. One little boy had his pinny draped around his neck in a long cape. A choking hazard, thought Maisie, wondering when one of the trainers would notice.

"They looked brave," said Carol. She paused, staring straight over the field like a seafarer's wife on a widow's walk, looking out to sea, "but they also looked pretty much scared shitless."

"Maisie!" Her friend Fran called to her. "Your bag!"

Maisie turned around. A large squirrel had its entire upper body hidden in the canvas bag that she had brought along.

"Hey!" cried Maisie, stomping her foot toward it. The squirrel took its head out of the bag and stared at her defiantly, flicked its plumed tail, then scampered away.

"The squirrels are bonkers this year," said Carol. "They ate our pumpkins in, like, a day."

"Neil said they're preparing for a rough winter," said Maisie.

"Well," said Carol, "at least someone's prepared." She sighed. "*I'm* certainly not."

Maisie rubbed her lower back and surveyed the field. The sound of whistles fell in pockets here and there. Cool sunlight flickered through the green grass like a hand ruffling a crew cut. Autumn was in full swing. The sun hung precipitously low in a glower, like a submarine scope, a monocle, watching, saying, *I may be low, but I'm watching you.*

Maisie looked up and down the sidelines. There were a few babysitters, a couple of dads, but mostly it was moms, all of whom had managed to get up, *again,* like every day, and whether they liked it or not, dress not only themselves but also whatever small human beings they were in charge of, finding the socks, finding the shoes, getting lunch packed for whatever older kids were heading off to school, some picky eaters with their lunches of rolled-up pieces of cheese and de-shelled pistachios, some not so picky, happy with pre-bought snack bags. Some of the mothers, surely, were up throughout the night, tending to an infant, nursing, feeding, changing, responding to every single thing. Others were up throughout the night arguing with their partners in the confines of their bedroom, exchanging nasty repartees or out-and-out name-calling over money, or their household's division of labor, or arguing about sex, jealousies, or extended-family dynamics. Still others were more than likely sitting up in the bathroom with a toddler or tween who was vomiting into the bathtub or coughing a croupy cough while the shower fogged up the room. Or they were sleeping in a kid's bed because the kid woke from a bad dream. Others surely slept solidly, after making love, holding each other. Most of these men and women had even worked already today, sitting down at their laptops or shouting orders into telephones before the sun was up. Many of them were gone into their workday, near or far, but not here. Yet some of them had made it—was it such a priority?—to this little kid soccer practice at this classic American park, even though the kids themselves might have been dragged along. They had all made it here, this practice, and were each looking out over the autumnal, suburban scene with their various thoughts in their heads. Maisie thought of all of them, looking here and there. Her mind wandered, slack with pregnancy, thinking of the lives of these parental figures, standing sentry like cut boxwoods, watching over their charges. Where had they all lived, up to this very moment? Where were they at twenty-five years old, when it was mid-autumn? At fifteen? Ten? Who were their parents? Was this better than before? Was it worse? Were they parenting as their parents had or were they avoiding the way their parents had parented? Who were all these people she knew and yet did not know?

She looked at her friend Carol. She knew Carol quite well, yet she barely knew where Carol had grown up. Near the city?

She thought of the hordes of men and women on the train every morning. It never ceased to amaze her that everyone, everyone she saw up and about in daylight, walking in the world of the upright as they managed to get on with their lives, whether they were in the mood or not, like soldiers dutifully following orders, were fulfilling what they expected of themselves to fulfill. It exhausted her, all this effort. Yet the poignancy of the effort itself, the purposeful and personal grace of it all, usually made her glad to be a human being. Just as, when she'd lived in the city, she was amazed at everyone's patience and self-control on the subway, particularly when it was markedly tight quarters, and hot, or smelly, and overwhelmingly irritating and uncomfortable. Only rarely did someone lose their mind and start yelling or acting rudely. Maisie, under such circumstances, often felt the urge to shove someone out of her way so that she could breathe some air. Post-children, really, she became much more moved by everyone's winning efforts. Just as, recently, when she'd slowed and pulled over slightly for a speeding ambulance, and everyone else had pulled over slightly as well, crouching aside like a choreographed movement demonstrating collective consideration and effort, Maisie had started to cry. The siren went wailing by and there she was, sniffling behind the steering wheel.

"What's wrong, Mom?" Xavier asked from the way back of the minivan.

"Nothing, sweetheart," she said, having no idea where to begin.

But then, worried Xavier might think she was upset about something else, or upset at him, she tried to muster something. "It's nothing bad," she said brightly, calling back to him. "I'm just tearing up because I'm worried about where that ambulance is hurrying to."

"That makes you cry?"

"It touches me how everyone moves out of the way so the ambulance can get where it's going."

"That's why it's good we're persons and not animals," Xavier said, not missing a beat. He paused. "But actually, Mom, I'm wrong because we *are* animals. And animals are really good at taking care of each other."

Care. The word somehow broke her into pieces, or, coming from Xavier's mouth, with its voice, broke her into little smatterings of life, like small furry unidentifiable creatures scurrying for cover, then scurrying to get close to one another once they were out of harm's way. *Care.* If caring was what kept life from getting lost, then caring for children was just care, care, care.

Harriet piped up. Her seat was directly behind Maisie's.

"What if we ever had a fire and some of us didn't make it," said Harriet in a statement, not a question.

"That would be . . . terrible," said Maisie.

"Yeah, Harriet, that would be bad," said Xavier. He snorted.

Harriet spoke quickly. "Then the left-behind people would miss all the other people. The other people that goed."

"You're right, Harriet," Maisie said.

In the rearview, she could see Xavier looking out his window, but with tender delight, smiling softly. "The people that *goed*," he repeated, loud enough for Maisie to hear.

→►◄←

This was her community now—the mothers on the sidelines, the partners, the sitters, with their dry-skin hands and treated hair, some with early wrinkles, some putting effort into their appearance while others put more of their effort into the snack bags that they've brought along.

"Mom!" a small voice called, and, in unison, a dozen women turned their heads in the child's direction. Even when Maisie was little, it had always astounded her that all mothers were called Mom, all dads were called Dad, and that there wasn't more confusion over who was calling who when the kids called out their names. Now that she was a mother, both front and center, pinnacled, but still somehow on the sidelines, it made perfect sense to her that a parent's name, who they were, was basically beside the point to every single kid running around on the field. All that mattered to the kid was who belonged to them.

Romeo was playing nearby under the bleachers with his little friend Luke, whose babysitter was watching them. He came running over to Maisie with leaves clutched in one hand and a stick in the other. "I a fireman," he announced.

"Good, honey," said Maisie.

He thrust his fist out. "This my crabs. This my bow," he reported. "I *big*!" he called over his shoulder, like a stormy actor as he headed back to his friend Luke and the sitter.

Carol kicked a stray soccer ball back toward the field and returned to her spot next to Maisie. "Can you tell me," said Carol, "what you do when Harriet has tantrums?"

Maisie sighed. "Tantrums," she said, as though exhaling a cigarette. The baby (Esme!) in Maisie's large belly moved precipitously, like a fish coming to attention, as if to say, *Tantrums? Did someone say tantrums?* and was eager to discuss.

The question made Maisie weary. It wasn't that she generally minded talking about kids, but most of the time, while largely pregnant or largely preoccupied with caretaking, she wanted to talk about something surprising or nothing at all. Something like the uncontacted tribe. But, as for the kids: Some days were fine, and it was easy to think that having small children was a plain and simple treasure of explosive love, pieces of your married hearts running around in the world, full of hope and wonderment, days brimming with happy chaos and burgeoning growth, a cuckoo house full of surprise, full of tumult. Some small moments made up for all the monotony and aggravation, even all the anxiety over things like money, like the time when she looked quietly around the corner into the living room and Harriet was sitting next to Xavier, smoothing his hair down tenderly, admiring him as he looked at a book. She leaned close to him on the sofa, looking at the book he was reading. He looked up at her gently, his face with a sweet smile.

"Want me to read to you?" he asked her.

She nodded. Xavier raised his arm up like a little man and put his arm around her as she wriggled in close to him. The next time Maisie looked, Romeo was out there, too, large on Harriet's little lap.

Or, when checking on them as she heads to bed, she finds all three of them asleep together in Harriet's double-sized bottom bunk, holding hands like a daisy chain.

It was slow, very slow, very mundane but also thrilling, watching toddlers toddle through the house, watching a baby try to fit a round peg into a square, the hilarious expressions at trying new foods.

Other days were not so full of warm calmness. Other days, it was as if Maisie saw nothing more than the shrill screaming coming out of Harriet's fanatical face for a full-on forty-minute tantrum. She was like an egomaniacal starlet who was losing her mind, headed toward sedation or an overdose. Harriet might screech and scream the same type of thing over and over, oddly reminiscent of the provocative bad boyfriends of Maisie's past: "You're making me not *know* what I'm *thinking*! You're making me *forget*!" lying on the floor and pinwheeling in circles with kicking legs, the terrible stuttered breathing as if she's about to gag, her little red face screaming: "You *know* what I'm talking about! You're just not *saying* you know!" Maisie might think, *If I was a Salem Puritan, I would think this child was possessed,* as Harriet flails uncontrollably on the floor, flopping around, almost convulsing. In her more adult moments, Maisie was aware that it was a very fine line between being very funny and very heartbreaking (a young girl distraught and crying!) and so downright aggravating that Maisie sometimes had to suppress the urge to kick her daughter as she walked around her.

"We don't scream like this in the middle of the kitchen," she'd say, through gritted teeth, righting Harriet up onto her bottom so that she might stand up. When Harriet reels around to squirm back onto the floor, kicking her legs and thereby kicking Maisie, Maisie shouts, "And we don't *kick*! *Ever!*" though Maisie, in the moment, has the urge to kick her daughter with a forceful lifting nudge that would fling her into the other room, like the poodle in her dream. The image is enough to halt any such thing, but there's the image, again and again, of a too-hard kick into her child. Then, Harriet might twist, and Maisie might grip her harder to pick her up to bring her upstairs to her bedroom.

Maisie might pick her up a little too gruffly so she won't lose her grip on the stairs. "Owww! You pi-*pinched* me!" Harriet might cry.

"Did I?" Maisie might ask, dropping her daughter on her bed abruptly with a bounce, turning dramatically to head back downstairs, the wails of her daughter behind her like cartooned wafts of smoke. At the bottom of the stairs, Xavier and Romeo are looking at her sideways.

"What's wrong with you?" Xavier might ask sourly. "You pinched her, Mom. She's only *five*."

"She's almost six, Xavier. And I didn't pinch her," Maisie might say, still flushed with distemper, her heart racing, feeling as if she'd like to throw a rock through a window. "Or, if I did . . . I shouldn't have."

"Exercise the kindness muscle, Mom," Xavier would remind her, on various occasions, "otherwise it'll never get strong." Xavier had been taught, in preschool, what seemed to have escaped mankind throughout time.

Exercise the kindness muscle, Mom, and it did need exercising! And so did the patience muscle, so did the focus muscle. All of it needed exercise and practice, just as much as she had practiced skating around the hockey net for a fake and then a hook shot, or slap shots, on the pond next to her house when she was a girl, the puck hitting the small squares of plywood in the upper corners of the goal that Miles and her father had made, hanging from little white teacup hooks. The puck, if her shot was hard enough when it hit the plywood, would leave behind a satisfying gash mark from the puck's black rubber, like what a black shoe sole leaves on a gym floor.

Practice, care. *Practice care.* Which came first, the care or the practice? And could they come at the same time? Sometimes practice didn't seem to make much difference; the reward of all her shooting practice wouldn't really pay off when she wanted it to in a game but rather when she hadn't played for a day or two and was just kind of loosely skating around, then—*bink! bink! bink!*—the puck would hit the little wooden placard targets every time, without any effort: *That's right!—bink!—Nice shot! bank!*

"The effort is what you already put in," her father, a hockey coach, would tell her. "The rest is just muscle memory. From all of your practice."

Maisie can see her father driving, gray New England sliding by outside the window next to him, rough snowbanks, leaden sky, his breath puffing out in front of him as he spoke. "If you didn't practice, you wouldn't even know how to skate!"

Maisie would think of all the possible talents latent inside of people, like fallow fields with their potential growth that might prick green through the surface like bristles of grass, but that never get fostered, never get worked on, never get applied: a factory worker somewhere who has within her the most graceful dancer of all time, a community leader who might have gone to a global level of leadership, who might have won the Nobel Peace Prize if his mother hadn't become ill, or his daughter hadn't gone blind, or his wife hadn't died in childbirth, or, simply, he hadn't preferred living a measured, intimate life more than a life on a global scale. She'd imagine people who had all the talent but never had the chance to practice their innate gift. The hundreds of millions of transformative writers who never learned to write, doctors who were never doctors, born leaders who lived and died in remote circumstances, statisticians with no stats, would-be psychiatrists who work twelve-hour days in a factory or gifted teachers who never got to go to school. And for all the people unable to tap a unique talent, there were the people who weren't interested in the particulars of what they might have.

"Just because someone has a gift doesn't mean they'll use it," her father would say. "I might have a talented player, but if he never practices . . . so what if he's got talent? I'll take the hard worker over the gifted any day of the week."

There were so many different pathways for life to take. Did a person lead a life the way they lead a child, a dog? Or was life like a rainstorm, or an intense sun, something that befalls someone? It seemed like a combination of the two, like walking the dog through certain weather. Maisie's mother dying was like a permanent kind of weather, and Maisie had found, over the years, that walking on one leg that was grief, and another leg that was gratitude, seemed to work pretty well. Too much grief imbued everything with dimness and resentment. Too much gratitude was another kind of contamination, like fake sugar or cosmetic surgery. Maybe it was more like one leg was pain, and the other was love. *Pain, love, pain, love*—the two legs couldn't move forward one without the other.

Maisie would often try to think of her mother as a person, which wasn't easy to do because her mother was more like a movie star or a celebrity, intensely familiar but condensed, flattened onto a movie screen. When her mother died, all the choices her mother would ever make had died with her. All the interactions that her mother would have had with Maisie, or with Maisie's children, all of that had vanished as well. Maisie thinks of all the things that her mother would never get to see, that her mother would never get to do and say, that her mother would never get to feel and learn. When Maisie thought of her mother missing in this way, of all her mother's prospects, interactions, choices, and decisions dying as well, the two-dimensional movie star person lying flattened on her death bed seemed to fill out into 3D as though not just blood but life's vitality was suddenly circulated to the tips of her mother's fingers, the tips of her mother's toes. The possibilities and realness of her mother's actual existence came alive, as did the possibilities and realness of her own life—*it could all end, at any moment*—Maisie could grasp it for a second, and then it was gone.

Her nana said to her once, "When someone you love dies, something starts praying inside of you all of the time."

She thinks it was Nana who said that.

"And that," Nana said—*was* it Nana?—"is an extraordinary thing."

→►◄←

Practice. Care. They sounded like prayer, and they were like prayer.

She thought of the patience and care that her nana displayed when she came marching down the main dock in town on that day when Maisie sat frozen on the edge of the float, unable to jump into the ocean like all the other kids who were splashing around on the first hot day of the year. Usually, Maisie loved to jump into the ocean, especially for the first time after the winter, but on that day, the water looked different, like dark green paint that was waiting for her to jump in so it could smother her.

All winter long, leading up to that first hot day, Maisie had regular nightmares about drowning. Sometimes, it was her mother who was falling overboard from whatever lobster boat they were on, over and over. Sometimes it was her brother, Miles, or her dad, or herself—the cold crashing sound, the cool saltiness enveloping her. Sometimes there was no one driving the boat. Unmanned, it went in broad circles that got tighter and more severe, and Maisie tried to right it with the wheel, imagining that at any moment the boat might run over her dad, or Miles, or a stranger.

"Just jump in," said Miles. He was shiny from swimming. Kids thrashed happily in the water in front of them. Explosions of splashes erupted all around. "Just jump." Miles started to touch her shoulder with his wet hand and, in reflex, she elbowed him in the stomach. He frowned at her and walked away up the dock's ramp.

Shortly afterward, Miles returned with their nana. Once on the dock, Nana took off her sundress. She was wearing a bathing suit—a navy-blue one that had a little skirt attached to it. Maisie had never in her life seen her nana in a bathing suit.

Nana made no mention of anything and instead walked silently to the float's small wooden swimming ladder, kids swimming all around her, and promptly slid backward into the water.

Maisie and Miles began to laugh. They had never in their life seen her swim before. They had never even thought about if Nana *could* swim.

"What heaven!" cried Nana, and her head bobbed up and over a small wave. One of her kicks produced a straight splash that reached impressively high and glittered in the sunlight.

"Glorious!" shouted Nana, and Maisie felt a warm feeling relax in her chest.

→►◄←

The small soccer players cheered at the other end of the field.

"Tantrums are tough," Maisie answered Carol.

Carol's daughter, Maddie, jogged past them. Her shin guards had rotated around to her calves. "These are too big, Mom," she moaned.

"You're okay," Carol told her. "It's almost over."

"I try to ignore the tantrums," said Maisie.

"And can you manage to do that?"

"Sometimes—it's a bad habit—I get sarcastic," said Maisie. "Then I hear them being sarcastic with each other. Or to their friends."

Xavier might say to her, mildly but caustically, as she walks past him on her way to the laundry room from the kitchen: "Oh. *Okay*. Well, I guess, *Mom*, you don't *want* to hear about what happened at school today since you keep walking *away* from me." Or, worse, Harriet, hands on hips and bobbing her head back and forth in a sideways figure eight, speaking to her playdate, singsongy taunting with a touch of street: "Oh. *Well*. I guess you don't *want* to play with my LEGOs since you're not letting me hold your *pony*."

Carol and Maisie watched the kids, all in a balled group, run to the center of the field.

Carol sighed. "Sometimes all Maddie says is *No*—*no no no no no*—and I just don't have it in me to take it in stride." Carol yawned, a bloodhound yawn, her pretty face looking drawn and spent, water coming to her eyes. Carol wondered aloud, "Why do sitcoms and everything make it all seem so warm and fuzzy?"

"Make what seem all warm and fuzzy?"

"Kids and stuff. *Family life*."

"Sitcoms are TV shows," said Maisie, thinking of the previous morning. She had been trying to tidy up the kitchen—crumbs and scraps of paper on the floor like a busy children's restaurant, needing to be swept and cleaned up, but her stomach was so large that she couldn't bend over, and it was very hard to squat. Squatting felt like she'd induce labor. The dishwasher still hadn't been unloaded, and the sink was full of plastic dishes. She pulled the overstuffed garbage bag out of the can and the bag split, wet leftover cereal and pasta like vomit clumped onto the floor.

"Eeeew," said the kids, but Xavier wanted to know where his library book was, but also would she please heat up some soup (for breakfast!), as well as locate his *library card*, Mom, since they were taking a field trip to the town library the next day and he had a *great idea* of what book he *needed* to get to show the whole class, and he also *really needed* a five-dollar bill because his friend Sophie was going to be coming to the door to deliver the Girl Scout cookies *any minute, Mom,* and he needed to be ready with the money because she had to go quickly to her bus stop.

Romeo came whirling out of the living room, a hand over his eye, screaming, "Mine eye! Mine eye!" and then tripped into the stairs, hitting his forehead on a stair's rim.

Maisie picked him up, holding him for a moment, while Xavier shouted from the front stoop, "Mom, do you have *ten* dollars? I need *ten* now!" Romeo tucked his nose into Maisie's neck, crying, while Maisie picked up a stray baby carrot off the floor and ate it. The phone began to ring, the soup started to foam over in the kitchen. Was a bath running upstairs? From the downstairs bathroom, just as Maisie answered the phone, Harriet yelled, "Mom? Will you wipe me?"

It was perhaps slightly like a sitcom, but not a fun one to watch. Maisie could deal with that kind of slight tumult, could happily deal with the practicality of meeting ongoing demands, and that was generally what her household was like, bubbling and percolating with children's personal demands, then looking up to see Neil as he cooked something in the kitchen, resealed the driveway, or walked into town with the kids all hanging off him. It was the grown-up stuff that was hairy and hard to deal with. Like how to remain patient and composed when a child is screaming in your face and throwing a fit, when even someone relatively patient like herself would have the urge to shove the child backward. Even a poor sick child, or a hurt child . . . often she was helpful and sympathetic, yet sometimes she wondered, *Well, now what kind of ailment is here to so annoy me today?* Or how to manage money properly. Or how to communicate with her husband when her mind had gone blank or she's resentful of something, something vague, something large, and something, admittedly, that she was unable to distinguish. Or how to be still long enough to absorb the very grown-up idea of how to rev up and *focus,* for God's sake.

Maisie thought for a moment and thought, well, yes, however, actually, sometimes, it *is* warm. Maybe not fuzzy, but far warmer than a TV show. She thought of the evening prior, just yesterday, the kids, post-bath, all clean like peaches, as Maisie sat on the couch in the little living room with the newspaper on her lap.

Harriet propped some pillows up on the nearby armchair for Maisie's feet. "Put your feet up, Mumma. Your big feet—look how big!"

A box had come from Neil's mother, and the kids tore into it. Xavier put on a home-knitted hat and slippers. Harriet unrolled a clothing item in the package, a gold T-shirt with gold stars on it, quickly put it on and got right down to business, blue latex gloves on, the clip in her hair, a miniature clipboard, just her size—"I think nurses wear this when they're nurses—"

Neil lay down on the ottoman to let Romeo brush his hair with a tongue depressor.

Harriet, with clipboard: "Do you have a headache, Daddy?"

"Little bit." Neil closed his eyes and took a deep breath.

"Dad, does anything hurt you?"

"My knees."

"Open your mouth up. Where are the scissors?"

Romeo stroked Neil's knees gently with the tongue depressor. "You like a massage, Daddy? You like a fen-tine [clementine] to eat, Daddy?"

Maisie smiled as she watched Harriet first consider Neil's body lying there on the ottoman like a mattress and then abandon her clipboard on the floor so that she could climb onto him and nuzzle into his chest. Like an adult, Harriet sighed deeply, breathing him in.

"I don't like music class," she said.

"Why not?"

"Hey, Dad! I hear your heart thumping. . . ."

"Why don't you like music class, Harriet?" Neil's eyes were closed, resting. He put his arms around her.

Harriet sighed again. "The room smells." She closed her eyes, smiling, relishing him, like a woman might do in an advertisement for phenomenally soft and wonderful-smelling sheets.

"The music room smells?" Neil asked her.

"Yeah. Like Vaseline."

Or a moment last winter when Maisie, early pregnant and

nauseous, had fallen asleep on the couch on a Saturday afternoon. She woke to a darkish living room with a blanket over her. Neil was on his knees in front of the fire, adjusting a log. He sat back on his heels and stared into the fire. Romeo wiggled onto Neil's lap. Maisie watched their similar profiles, father and son, big and small. Maisie could see the muscle of fire reflecting on their faces, the flames licking up and down. She could hear the ghostly sound of the flames burning the wood.

"Dad," said Romeo.

"Mmm?"

"Did cavemen's fire look the same as this?"

"Mm-hmm."

"Dad?"

"Hmm," answered Neil.

"Declan's dog's mouth? On the sides it look like octopus." Romeo tried to reveal the inside of his lips.

"I know what you mean," said Neil. "Those bumps on a dog's lips."

The fire crackled; embers popped.

"I see a face in the fire," said Romeo. "Dad."

"You do?"

"Right there. See it? Now it burning up."

+>-<+

Oh, so what if while mothering there was constantly the background feeling that everything she was doing was spread thin, that she couldn't get purchase anywhere, couldn't get traction on anything, in the same way that with a bad tickling cough one can't get behind the tickle of the cough enough to hack out what's causing the hacking, or when the pump of shampoo or hand soap never sucks up the product, regardless of how much the pump is pushed.

Most days were in between, easy enough and demanding enough that they left Maisie feeling both exhausted and filled, but very generally there was always a feeling of worry, mostly about money, a depressed sort of realization that begged this question of her: If I am trying to get through these days, to what end am I trying to do that? What if I stop trying? Though there was, yes, that urge to run for the hills sometimes, there was the panic of whatever would happen if she *were* gone. Who would ever know where the tiny plastic, and central, action figure of Romeo's play-life was? (In the bowl in the living room, underneath two paperbacks.) Who would ever know where the backup winter gloves and stuff for Harriet was (on the top shelf in the downstairs closet) or that the insurance company needed to be called back because clearly both claims hadn't gone through—*again;* Xavier's lunch account needed to be replenished; Romeo's rash had been coming and going for six days now, not two; Harriet's hat was sitting on the radiator at the library, and it needed to be collected before she had a spontaneous fit about it some morning before school when she realizes that it's missing.

"It's an entirely different world when they're becoming baby adults," her friend Freya had told her over the phone. Freya lived across the country, and across the figurative country of mothering in that her kids were almost all gone from her house. "It's less about little monitoring logistics, but you worry more than ever about mental health. Like my Julius . . . he's doing great, but where does my mother mind go? I don't want to be, like, breathing down his neck, so sometimes I don't call him for a pretty long time. Then I imagine he's a heroin addict, some derelict, or suicidal, or devolving into a cruel and awful person. Then he calls, or he comes home, and there he is . . . wonderful, healthy, you know, fully *him*."

If it weren't Maisie, who would watch her kids all the time? Who would *see* them and know that something about recess is bothering Xavier; something at Jessie's house terrified Harriet, and Maisie's pretty sure it wasn't just their strange one-eyed cat. Who would keep track? Who would *follow* what was happening? Neil, of course, but he needed to work. Did Neil experience a certain contour of the children's minds in the same way that she did? She believed he did understand their children, yes, closely and with tremendous love, but why, as a mother, did it feel to her that hunks of her brain had been gutted out and dribbled jellylike into theirs, a shared soup of sweetbreads, something transplant-like about it all, something like an organ donor and they were sharing organs.

The way her milk lets down at the sight of her baby, the way she might get a sense of foreboding for a moment—*Xavier*—and then the phone rings and it's Suzanne saying that Xavier, at Suzanne's house for a playdate with her son, is fine but unfortunately is locked in their garage, alone, because the kids were messing around and now the automatic door won't open.

"I feel terrible, Maisie," Suzanne said to her, as if the entire event was over and Xavier was lost to the garage forever. Just as Suzanne's voice started to get shriller, she suddenly exclaimed, "Oh, thank God! He's out. He's here. He's here in the kitchen."

Maisie could hear Xavier's friend Aden in the background. "It opened a little bit," he said.

Then Xavier, maybe from the other side of the room. "The door went up a little, so I crawled out underneath."

The quick image of her Xavier shimmying in a marine crawl under a slightly open door, the mechanics of the automatic door surely menacingly humming, stuck, made Maisie feel slightly ill as she pictured the heavy door malfunctioning, methodically closing down on her son to crush him.

Maybe it wasn't her brain or her body at all but something no one understands, some other element that no one will ever be able to explain. Maybe souls communicate with each other, unbeknownst to the persons, or maybe simply it was a tether of death, or a tether of life.

What was so different about life and death, thought Maisie, when they flew so closely together always, hand in hand, like two waters in the same stream? When a life gets formed inside of a body—the tiny chambers of a tiny heart, the tiny earlobes and folds of a miniature small intestine, a heart the size of an apricot, organs that Maisie didn't even know the names of, all the parts of an eyeball, the tiny bones of a hand—ever since all those pieces mysteriously got formed *inside her body*, the prospect of death has had its cool hand on the back of her neck all the time, like a concerned grandmother.

Having children was being at a blurred precipice where living and dying meet, *all the time*, the bounty of fragrance and motion and light getting rubbed up, *all the time*, shoved up against the dark, sleek velveteen storm of night's valley. Being a mother was the most open and closed she'd ever felt. It was the most alive and dead, there and not there. Her heart was open, and she was completely *of the world* and *in the moment,* as they say, but at the same time she was shut off, closed off from the daily industry of the world, no longer a function of society that earns money but instead was a participator only by making the small citizens who would become big citizens to make the money and learn to consume. Oh, she needed to earn more money, so that they could all be—*They will learn love!* interjects Maisie, shouting at the money-man thoughts, slinking around like a boogie man.

→►◄←

Very suddenly, a commotion of mothers gathered around the young Europeans who ran the soccer program. The women were elaborately filled with gesture, like mimes, arms up, arms down, pointing toward an area in the park where the baseball diamond met up with a playground. A man in a gray sweater was shuffling away hurriedly.

Carol and Maisie watched as one of the soccer trainers, Coach Nigel, exclaimed in his jaunty brogue, "No! He can't do that!" and bounded after the shuffling man.

Leslie, who'd recently moved in, approached Carol and Maisie to explain. "That guy was taking pictures. We think he's a creep."

"Pictures of the kids?" asked Carol, aghast.

Maisie sniffled angrily. Her waterlogged pregnancy inertia was replaced by a maternal disgust that suddenly overwhelmed her. Whether this man was taking pictures or not, the fact that her addled brain had to entertain the thought of her daughter in some sort of fetishistic placement made her want to bound after him, push him over, and step on his face.

The three mothers watched from a distance as the soccer coach confronted the man. They could see the man shrug and then pull his camera out of his bag. They could see that Coach Nigel was watching the man delete the pictures from his camera.

"Maybe he's totally harmless," said Leslie. "But either way, you don't go around taking pictures of other people's kids."

By now Sydney had joined them. "I was *talking* to him, too. And even while I was talking to him, I was thinking, *This isn't right*. Why didn't I say anything to him? Why didn't I just say, 'I don't appreciate you taking pictures'?"

"Or just: 'Stop taking pictures, please,'" suggested Leslie.

"Yuck," said Sydney, staring off and shivering her shoulders. "Why didn't I say something?"

"He might be harmless." Leslie shrugged. "Just taking pictures."

The hormones, the weepy but now hyperprotective hormones, coursing through Maisie's bloodstream made her want to roar. If her stomach wasn't so large she might have sprinted after the man and knocked him to the ground. She reached into her bag for her flip phone.

"Something's not good," Coach Nigel said simply as he headed back toward them. "Anyone have a phone?"

Maisie handed him her flip phone. The group of them looked between Coach Nigel and the children shrieking and running, the silver soccer balls bounding and bouncing around them like firing neurons, the grass of the field thick and green like a grosgrain ribbon.

The mothers did their best not to interrupt Nigel while he called the police. They listened closely and did a fine job of not interfering as they would have with their partners, interjecting suggestions of what the man was wearing, which direction he went, and where he might have gone. Somehow, Nigel managed to get all the details right.

He handed the phone back to Maisie. "Right, then, thanks," he said, and jogged back onto the field.

"One day," said Sydney, "those flip phones will be obsolete. We'll all have phones like iPhones. Miniature laptops in the palms of our hands with the internet, cameras, music, everything."

"If I can check my email on my phone, my life is over," said Carol.

"Does that mean I'll have to check my bank balance, *on my phone?*" asked Leslie.

"Oh my god," said Juliet. "That all sounds too exhausting for me."

Sydney continued. "People will be able to read the news immediately on their phones. There will be so many sources that most people won't have any clue how to know which news is true."

"Nightmare," said Octavia.

"Even now," said Sydney, "most people don't have a clue about what goes into solid reporting." Sydney had been a war correspondent before having her kids. "Some people assume that journalists just casually write down whatever they want, or that they're being told what to say."

Octavia, a pediatrician, sighed. "Some people assume doctors are just working for drug companies and that we're not here, after years and years of grueling study, to actually serve, to save lives and heal people."

A handful of faces turned toward her.

"I'm sympathetic to the neuroses of new moms, but I've got to admit I have difficult feelings for every smug face who wants to 'think about' vaccinating their kid. Really makes me sick to my stomach. I'm calm and understanding in my office—I have to be!—but I'm about to tell them all to find another doctor."

Maisie looked around. After she and Neil decided to throw caution to the wind and toss her birth control pills, she had a checkup to prepare for life as a prenatal person. Looking over her chart, the doctor asked her if she wanted a booster of the measles, mumps, and rubella vaccine. Maisie brushed it off, worried that the booster might not be covered by her insurance. As she was about to leave, the doctor came back into the room and told Maisie that when the doctor herself was a girl in second grade, she'd gotten the measles. She gave the virus to her teacher, who was pregnant, and whose baby was born deaf as a result of the infection. Maisie and the doctor looked at each other. The doctor's two sentences not only pointed to Maisie's foolishness but also probably summarized a certain trajectory of this doctor's life, like why she became a doctor.

"Yes," said Maisie, "thank you. I'd like that booster."

"I feel for you, Octavia," said Jackie. "I was caught up in the autism paranoia. Honestly, before I had my second kid, my head was so far up my ass that all I could really see was my own shit."

"Jackie!" laughed Leslie.

"My sister said it to me. She's a doctor like you, Octavia. She was on a measles-and-rubella vaccine initiative with the Red Cross in Ethiopia. They've prevented millions and millions of deaths. She saw such horrible circumstances . . . babies . . . moms. When she came home and I was all pussyfooting about vaccines she told me my head was so far up my ass that all I could see was my own shit." Everyone laughed lightly, like skipping stones. "It definitely reminds me to think beyond my, like, butt. Narcissists are up their own butts. Sorry, I keep saying the same thing. But I know because I'm basically a recovering narcissist."

Nina said, "My cousin's son has asthma. She's completely convinced it's because of his vaccines."

"It's tough," said Sydney. "Skepticism is such a good thing, but so counterproductive when people don't take the next step of actually being curious enough to follow through to reality."

Jackie continued. "And reality is exactly where narcissists are *not*, because they are in their own little reality. In their own butt."

"Isn't everyone in their own little reality?" asked Maisie.

"Absolutely. But self-centered people are overconfident and less empathetic. They only see what they want to see. I know because I've been there. I didn't trust other people—I never did—and I wasn't emotionally smart enough to know that trust is what would bring me meaning and peace." Jackie said it again: "Self-centered people don't trust other people. I never used to."

"Then what happened?"

"Then my baby turned into an actual person, and when a *second* human being came out of me, something just struck me that we're all as unique as the next person. Most important, my kids taught me that humans tend toward kindness. Not big news for most people, I realize, but before being a mom it was hard for me to really feel how every single human being is as much in their own life as I am in mine. When you don't trust anyone, your whole world is just you and only you, so that's how I thought everyone else operated, too. There's no growth there, just raw survival and ambition. It's friggin' lonely."

Sydney asked, "Are you still ambitious?"

"Maybe one day." Jackie laughed. "Mostly now I'm ambitious about being present. Trying to stay on my toes in terms of *being alive*. It's all such a short ride." Almost everyone listening knew that Jackie's brother had been shot and killed in a mass shooting at a bank about a year earlier.

Everyone was quiet. "Yeah," said Solange. "My mom once said that she learned the most about being alive when she had me and my brother. My mom was just randomly getting something out of the fridge once when she said something that I think about almost every day. She said, 'Learning how to love teaches you everything that you need to know.'"

Jackie asked, "Have you ever told your mom that you think about that statement a lot?"

"No," said Solange. "I never have. I can imagine exactly how she'd respond though if I did: 'I said that? I didn't say that. Did I say that?'"

Jackie said, "I mean, it's true, isn't it? The people who drive me the craziest, and who I love—my sisters, my brother, my husband, even these kids!—I definitely learn the most about, like, everything, from interacting with all of them."

"I read something the other day about how our kids are mirrors of ourselves," said Melissa.

"Cool," said Octavia. "I definitely am trying to give my kids things that I didn't have growing up. Like consistency, for one."

"If our kids are a reflection of ourselves, isn't the whole world a reflection of ourselves?" asked Melissa. "Like, how we view the world is pretty much how we view ourselves?"

"Heavy, Melissa," said Leslie.

Melissa shrugged. "What's that thing that's like how you feel about your mother is how you feel about life, and how you view your father is how you interact with life? Or, maybe it's more like your mother is the one who shapes how you see yourself . . . your father is how you see yourself in your life . . . I can't remember."

"I don't know that thing," said Sydney. "But my dad took off when I was two." She raised her eyebrows. "So . . . a complicated relationship with life."

Everyone laughed.

"I think I know the thing Melissa's talking about," said Nina. "You look out into the world and you'll see what's inside of yourself. You look inside of yourself, and you'll see what is out in the world. Something like that."

There they all were, parents and caregivers, laughing, huddled near one another on the sideline like a team, these people who Maisie knew and who she hardly knew, sharing things that seemed personal but were surely only scratches on the surface of their lives as they converged in places that most likely none of them had ever considered much before they had their children—the community pool, the sidelines of mini fields, playgrounds hither and yon, parking lots of themed restaurants for birthday parties, places full of trampolines, curbsides, pediatricians' offices, bus stops, hallways of schools, of music classes and ballet—and had conversations they likely had never thought about having.

At Emerald Gymnastics, the five- and six-year-olds prance about in sparkly leotards and spandex while the waiting parents watch them glumly through a plate glass window in a waiting room that resembles a school cafeteria.

A woman named Brenda, who Maisie had only met at the start of the gymnastics classes, was telling Maisie about how it happened that she never went back to work. She'd always thought she'd return to work in the city once her first baby was six months old. Instead, she went on to have two more kids and never went back to the city. She cuts hair at a salon, part time, Brenda tells Maisie, "Because I like to listen to strangers. I should have been a therapist. I still might do that, in fact. Look, I'm glad to not work anymore. At least, for now. Never in a million years did I think I'd stay at home with my kids. But it was like quicksand, and after a while it seemed like I'd be paying someone just so I could go back to work, not so I could make money. Three years ago my husband's dad just dropped dead of a heart attack in our driveway getting out of the car to visit us. He wasn't ill, wasn't obese, no high blood pressure—a healthy guy! News flash, folks! People drop dead. You only live once!"

Brenda continued. "Check in on me in like ten years, though.

I'll probably be annoyed that I'm not in the system anymore. I'll probably be resentful that I didn't stay in the game. Someone just told me the other day that resentment is actually envy. Makes sense, right? My sister's older than me and she feels annoyed with herself that she lagged behind in her career for so long. She takes it out on her husband. But I have another sister who loves her kids and everything, but she *totally* prefers being at work. She does *not* like the annoyance and worry of everyday parenting. And I can understand that. But I like it, for the most part. Ha! Look at me! Look at us! Watching these cute kids tiptoe around out there on the mats with their long ribbon wands. I mean, it's like we're in a cartoon, isn't it? Like a *New Yorker* cover. All the colorful, playful kids out there, and then all of us drab parents and nannies just standing here with our heavy jackets on in this bleak little room, looking through the glass."

"Did you just say you read somewhere that resentment is actually envy?" asked Lisa.

"Yes," said Brenda. "Isn't that interesting?"

The handful of them were quiet. Their parkas swished as they thought about it.

Brenda continued. "Something else that I read that's interesting: Most of the suggestions that you feel like you have for other people? Most of the criticisms you have, or advice that you want to give to someone? It's really advice that *you're* meaning to give to yourself."

Again, the parkas swished.

A woman named Joy said, "It's true that at this point in my relationship with my partner, it's really like we're talking to ourselves. I mean, when I feel like whining, 'You never appreciate me or thank me anymore,' I know it's time for me to start saying how much I appreciate her, and to thank her."

"That's very grown-up of you, Joy," said Astrid. "Last night my husband and I were having our standard division-of-labor argument."

There were murmurs of recognition from the group; with this argument, all were familiar.

"This time, we were specifically arguing about who grocery shops more. We literally stood in our dark kitchen, looking into the refrigerator with its bright light, pointing out who bought what."

The women laughed.

Astrid playacted the scene, pointing high and low. " 'I bought this,' 'I bought this,' 'I bought this. . . .' I guess, like Joy says, I could have just turned to him and said, 'Thank you for grocery shopping so often!' "

Everyone laughed again.

"And I'd really be talking to myself!"

"Listen, my partner is a woman, and I could say the same things," said Joy.

"Me too," said David.

Brenda sighed. "Gosh. We hardly make ends meet. If I were to work full-time, and pay for childcare, we'd lose money."

"But isn't it worth it to keep your career alive?"

Many of them murmured in agreement. But, they said, well, the kids were only kids once, right? More agreement murmurs.

Astrid said, "When your husband starts working more than you, he probably starts becoming a boss of other people. After a while, he comes home speaking like a manager to me and the kids. I ask, 'Do you talk to the people who work for you like this?' He'll say, 'No. I only talk to you like this.'"

"Hmm," said Angelique. "You know, I think I *do* talk to my husband like he works for me when I get home from work."

Chrissy sighed. "I haven't worked in so long."

Dawn said, "I don't miss work. I hated it. I like being home with the guys." Dawn rolled her eyes as she said it so that the other moms laughed. A large baby that she was carrying in a backpack peeked over her shoulder. "Right, Jack-o? Don't we have fun at home?"

Jack bared his teeth like a dog. There was one tooth.

"If you break it down, the person who's working is keeping everything afloat. But so is the person who's home. A whole different kind of float. If there's nothing to keep afloat in the first place, well . . . I mean, where does someone place a value? It's not a zero-sum game. Why are Americans always trying to place *value* on everything: better/worse, more powerful/ more weak, stronger/weaker, either/or? Or maybe it's not just Americans, maybe it's humankind."

"Confident and kind, that's what I'm after. For myself and for my kids."

"I used to think confidence was overrated, that it kind of meant someone was arrogant. So childish of me! If someone's truly confident, they're just solid enough in themselves that they don't act like an ass. Right?"

"Exactly."

"Can we just address the stupidest idea of all around raising kids?"

"Might that be the myth that married people don't have sex?" asked Maggie.

Laughter.

"The stupidest is the question of," Angelique mimicked an earnest TV interviewer, "'Can you *have it all*?' I mean, all of what? No one can swim and sleep at the same time. Who in their right mind wants everything at once? You want to eat a birthday cake and pickles at the same time? I mean, isn't all of life, for everyone, figuring out how to balance all the things that you find important? *Not* having everything at once, and figuring out what to prioritize?"

Regina was untangling her younger child's hair from a lollipop as she said, "It is true, though, that since I became a mom I feel solidly mediocre at *everything*."

Murmurs of agreement, like they were in the UK Parliament.

Michelle finished, "That's very true. I'm just spread thin all over the place. I used to be very focused, very compartmentalized. I was an athlete, and that was something that was fairly easy for me to excel at, as long as I put the time in. It was also easy to finish briefs at work, then go back to my little apartment. Oh my god . . . now? Now it's like I'm a feeble kid watcher, feeble housekeeper and cook, feeble money manager, feeble dog owner, feeble lover, feeble mother."

More UK Parliament agreement.

"I'm a writer, supposedly," said Amelia, "and I actually had no idea how much of writing had to do with actually spending time alone. It's like the writer in me is an entirely different person saying, *Okay, lady, let's get down to business and sit your ass down*, but then there are all of these little thoughts about kids' moods, or rashes, lost shoes, something at school, maybe even married life, how to communicate something and blah blah blah and the writer person, who used to be there all ready to get to work, says, *Ummm—see ya!*"

Noelle said, "Every job requires being alone to do it. Some people can work with their kids around, but talk about spreading things thin! You might be *alone*, away from your family, but figuratively you're never *alone* alone," which she amplified by delivering it like a flourish in a ghost story.

"Which is also the wonderful thing about having a family," said Ginger.

Everyone was quiet.

"Yes."

"True."

"If anything happened to any of them . . . I just don't know what I'd do."

They were all quiet for a time until Shannon spoke up. "I was working in Paris and my supervisor killed herself."

The moms and David all looked at her.

"I'd only just started. I mean, I worked with her every day, mostly just the two of us, plus another assistant. I'd only been there like a month. She had a husband, and kids, beautiful apartment, successful career." Shannon looked up at everyone. "She jumped out of a window. Her daughter's bedroom."

There was an audible sigh of pain. Shannon looked down at her son sleeping in his umbrella stroller.

"I came home to my parents," she said. "I couldn't really deal."

Everyone was quiet.

Shannon kept talking. "I just hope my kids can rely on me the way I can rely on my parents." She was starting to tear up. "It wasn't really until I had these little kids that I realized what awesome parents they are. It's because of how they loved me that I know how to look for nurturing places in my life. The other girl who was an assistant with me when it happened? She completely fell apart."

→►◄←

Once, Maisie's friend Gabriela had said, "I'm not sure when my *new* family will really feel like my *real* family," and they laughed, because Gabriela's "new" family consisted of a husband, twin sons, a baby girl, and two dogs. "Maybe . . . twenty years?"

They also laughed because they knew that, as mothers to young kids, both Maisie and Gabriela were like toddlers in the realm of parenting. They knew they knew hardly anything, having only been at it for a handful of years. Maisie's father had told her once that only experts realize how little they know while fools are full of false confidence. Yes, they were learning the basics, practicing the basics of parenting skills, but given the splat wackiness of having little kids and being young parents, they knew very well that, in the grand scheme of their children's lives, in their lives, this was (hopefully) the very, very beginning. In so many ways, they knew so little.

→►◄←

Once, Maisie's nana was showing her a picture of her wedding day to Maisie's grandfather. They were dressed for their honeymoon to Montreal, in regular clothes. Nana carefully held the photograph at its tip, between her thumb and her forefinger, as if the photograph were a match. Nana's young face looked up at them out of the black and white. Maisie's pop looked up at them, too. He had his arm around Nana, and his hand gripped her upper arm with a hardy, athletic squeeze. They weren't just smiling; they were full of a happiness that brimmed out of the photograph. Maisie could almost hear the laughter.

"Look at us . . . ," said Nana, smiling at the picture. "We had no idea about anything!" She put her arm around Maisie and squeezed her, mirroring the photograph. They stared at it together. Nana's younger face looked game, ready for anything with her twinkling eyes looking up and off to the side, her smile wide and open-mouthed. Pop's eyes looked right at the camera as he pulled her close. He looked not only completely delighted but also grateful and amazed, as if to say, *Can you believe that life is this good?*

They stared at the picture, looking back in time. Maisie wondered who took the picture and was about to ask when Nana said brightly, "Boy, do I miss him!" She squeezed Maisie again with her arm.

"Just remember," said Nana, "wherever you put your focus, that's what will grow and grow and grow. It will be your treasure, whether you intend it to be your treasure or not. If you look for disappointment, you'll grow disappointed and resentful. If you look for things to be grateful for, you'll grow grateful and kind. Look for things to be amazed by, Maisie, and you'll be full of amazement and curiosity."

Nana put the picture on her fridge, held up by a magnet in the shape of a lobster pot. She touched the face of Maisie's grandfather with her fingertip tenderly, then she flicked it, with both annoyance and humor because, as Maisie knew, it had not been an easy road with the man; her grandfather's wondrousness had brought a lot of difficulty. Maisie never met him, but she knew that her grandfather was dying of liver failure when he had a massive stroke and died, in a bar, when Maisie's father was thirteen. According to Nana, he was a kind, thoughtful, and magnificent man when he was sober, but a cruel and tortured person when he drank too much.

Maisie never saw her own father drink, and it only occurred to her as she got older the tremendous strength and effort that her father must have exercised, under the circumstances of his own childhood, to be the father Maisie knew: a patient and predictable man who never drank after her older brother, Miles, was born. When they were bigger kids, Nana would leave pamphlets lying around for Maisie and Miles to find: *Alateen* or *Alcoholism, A Merry-Go-Round Named Denial.* In Nana's bathroom hung an embroidery of the Serenity Prayer: *God, grant me the Serenity to accept the things I cannot change, Courage to change the things I can, and Wisdom to know the difference.* Maisie always fixated on why certain words were capitalized. Spelling mistakes and grammar oddities, in general, always bothered her. For most of her life, the prayer's words were so abstract that they had no meaning to her. But, as words and prayers and mantras are wont to do, they were robotically noodled into her head, and the more their memorized words coursed into her blood and brain, seemingly sinking into her DNA and into her formulation of emotions, the more any pain and confusion dissipated. Just as beauty is empowering because it reminds us of the absence of pain, so, too, words, like an inoculation, can prepare our body for strength. Maisie never even realized she knew every word to the Serenity Prayer until it came quietly out of her mouth, like a song, one day as she stood in the shower when she was no longer a child but not yet a grown-up.

Her nana would say, "It was your father who turned the tanker away from generations of dysfunction."

Her father would say something similar, but about Nana. "Your nana taught me that it's every generation's job to learn how to live better and love better. Some generations drop the ball. Change takes time and effort."

→►◄←

At Mass once with Neil and his sister's family the priest said, "So I ask myself, how will God's love be revealed to me today?"

For a while, Neil would repeat it in the mornings, jokingly: "How will God's love be revealed in me today?"

Was Maisie loving better than the generation before her? She had no idea. Who was around to keep score, to keep tabs? Where was the feedback? The two times that she was given direct feedback, she'd burst into tears: once when her pediatrician said, in earnest, "Good job, Mom," and another time when the preschool teacher said, in Maisie's first ever parent-teacher conference: "Well, first off, you must be a wonderful mother."

Around town, it was the older moms that Maisie wanted to listen to, though some information was jarring. "You just wait," said Barbara at a Halloween party. "My oldest son drank too much at college and slept with a girl he barely knew. Well, she drank too much, too. She was also from a strict, Methodist family. It worked out, considering. We now have a two-year-old grandson who lives with his maternal grandparents. A Methodist minister and his wife. Our grandson is adorable."

It was the older moms that Maisie wanted to listen to. Where else was there to find real guidance? The young mothers were often full of ideas, but honestly they were all the blind leading the blind.

"Aren't we all the blind leading the blind, all the time, anyway?" an older mom friend, Mary, had said to her once. "That's partly why I like photographs so much. I can stare at them and see new things."

Maisie first met Mary at the preschool. It was Romeo's first year. A coven of mothers was waiting for the three-year-old class to get released from the large classroom on a rainy day. Many of the parents didn't know each other yet. Most of the mothers were newish moms who nonetheless felt seasoned because they'd been mothering for a few years. A straggly haired woman whose hair grew out from her head in a sort of fluff with no precise ends was talking animatedly as she wiped the mouth of one of two babies (twins) that were in a double stroller made like a train, one seat in front of another rather than side by side. She was loudly regaling another mother with an ear-infection story, then giving advice on putting tubes in the ears, which turned into a sort of sermon about sleep training and co-sleeping, which didn't seem directed at the original interlocutor but rather everyone within earshot, at which point Maisie turned away to read flyers on the bulletin board, one about a food drive, another about welcoming a family into the parish where the preschool, unaffiliated with the church, was held.

Janet, the preschool director, came out into the hallway from the classroom. Everyone hushed at her appearance, including the ear-tube regaler, and watched Janet start to remove pushpins and flyers from the bulletin board. Most of the mothers, including Maisie, hung on Janet's every word. Here was a woman who had taught preschoolers for longer than some of the new mothers had been *alive*, for crying out loud, and who had her own grandchildren. Even when she seemed wrong, she was usually entirely right. When Xavier was in the three-year-old class, Janet had told Maisie, in passing, "This child doesn't respond to no," after she'd overheard Maisie say, "No, Xavier, we don't have time for that." As Maisie headed to the car, holding Xavier's hand, she was annoyed. *All children need to hear no,* thought Maisie. *Who does this Janet think she is? She doesn't know me! She doesn't know Xavier!* But, by the time she was starting the car, Maisie realized that Janet was entirely correct. Each child, like each adult, was entirely different. While one might love precise instruction, another might be entirely annoyed by being told how to do something. It was true that whenever Maisie started something with *no*, or inserted a *no*, Xavier would inevitably tune her out. At the sound of *no* he would immediately disengage and stop listening. It was just as easy to say, "We're running late. Can you get your shoes on?" and Xavier would've likely happily scampered into his shoes and off they'd have gone.

As Janet rearranged the bulletin board, holding pushpins in her mouth and papers pressed between her knees, she asked

Mary, who was standing near her, how her children were. Presumably Janet had taught all of Mary's children at the preschool, and this of course was of interest to all the bystanders as well. The collection of people present listened in to hear how Mary's oldest was in college, her next child, a daughter, was a senior at the high school, another daughter at the middle school, and her son Tyson was at the elementary school.

Janet removed the pushpins from her mouth and pressed them into the bulletin board. "College, high school, middle school, elementary school, and *preschool*. . . . That's something else, Mary." She smiled. "One in each."

They laughed, and Janet went back into the classroom.

The loudish woman who had been talking about co-sleeping and ear infections looked almost as though she might punch Mary in the face. "You have *five* children?" she asked Mary.

"I know," Mary had said. "I mean, to have them so spread out, can you imagine?"

Maisie could not imagine any of it. Nor could the other speechless parents. They stood quietly as rain thrummed loudly on the roof. It was because of the rain that they had all gathered in the hallway outside of the classroom rather than at the low iron gate of the playground that was the customary spot for pickup, and where parents were discouraged from arriving early to stand and observe their child's play on the playground because their presence occasionally caused misbehavior: haughtiness in the sandbox to display bravado, or a sudden display of meekness or intense homesickness from the child who had been happily adjusted for the previous hour and a half.

"Wow," Siena said to Mary. "Five. That must be really hard."

Mary shrugged. "Hard would be never having them at all."

→>◦<+

The first time Maisie went to Mary's house it was to pick up Xavier, who, without any mom arranging, had made friends at school with Mary's fourth kid, Tyson.

The front door opened directly into a bright living room. A staircase was straight ahead, its risers painted a glossy dark blue. To the left was a bright living room, and to the right was a dining room, both of which were informal and inviting with the general refuse and wear of a family with teenagers.

A large black dog gave a bark and greeted Maisie as though they'd met before. Maisie patted it, and the dog leaned into her and then collapsed, rolling onto its back at her feet.

Mary's voice called from upstairs. "I'm here! I'll be right down!"

Maisie scratched the dog's belly and looked around. The living room was white and ran the length of the small house from its front to its back. Large windows looked out onto the street at its front, and the back overlooked a small yard that was covered in snow. Above the mantel, above the fireplace, was a large framed print of a black-and-white photograph of a still, snowy scene. A large willow tree, encased in ice, hung in the frozen position of a firework in its free fall. Beneath its branches was a large frozen pond, with black ice in areas where the snow hadn't gathered. Behind the tree was more icy enchantment, but also darkness, with areas so black that they made the white brighter.

Xavier came partway down the stairs, looking as though the air in this house of older children, with its mysterious teenage bedrooms and large shoes tossed in messy piles at the door, had caused him to grow. He smiled at Maisie—"I'll be right back"—and ran back up. The black dog scrambled to his feet to follow Xavier up the stairs.

Maisie's boots had snow on them. She kicked them off on the doormat so she could go look at the photograph better. She moved closer to look. In the snow and the ice, there was menace and danger. Was the pond's ice thick enough to hold anything? The ice encasing the branches was jewel-like, beautiful, and the tightest sparkles of the snow seemed to emanate the same cold-air scent that got trapped in the fur of Maisie's childhood dog, Major, when he came inside from a cold winter day. She'd shove her face into Major's thick, cold fur to breathe it in. She has smelled the same combination of frigid exhilaration in Xavier's hair, and Harriet's, when they've been outside in the cold. She's inhaled it as she's taken off their coats, the cold air still rosy-cheeked on them. *Why you doing that, Mumma? Why you smell my head like that?*

How could she explain that the smell brought her to her dog, to her mother's deathbed, but also to the frozen pond near her house where she'd shoot pucks at the makeshift goal with its plywood targets?

Closer up, the photo was more abstract. Shadows looked like faces in the bushes, in the angles of the branches and the snow-lumped white leaves. She saw one smiling face, ghostly, of a woman. Another face was angry, a man in profile, and another looked like a face that was turning into a wisp of smoke, its eyes completely hollow. A snowy bush looked like Minnie Mouse. She was not the best at drawing, but she could copy things very well. She took a drawing class in college and often when she saw distinct faces and shapes in things—in puddles, in branches, in wallpaper or something like these snow-covered branches under this tree in this picture—she learned that if she just copied this little thing that she saw, the strange shape, it would make the picture come alive differently than the thing itself.

Mary's voice was behind her. She was straightening the mess of shoes and boots near the front door, marrying them to their mates, placing them in neat pairs. "The best is when a fire is going and it looks like it'll melt the picture," said Mary. "I'm getting tired of looking at it, but I kind of treat it like a mirror."

"Like you see your reflection in the glass?"

Mary smiled. "That, too, I guess, but it's more like it reflects my general life."

"Like how?"

"Totally depends how I look at it. The picture can feel great, and the picture can feel . . . restrictive. I often feel like a big bendable tree, frozen in ice."

"It's really beautiful," said Maisie.

"Thanks. Since I took it, it doesn't look that beautiful to me, unless I imagine that someone else took it."

"You took it?"

"Over twenty years ago. I still take pictures, but professionally they're of weddings, bat mitzvahs, family portraits, dogs, stuff like that. This photo, though . . . it's all sorts of things . . . my whole world before I moved into this house and had this whole family. Or some part of me that's been kind of frozen over? Or maybe how sometimes I'd like to *freeze* my life and make time stand still? Sometimes I don't notice it . . . sometimes it enchants me like someone else took it. Sometimes it irritates me because I'm not sure I even like it. One night, sitting right here in this chair, years ago—I was actually nursing my daughter—I was looking at it and I had this mini revelation that felt way more important to me at the time than it does now." She laughed a little. "I thought, *How I look at this photo is how I look at my* life."

"It's beautiful," said Maisie. "And, like, impressive and arresting."

"Well that would be a nice way to look at life, wouldn't it?"

The large black dog sauntered in, came next to Maisie, wagged his tail in greeting a couple of times, and then lay down with a groan. The white winter light cast an oily sheen over the dog's dark fur. Maisie leaned over in her seat to pat his head.

Mary watched Maisie pat the dog's—Boris's—head. "We had another dog before him who was sort of the love of my life. Bruno. I recommend a dog."

"Too much to take care of," said Maisie.

"The dog is like a big Xanax when you pat him," said Mary. "And I've never taken a Xanax, so . . . maybe I don't know."

Maisie was patting Boris's ears, which had some silky threads with tiny little kinks in them. "I'm feeling that a little bit right now," said Maisie. It was not unlike nursing.

→-◄-

Esme's suckling slows. Maisie thinks of each of her own children's faces, the quiver of mystery, like a halo that has descended and been absorbed into their skin, in the curve of their cheeks, the squinch of their lips, that remind her of total hope, total joy, and then, fairly quickly, their young faces cause her to remember the recent *state of affairs*, and she feels the financial woes all over again—how could she have come this far? With all these kids lining up behind her, dutifully, faithfully, and blindly following her into . . . what? Debt! How could she have been so selfish, so pathetically hopeful while really acting hope*less*, so misguided as *this*?

She considers the classic standard of dutiful parenting: work work work in the name of the kids, sacrifice sacrifice in the name of advancement: loving couples living apart, loving families living apart, illegally crossing borders, scrimping and saving and forgoing whatever needs to be forgone so that their children can have whatever it was that the parents weren't able. What was wrong with her? She wasn't by any means out there charging fancy shoes on credit cards or shopping her butt off at the fancy mall. Okay, so she wasn't a great price comparer at the supermarket, it was true, and, no, she didn't clip coupons much, but she was a whiz at finding items on sale.

She has the urge to wake up Neil. How dare he have a moment's peace (sleep!) while she sits fretting as Esme gnaws at her. They have already had so many fights about the handling of money that now they tiptoe around it gingerly, a little angrily, but mostly carefully, since they both know it is their own faults together, combined with the world at large. A typical, brief exchange:

"I'm going to pay off the miles credit card from that equity line again."

"Well . . . sure. I already transferred money to pay for the preschool deposit and the rest of that stupid tax bill and that other credit card we wanted to close. . . ."

"Did you close it?"

"I . . . think so."

"You *think* so?"

"Look, why don't you take care of it to begin with if you want it taken care of?"

"Well, I don't want to get involved with it if you already took care of it. Which is why I'm asking. Did you close it?"

"No. In fact, I used it."

They look at each other sadly, disappointed. "For what?"

"For the utility bill. And also for Xavier's soccer uniform."

At the name of their son, they walk away from each other, deflated, to go sigh alone, Maisie in front of the sink and its running water, Neil at the back door, surveying the miniature backyard.

What happened to her that she can't manage the cash? She thinks back to college. She thinks back to school. She was preoccupied with painting and books. What a waste of time! What a stupid luxury! Who did she think she was? As if she'd make loads of money (*someday* . . .), or was she always expecting some man to buy everything that needed to be bought? Of course not! Where was the fire in her belly to tenaciously keep at her career? She had worked! She had always worked! And now, trouble everywhere: on the newspapers lying around the house, on the welcome screen when she logged on to her email, all headlines full of grim financial undertones—*Stocks Volatile After Rate Cuts; Unemployed Father Kills Self and Family; Bleak Retail Sales Reflect Downturn*—she barely understood what was happening, but it was clear there was trouble at every turn: *Household Debt the Highest in History; Global Markets Have Worst Day Ever* . . . The money page headline tells of a British financier who jumped in front of a train after having breakfast with his wife and six-year-old daughter. . . .

She had a good education, and no one thought to teach her about finances? (What about *parenting*?) She didn't think to seek out some financing tips? All the classes were there, surely, but shouldn't it be a requirement for an American like her to know about money and spending and saving before she was let loose into the adult world? She had always managed. She wasn't crazily irresponsible. She worked, sure, she worked all through college—waitress, waitress, clean, tutor, babysit, work study, waitress, filing, and then tutor some more—and she always worked after college. She taught. She got a job with a curator, then with an interior designer. She managed props for a theater company. The PR stuff came after that, then the PR for the nonprofits, then the nonprofits themselves. She worked every day, all day, and paid all her bills on time. So she didn't *save* much money, but she didn't spend money like crazy, either. She always made enough to make her ends meet, and, well, use her credit card sometimes when she needed it.

But the last few years . . . it wasn't just her family life, it was financial stuff, national, global, that she'd read about and barely cared about, barely understood. A two-page graphic in the newspaper made it clear to her. Household debt was literally off the chart that was keeping track, skyrocketing into the upper-right-hand corner of time. Foreclosures were speckled about the map of the country. Driving around, Maisie had seen the foreclosed houses: homes that had been lively with families—lamplight and curtain curves like smiles in the windows—were transformed into stunned structures with fore-closed eyes for windows: matte and abandoned.

"You Americans," said Bernadette, a transplant mom from Ireland, "you're always sort of late to the problems, aren't you? But then you really do pull it together really great."

If only Maisie had *given it more thought,* she thought, and planned out a plan like sensible people do (i.e., picked out a more specific profession—a doctor, maybe, or an engineer) and just got on with it and followed the necessary steps et cetera, et cetera. It was almost as if she felt passive aggressive about it, as if not caring about money was a way to get back at the money world itself, the dog-eat-dog world of mostly men, mostly greed, mostly consumption. Sticking it to the man! Idiotic! As if her ambivalence was rebellion, when all the ambivalence was doing was holding her back from moving ahead.

Oh, it was too much. She had to get her effing act together. But what if, even with her act together, it wasn't enough to sustain this middle-class life that her family had been living? Then what? Then where do they go? Head for the hills? Every day, in the squalor of her life—oh, she loved her family, her kids, her husband! The toss and turn of it all! Still, every day in the tumble of her daily life, even if only for a moment, she had an overwhelming desire that appeared, and then disappeared just as quickly, but stayed long enough for her to recognize it, like phosphorescence in a small, tidy wave—a small pop of a cork with the noise wholly there and then gone, but still in her ears—the urge to go—but there was nowhere she wanted to go—the urge to disappear. But then she'd miss her family. She'd bring them with her. To simply begin anew, all together and with them, somewhere else. A clean slate. A do-over.

Maisie tells herself she's tired, for crying out loud. She's nursing, after all, having the energy literally sucked out of her by this petite human appendage at her bosom. After some solid hours of sleep she'll feel less hopeless. Things will somehow seem manageable in the morning. After all, it was all only money. After all, they had their health, right? They had health insurance! And a lot of love! Right?

Might she really vomit? Is this worry? Or is this postpartum blues? Maybe it *was* hormonal. A stomach virus? Though the situation was, let's face it, dire. And true. But either way, money or no money, the sun would still come up, Romeo would hug her with his little arms shoved under her armpits, and Harriet would still stay completely fascinated with every single new thing that she encounters. Wouldn't she? *Because earwax, Mumma, tastes like dandelions. Ladybugs, Mumma? They smell like peanut butter.*

Some nights, the dark outside of their box of a house, things scrape at the corners, at the walls, at the window frames and the glass. The wind shudders stuff, and the clicking around them might be from something as lovely as a delicate branch of the enormous rosebush, its thorns grating against the house paint like claws. The roses in the dark are unidentifiable light blobs of lushness, clumped and almost indistinguishable from the overall dark night save for their sweet fragrance and cloud-like puffs. Anything can happen, outside, in the night. The roses might break off and float off in the wind. They might unfurl into yellow-eyed demons, little fangs, and claw their teeth all over the house as they leap over and around it. Is that the wind or small creatures that transmogrified out of the roses, leaping, silently squealing from the rooftop?

Maisie is on a wooded path. So much moss! There are lacy patches of light at her feet, the smell of spruce, and her arms are floating up. The air is so still it's as if—*oooof!*—she jerks awake as though someone punched her in the stomach. Her abrupt movement causes Esme to unlatch and begin to cry.

Maisie snaps to, rearranges the infant, sits up straighter. She gives up trying to sleep and decides to read her book to knock any ill-feeling thoughts to the back burner. She lights a candle so as not to disturb the baby or Neil.

But even books lately have left her hemmed in and wanting. Even while reading, she is chasing her own tail, retracing territory that's already been covered. Her brain won't seem to expand as it used to. It stays in the same confines as though she's in a large, ancient arena with an enormous sky above her, but no exits. The train station in a story about two young lovers and the train station in a story about a child that is lost is, in her mind, *the same train station.* The houses in a novel she read recently where a young couple move in next door to an older couple are the same two houses that were in a novel she read about a working mother living next door to a stay-at-home mom. Not much new was breaking out of her head. She was heading down the same path, the same setting, the same terrain. Even a historical novel where lots of cooking was going on seemed to be somehow set in the kitchen of the suburban house where the stay-at-home mom of the aforementioned book was living.

Which explains her breakout reasoning behind her most recent read: a thriller about two young couples, able-bodied vacationing Americans who carelessly venture into a Mexican jungle in search of a new acquaintance's archaeologist brother. Needless to say, things go badly.

As the candlelight flickers and Maisie reads about the young travelers getting eaten and taunted by a demonic vine, she considers something she read somewhere in a book of old wives' tales: that the creepy energy she's absorbing from the book might somehow get absorbed into her milk and thereby get into her nursing baby. For a moment she acknowledges the strange sensation that she is actually completely *nourishing* someone, and yet, close as she is, baby Esme can't somehow taste what Maisie is thinking. *The jungles inside of me,* a part of herself says.

Maisie is quickly absorbed in the soap opera machinations that are beginning to emerge between the lost couples in the novel. She is utterly swept up in a particularly gripping passage—one of the girls is missing, presumed dead, and then appears in the distance in the dark woods—when Maisie is all at once aware that Esme has stopped nursing and has stopped making any sort of noise whatsoever. The room is completely quiet. There is Neil's steady breathing, like ocean waves, the drone of a distant airplane through the cracked window, and a siren so distant that it sounds comforting rather than worrisome.

Maisie glances down at Esme, expecting her to be sound asleep, a sealed-up face, peaceful and ready to be put back into her bassinet. Instead, Maisie is startled. Esme is wide awake. Her small, candlelit face is turned on like a light bulb. Her dark eyes stare plainly, intently, up at her mother. Her small unsmiling face is pure frankness, the plain unconscious, popping like a flower bud out of the swaddled white flannel blanket. *Quiet alertness,* thinks Maisie, watching her baby's shiny eyes. A small splash of milk on Esme's cheek is the only trace of the earlier feeding's hubbub. The hushed radiance of the candlelight makes the infant's face look as though she is inside a hut made of hides, or a firelit cave, rather than a suburban bedroom. A face in miniature, looking squarely at her mother. *So that's who you are.* A life in miniature, thinks Maisie, only her fourteenth night alive.

"Hello," Maisie whispers to her. "Hi."

The candlelight flickers. Esme's small dark eyes—medicine man eyes, shaman eyes—seem to hold weighty information, as though they contain completely the mystery of where she just came from. Was it vast? Was it nowhere? Was it simply a belly?

The human race, thinks Maisie, but she's getting lost in something else in her baby's eyes that gleams soberly back up at her. Maisie feels a dull ache, something as tiny as a taste bud but as huge as a taste, that courses through her chest at the sight of the baby eyes, the rounded baby cheek, the soft shaded baby line that divides her upper lip from her bottom lip. Maisie recognizes that her own face is like a satellite, a moon, to this baby's thoughtful face. She beams herself down at the infant, full of yearning, full of might, all the origins of love coursing through the air between them.

Baby Esme huffs a small sigh in the quiet. Through the open window the night air speaks up and the slow whoosh of a breeze turns into a hush of loud rain. Maisie smiles at her baby, since it seems to her that Esme, along the shaman lines, has somehow magically made the rain begin, pointing out, amid Maisie's flurry of man-made money worries, that workhorse nature is wearily hoofing it along, blowing seeds and sprinkling rain, supplying milk and hormones and rapturous motherly love.

A car slices by. Mother and daughter sit in the candlelight like a La Tour painting, listening to the distant stadium sounds of the cheering rain: louder, softer, all of it saying *ahhhhhhhhhhh*... and then the wind tosses the trees around and the pull string to the wooden blinds swings panicky back and forth, back and forth, tapping on the windowsill as Esme stares thoughtfully up at her mother. In the distance, through the rain and the close wind, is, again, the soft plaintive wail of a siren. Trouble, somewhere.

Maisie always loved this age with her other babies: the pre-smile phase, so solemn and plain-faced. The general consensus, she well knew, among most mothers was that they were waiting with bated breath for their infant to finally smile at them. But Maisie got such a kick out of this early time, the tiny expression so fully no-nonsense in comparison to all the goo-googahing going on around them.

Maisie would try for a laugh. She'd jump up from beneath the changing table, knowing that the startle reflex was usually the one that did it. "Boo!" and the baby would look at her sidelong, skeptical, *Is this something I need to learn?* Maisie would look away and then turn her face quickly back—"Blah!"—and their little body might jerk in reflex for a moment, then look demurely past her ear.

But mostly what she loved about this phase was the idea that the baby was here, and she, the mother, was completely responsible, completely on point, completely able to study every little thing before seeing the new person's character (the smile!)

emerge. It was almost like still being pregnant, carrying around a being within her, but the baby was *out* for her to study and get a handle on before its nuanced person (with its smile) arrived.

Gradually, in the candlelight, Esme's face starts to look uncertain. Her small brow starts to furrow and her elastic mouth purses to the side. She reddens and then pales and then reddens again, just as clouds change the shadows over rolling hills. Her eyes slowly cross. A deep, loud grunt is followed by a grumbling bowel movement that Maisie can feel like small, muffled thunder in her arms. The baby's face settles, eyeballs glancing in a steady gaze to the side like an adult calmly contemplating a noise, wondering, *Did you hear that? Listen. Wait.*

Outside, the sway of the wind makes Maisie think of a little bird she sees that shoots up and down their driveway, then flutters up under the eaves to disappear into a hole. It reemerges in a fluffy burst, out of the hole, twittering busily as it dips and rises then lands, in the middle of the driveway, to bounce across it, looking for little bugs, little worms. It stops and is still for a moment. Maisie sees it from the kitchen. Its head twitches left, right, up, down, as if it is a puppet, as if something is controlling it and making it move.

Maisie listens. Around the house, out there in the dark through the cracked open window, the simmering rain sounds like a pencil slowly scribbling circles, round and round the house like a spool of wire, tightening in. A gust of wind abruptly pushes the window shade into the room and then sucks it back out in a clack, blowing the nearby door shut, which causes another door to slam. Through the wall, just as she's about to rise to change

Esme's soiled diaper, Maisie can hear the cries of children, stirring from the slam.

Their indeterminate cries and moans at first sound promising in that the kids might fall back asleep. But no, Harriet gets louder, calling, "Mom," mildly in the dark, and it is escalating to "Mom?" and then pressing, "*Mom!* I *need* you!"

Through the wall, Romeo speaks up as another door downstairs slams shut. Romeo calls bravely, "Who dat? Who dat, Mumma?" Then, sounding terrified, wailing as if he's on a roller coaster, "Who *dhere?*"

Xavier chimes in from his far corner of their room, hollering over the storm of his little brother. "Mom?" sounding deep-voiced and tired, a teenagerish sound of impatience amid the squeals and shrieks. "Mom? They're all *needing* you, Mom. Don't you *hear?*"

➺–◅

It had been, needless to say, a jumbled remainder of the night: switching from her bed to Harriet's, then onto the rocker in Romeo's room as she half dreamed about sledding on a hill that didn't have enough snow for the sled to move, then on to calming small nerves back with Harriet as Maisie waited out a night terror with Harriet senselessly screaming, "No, Mommy, *No!*" and looking petrified past Maisie's head as if Maisie weren't right there in front of her—"Don't *do* it! No!"—while her brothers slept right through. The night terrors always made Maisie go back in time, wondering how her ancestors interpreted them. Were they gifts or forebodings? Danger or cathartic? When the terror was over, Harriet snapped out of it and woke up, nonchalant but thirsty, but with no glass of water next to her bed.

Maisie brought her into the bathroom. There was no glass in there, either. Maisie ran the faucet and cupped water in her hands at the sink for Harriet to drink. Harriet looked at her mother, in the buttery glow of the night-light, as she slurped the water from Maisie's hand, her little-girl eye raised an eyebrow at her mother. *You can make a cup out of your hand?* Maisie ushered Harriet back to her bed, where the child dove into her pillow and instantly fell asleep as though she'd been put under a spell.

Then, back to the master bed, the mother ship of beds, into a sleepy blur of falling asleep lying sidelong, as though she were doing the sidestroke, with Esme plugged onto her breast.

In her sleep Maisie can feel the animal presence of her infant next to her, warm against her torso, and she can just as well, in her half-sleep state, feel the presence of her other children as though they are inside of her pillow, or inside of her arm or shoulder, with their smells of yeasty grass and chicken noodle soup, with their breathlessness after running and the glow of their cheeks, with the alertness in the whites of their eyes, as white as the chest of a swan that seems to want to be stabbed. The darkness is right behind them. The darkness is always right behind them; it brightens their eyes and their faces. What *is* the thing, the clear membrane that is between being born and not being born, between living and dying? Between a body's glow, and a sudden shutdown of the whole operation? How was it that a whole life was bound up in a life?

As a girl, she held new kittens and baby rabbits cupped in her hands like liquid. Through their soft fur, a racing heart would blip lively against her palms, like a strobe light, a frenzy of warm furry pulses.

Here come the sounds of little feet running up behind her, then pattering past her head. Maisie walks into the kitchen, and the cabinets are open, drawers are ajar, as if a poltergeist has manhandled the place, as if the kitchen has been ransacked and pillaged.

When Maisie and Neil sleep in their bed they can hear rustling against the plaster wall at their heads. It sounds like it is birds, or mice, living in the wall. It is birds. They are nesting in the English ivy that has spread all over the chimney and the side of the small house like a lush green wall hanging.

When Maisie hears the rustling, half asleep, she imagines a large-paged, illustrated children's book that's in the kids' room, *The Burrow Book*. Half of the large page is above ground and, satisfyingly, half of the page is underground. All the kids, from small Romeo to mystified Harriet to delighted Xavier, become mesmerized by it. So does Maisie. The four of them, reading together at night, nestled in Harriet's bed, stare at the pages in silence. There are the prairie dogs aboveground. They stand upright so cutely with their neat little wrists bent, keeping watch. Underground there is a wide network of cross-sectioned burrows, long fingers of tubelike paths that lead to inviting, circular dens full of curled-up prairie dogs, sleeping foxes with their dramatically fluffy tails, or a dormant spider. A rabbit hole heads diagonally into the earth, the tube of it opening at its warren. It looks remarkably like the illustrated cross-section of a woman's vaginal passage; the mother rabbit and her little bunnies occupy what would be the uterus. In the womb-shaped rabbit warren, the baby bunnies and their mother are all bunched together, resembling a soft pillow of furry warmth and extreme coziness. Inevitably, after staring at the picture for a while, one of the children points at the round rabbit warren. Out of the quiet concentration, a small finger, perhaps unplugging with a pop from a thumb suck for a moment, points to the bunny den, and taps it. *This,* the small tapping finger seems to say. *This. Right. Here.*

Maisie hears the rustle near her head, and she is inside a burrow. Her hair is tangled in roots above her head. There is a fox family down a round brown hallway. Maisie hears the rustling near her head and thinks of this burrow book, the mammals all in there, in the book, in the beds, in her belly, in the wall by her head, but in this case they are birds, just beyond her head, just beyond the wall in their nest—*Are they in her head?*—crackling leaves and then a nest, her sleeping, combining sleep and the sounds and the books and waking life, and then her belly and the imaginary rustling feeling of a baby, rustling like bird feathers inside of her stomach, how the baby's feather rustling would turn to rounder movements and then the fetus would wriggle in there, in her own burrow. Sometimes the baby's movements in utero would feel like gas bubbles, little pops, and then sometimes the entire baby would roll dramatically, like a small log in water in a quick spin, which would cause her to startle as though she'd quickly sped over a small hill in a car.

In her semi-sleep, Maisie cups her baby's bottom with her hand and curls around it as though it is a heating pad. *Is the baby sleeping? Is it a boy? A girl? It is curled in a nest.*

"I'll tear those vines off," says Neil, murmuring into his pillow.

Neil has pulled her close. Maisie sinks into her husband and back into sleep. The sheets are delightfully warm, so nice to have flannel back again now that it was getting colder, and who is this little baby boy next to her, its little bottom curved like a puzzle piece against her stomach? She refers to it as a *he* in her mind, but it is . . . Esme! Her newborn daughter! Her baby, here, with her white velveteen kimono top, her baby, who had been looking up at her earlier in the midst of thick nighttime, channeling mysticism with milk dribbled out of the corner of her mouth. Now here she is, her cotton waffle knit blanket swaddled around her, her small hand mushed up against her cheek, the lint getting gunky in the tiny webs between her fingers, her fingernails as small as baby lentils.

Porous sleep! All these childbearing years she had been unable to completely give herself over to the blackout sleep that she so enjoyed when she was younger. Even when no children wake her, she is up and down throughout the night, perhaps not getting out of bed, but almost always shifting and rising for a moment here and there, hearing her name called even when it hasn't been, often aware she's dreaming, often having vividly annoying dreams, such as the one having to do with the bank, the mortgage, and the kicked poodle. Becoming a mother—she'd had no idea!—she had crossed over into a new country where she was forever on call, forever at the ready, forever about to be interrupted or held up in another room. Other voices and other lives called her away from her own voice, her own sleep, and took her hand tightly as if to say, *Mine*.

But wasn't it all a part of herself? These children and these demands? Wasn't everything about life pieces of one's own self calling it back to itself? She had read something once in a book about dream interpretations where the dream researcher suggested adding the phrase "part of myself" after each noun when recounting a dream, or summarize the whole dream with "part of myself" tagged on: *The garden (part of myself) needed some water.*

Well, got to see, got to know, got to keep it together . . . Where are the kids? Did they go downstairs? Maybe they are in the tree (part of myself). Hopefully they are not in the car (part of myself). No, but we're on a beach and the water is so *sandy*—why is this crazy drop-off so deep? And now there are so many tiny clear jellyfish it's like we're swimming in clear Jell-O that someone's been pulsing in and out through their teeth. Everyone get on that red serving tray over there instead of a towel! Serve 'em up! Kids and more kids! Let's head to the kitchen! The small children jump into the toaster. She is about to turn it on. "We're ready!" they say, waving at her through the toaster's glass. "Press the button! Press the button!" There is a lilac bush, half underwater, in a rough, churning Atlantic. Is it a flood? Why is the tide so high? She grabs one of the lilacs that's trembling just above the surface. She takes one of the small flowers, the color of black raspberry ice cream. She squishes it between her fingers, grinds it between her finger pads, then smells it, grassy and sweet with the undertones of salt air. She wipes the squish under her earlobes, like perfume.

→>-◄-

It is fully light out when the bedroom door explodes open. "She forgot," says Xavier, smiling as he comes in.

Maisie looks at him. Had she been sleeping, and he woke her? It was hard to say.

"Tooth fairy," says Xavier. "Forgot my tooth. Forgot to leave money."

It is definitely morning. It is Saturday. Maisie glances at the clock—7:56. She was definitely asleep. It is a small miracle that Esme has slept in her bassinet for a full five hours. Maisie looks at the bassinet. There is no baby in it. The curve of light blue sheet, framed in the straw basket's arch, seems to be a mouth shouting, *Where's the baby?!* A surge of panic regroups and settles just as she sees that her infant is settled right next to her, sleeping like a puppy.

"Hmm," creaks Maisie. "Maybe you didn't look carefully."

"I looked," says Xavier, flaring his eyes at his mother with a grin that clarifies that he does not at all believe that an actual fairy slips money under his pillow. "Is that Esme? I thought she was your arm! Awww . . . don't you wish you could just curl up and be as small as her, Mom?" He looks at his baby sister, a small smile on his face like an adult's. "I mean, I'd like to curl up all little next to you."

Harriet clamors in, her blanket clutched in her hand, her hair all over the place. She smiles at her mother, and then gets serious as she looks at Xavier. "Did you get money or candy?" she asks. She dabs her blanket at her nostril as she looks at him, a habit from her babyhood.

"The tooth fairy didn't come," Xavier tells her, matter of fact.

Initially Harriet's face fills with fear, and then she scowls. "You didn't put your tooth in the right place, *Xavier*," she says, disgusted, pronouncing his name *Safer*. "You didn't—"

"Be nice," murmurs Neil from his pillow. His head is facing in the other direction.

Maisie clears her throat gently. "This happened to me once," she says. "This happened to me once when I was little. . . ."

"It did?" Harriet dabs the nub of her blanket at her cheek.

"It happened to me, too," Neil says, muffled.

It took Maisie a few years to discover the power of referring to her own childhood when reasoning with her children. The tool of *commiseration*. Now it was such a regular tool that six-year-old Harriet often, out of the blue, comes to her with questions about it, questions that are there for Harriet's own contextualizing: Harriet might come floating into the bathroom as Maisie's cleaning the sink. "When you were little, Mom, did you ever wish that *your* mom would just *get out of the way* so that you could look in the mirror and sneak some of her lip gloss on?" Or "When you were little, Mom, did you ever maybe wish that *you* could be a little pig?"

"She probably wasn't expecting your tooth to come out until tomorrow," says Maisie. "Or something."

Harriet is puzzled.

"I did kind of feel around the edge of the bed," says Xavier, for Harriet's benefit. "Like if she got stuck."

Harriet is horrified.

"What do you think she looks like, Mom?" asks Xavier, but directing it toward Harriet. "Does she fly around like a bee?"

Harriet is riveted. Her brother is brilliant, imagining fairies, trying to scoop them out of his bed. "I—I—I—" starts Harriet, too excited by the topic to get anything more out.

Again, Xavier helps out. "I think she's this big"—he pinches his fingers to the size of a silver dollar—"and she wears a little tutu. The one here, around here near the city, is probably a little city fairy. Or maybe the one here is kind of country, too." He shrugs. "Maybe there are two here. A city one and a suburb one." He shrugs at Harriet. "Maybe they go around together."

"Like me and Jada," whispers Harriet.

"I know what the problem was," says Maisie. "I was in your room last night. I was in Harriet's bed for a little while—*that's* why she didn't come."

"You weren't in my bed." Harriet smiles.

"You had a night terror."

"I didn't have a night terror," says Harriet.

"Yes, you did."

"No, I didn't," says Harriet.

"You did. You were—" Maisie stops herself when she sees Neil is shaking his head at her kindly, a reminder: *Let it go. Don't argue with a six-year-old.*

"I'm hungry," says Harriet. Then, after a pause, "Who's ready for breakfast?" she asks loudly. "Anyone ready for breakfast?" Her kindergarten experience has gone straight to her lexicon and playacting, pretending that she is her teacher Ms. Ward, a friendly, loud woman who uses a bullhorn to call the kids in from recess. Harriet moves around the house with a pointer stick: "When I call your name, get into the bath." Or "Does anyone see what I might be talking about? Anyone? Can anyone *guess* what might be different on this page? Anyone?"

Romeo wanders in, entering like they are all in a play and he is the final character to appear. He plunges his head toward Maisie's leg and then rests his head on it like a pillow.

Harriet nudges him aside. "I was here," she tells him. "I was here first."

"*I* was actually here first," says Xavier.

"No," says Harriet snippily, "I wa—"

"Easy, Harriet," says Neil, without opening his eyes.

"Maybe the tooth fairy is a regular person," says Xavier. "Mrs. Popp told us that Greek gods could be anyone."

The faces on the bed are interested, waiting for more.

Xavier continues. "People were really nice to strangers because they might have been a god, undercover."

Everyone is quiet.

"What undercover?" mumbles Romeo.

"Like a person who looks like a really poor person was actually a god like Zeus, just in disguise."

"Who Zeus?" asks Romeo, saying the name so it sounds like the all-familiar Seuss.

"He's the head god. Like every person you meet might actually be a god here to teach you something."

Quiet on the bed while everyone absorbs the general idea of people not being who one might think, and how one might treat people differently if one assumes everyone is here to secretly teach you something, if one assumes that everyone is smarter, kinder, and more powerful than one's self. What can be learned from every interaction? Everyone is a messenger. Everyone is a teacher in disguise.

"Ms. Vanessa," says Harriet, referring to her gym teacher, "told us *she's* the tooth fairy." More quiet thought, punctuated by small mewling noises from Esme, which cause Harriet and Xavier to smile.

"The ancient Greeks were clever," says Neil sleepily. "Be kind to everyone you meet because you never know who might actually be"—and he raises his sleepy head like a monster—"*Santa!*"

When Xavier was about six, he announced to Maisie and Neil in the kitchen that he knew Santa didn't bring all the presents. Harriet stood next to him, his attaché, all business, present as a witness. Neil said, "You think Mom and I get *all* that stuff under the tree?" Xavier thought about it for a second, then smiled as if to say, *Of course not!*

Maisie is pinned in her place by the kids all over the bed, holding down her covers like paperweights. "Get up, guys," Maisie tells them. "I can't get up until you get up."

"Look at Esme's head," says Xavier. Esme is sleeping, but the fontanelle on the top of her head is pulsating. Her baby hair on the top of her scalp flicks up and down with her heartbeat, as if she is doing it on purpose.

Romeo laughs. "Her hair moving."

Harriet giggles.

"That part of her head doesn't have the bone there yet," says Maisie. "It's, like, open still."

Maisie thinks of the skull itself, the stitched-looking lines in the bone where the skull fuses together eventually. "Suture lines," she says out loud, but no one answers her.

Out of nowhere she thinks of something her own mother had written down on an index card and that her father had left on their refrigerator for probably ten years, until they moved. It was from *Romeo and Juliet*, and Maisie had read it so many times, in her mother's boyish script in navy felt tip, that it was almost like a mantra since she would say it by heart in her head as she walked, as she sat on the toilet, as she waited for things, as she fell asleep. Like many things said over and over, it was comforting on a level of rhythm, on a level of familiarity similar to liking a certain room, or closet, simply because you know it and it is familiar, though the actual contents, and in this case the actual sense of the words, seemed to kind of elude her:

The earth, that's nature's mother, is her tomb,
What is her burying grave, that is her womb.

Maisie imagines the delicate suture lines along Esme's tiny skull knitted together in quadrants of a cross, and then Esme as a curl-up of a tender skeleton inside of Maisie's womb, while meanwhile there are wildflowers, all across fields, all over the world, and there are forests with towering evergreen trees dropping pine cones and seeds into the earth, all of it dying, all of it turning to dirt, and the tunnels of animals, their nests and dens, buried deep in the ground like the dead. Living and dying were one mother, her inside and her outside, her physical and her spiritual, her night and her day.

Day by day she was seeing herself in the things letting go, dropping seeds, and the regeneration that was sure to follow. Day by day she was seeing herself along the edges of things, the perimeters, looking onto a world at a remove. The body was everywhere. It kept going, and going, and going.

Neil talks again without opening his eyes. "Should we go pick apples today? Maybe get a pumpkin?" Maisie imagines pumpkins and apples as heads and skulls of varying size, beheaded all over the ground. She looked at her kids; all were dropped fruits from her tree.

There are ripples of agreement among them.

"Remember last year," says Xavier, "the guy doing the branches thing?"

"What branches thing?" Maisie asks.

"Grafting," Neil says. "I remember."

"Remember, Mom? He had pictures and stuff—he was splicing the branches together. The little stump looked like it had horns coming out of it."

The man was demonstrating grafting in apple trees. A scion of one plant is stuck into the stock of another. Maisie remembers how the man kept saying the words *wound* and *healing* and *cut* and *growth,* and with words like *absorb, accept, blossom, adapt, bloom, fruit, join,* and *union,* the man sounded at first to Maisie like he was talking about marriage, then about having a baby, then, finally, like he was giving a life lesson on a person's interior life, and how emotional healing and acceptance will lead to fruitful expression. *Only attention, acceptance, and growth can bring about this unprecedented union.*

"To form a more perfect union!" Xavier exclaimed as they walked away after hearing the word *union* over and over.

"I forgot about that," says Maisie. She looks at Esme, then at Xavier. She thinks of a tree and its fused branches, and the nutrients it draws from the soil, tincturing every cell. In growth, nothing can ever be undone. The same was true in a body, and a mind.

Xavier says, "We can show Esme all around the place. She's never been to that orchard."

"No, she hasn't," says Maisie. She looks at Esme's squished face, her throbbing soft spot at the top of her skull, her minuscule mouth. She thinks of bringing Harriet or Romeo to the mall for the first time after they were born, the invisible stink of human consumption somehow sullying their tiny nervous systems. "Maybe she's too little still," says Maisie, but then she thinks of the fresh air, apples, grass, and trees, the wholesome outdoors on a fall day. Her mind goes further to think of wholesome and natural and deadly viruses and bacteria, looking wholesomely for easy, hospitable hosts. Yes, throughout time, infants have been out and about in orchards in the fall. Throughout time, infants have fallen ill and died. She thinks also of her own healing, her postpartum bleeding, the *lochia* that smelled like metal and pennies. She wasn't bleeding much anymore, but . . . "It might be too soon," she says.

Neil answers her. "I'll take these guys; right, guys? We can bring stuff home for Mom and Esme. Pumpkins, doughnuts, apples, cider . . ."

Maisie's stomach rings with nerves as she wonders what the balance is in the checking account.

"I want Mom to come," says Harriet.

"Me too," says Romeo.

Harriet asks Maisie, "What story are we on now, Mumma?" It was another influence from school. Harriet had come home after story time at the start of the school year with words from a visiting story time reader: "Everything is a story if you make it one," the visitor had told them, which Maisie had read in a school newsletter about the event. Now, just as everything in the house was having babies, and Harriet customarily parroted her teacher with her rhetorical questions, Harriet would also often ask, as Maisie imagined the visiting storyteller must have, or how Harriet's teacher maybe asks on the regular: "Now what story is this?" or "Is this a story?" or "What story are we on?" as though they had discovered a surfboard, or a train, and had gotten on it to slide along in a narrative that someone else (usually Maisie) needed to identify.

"You tell me what the story is, Harriet. But first you have to get up so I can get up."

Harriet doesn't move from her spot. She looks at Esme. "I think it's a tiny baby story," she says. She pauses. "And maybe something about what fairies eat."

→━◄━

The yellowed light of autumn comes dappled through the window, through the thinning glassy leaves that dangle like earrings. The light falls in small piles, spherical, blurred, pieced in bright patches here and there of concentric circles all over the wood floor, jittering from the wind in a way that could be no other season than fall. In spring, the sun comes into the living room like a pastel painting, dewy and new. In the winter, it is rose orange against the walls during a four-fifteen sunset. In the summer, it's cushioned like moss by the thick greenery outside. This October morning light, the jiggling shadows of the leaves on the floor, is enough to remind Maisie, for the time being, that there are other things—light and autumn, for one—besides money. But *money*, she thinks again, her stomach filling with shaky dread, *money, money, money*. The shadows of the leaves are suddenly shadows of bundles of bills, mocking her in their playful, pretty light.

Maisie parks the kids in front of the TV with cereal, then changes places with Neil in the shower. She puts Esme on the floor of the bathroom on a towel on the bath mat. When Maisie opens the shower curtain, the rattle of the rings causes the infant to startle, to dash her arms up quickly, turns her head to the side—the Moro reflex—like a Broadway jazz dancer, then looks like she's about to cry. Maisie says, "Shhh," and turns the water on, which is a bigger and steadier *shhhhh* that falls through the small room. The warmth of the steam is shrouded in the sound. Esme quiets, seems to fix her gaze on a spot on the ceiling just to the right of the light.

As Maisie steps into the shower, two dots of dark red blood fall out of her onto the porcelain. She pushes the splotches toward the drain with her foot, like foot painting, and their concentrated red-brown color blooms and then recedes in the trail of water that disappears down the drain. She stands still under the water, like a tree in the pouring rain, soaking in the luxuriousness of a warm shower. In the water's singing she hears her name. "Mom!" someone calls, but they are not calling. It is a figment sound, camouflaged in the sheer, steady volume of falling water, not unlike a figment limb, a by-product of hearing *Mom!* from downstairs, *Mom!* from across the park, just *Mom!* coming through the dark into her light sleep, coming from behind her at the store or across the driveway or through an open window. It is always, at any moment, as though one of her children might be calling her name.

There is a small, fogged-over window across from her. The bottom half of it is covered with frosted glass. Through the top half, from the shower, she can see the tops of trees, colorful and vibrant, orange and yellow like dress-up feathers, against a sky as blue as a forget-me-not, a sky so blue it seems to say, *Remember me?*

A speckled murmur of starlings, like gnats, descends on one of the yellow tree tips. Maisie watches the birds. She has a head rush and steadies herself against the wall tiles until she is clearheaded again.

If mothering a newborn was a combination of extended breadth versus the claustrophobia of being limited—so, too, was life, and so, too, was love. How can she touch all the things that she sees? How will she ever be able to trap anything, any moment or emotion, before it is gone into its slipstream, into the wind, the night, into the cool hollows of the heart where she may never find it again?

2

Farther away from the city and suburbia, in the maple-tipped reaches of farms and country, Neil coasts the minivan, an Odyssey, along dark, newly paved roads. The trees and their leaves are the color of school buses, the color of candy corn, persimmons and rosé, and the colors of all the apple varieties—the green Granny Smith, the yellow Golden, the ruby Red Delicious—their colors as sharp as pencil tips. The road, newly paved, curves through them like a racetrack.

"These roads are made for running," Neil says longingly. He grips the steering wheel and leans his body into a gradual turn. The leaves on the trees are the color of orange sherbet, lime sherbet, and butter.

"Romeo," says Maisie, "stop kicking my seat."

"I not kicking," he says. "Me just pushin'."

"Stop the pushing," she says.

Romeo pushes the back of Maisie's seat again, three quick pushes.

"Stop it, Romeo," Maisie tells him. She can hear the annoyance in her own voice.

"Why do people always say things are pretty all the time?" asks Harriet.

"Why you mad, Mom?" asks Romeo.

When no one answers her question, Harriet asks it again. "Why are people always saying, 'Oh, that's so pretty'?"

Romeo asks again, "Why you mad, Mom?"

When Maisie doesn't answer, Harriet echoes him. "Yeah, Mom," she says, "why you always mad?"

"I'm just tired," says Maisie, making an effort to soften some angry edges on her words.

Xavier announces to everyone, "Sometimes in the day it's like I'm asleep because I'm like thinking of something else."

"We call it 'daydreaming,'" says Maisie.

Harriet's right there, alert and on topic. "I was just picturing drawing an apple," she says. "Is it just a circle? Is it like a heart? I don't know how to do it."

Maisie thinks about the outlines of things. Where do the edges end? She'd read once about how chaos lives along every edge. If one were to zoom in on any edge with a giant microscope—the edge of a table, the edge of the earth along a coastline, the edge of a person's body along their skin, the edge of a wall—nothing fixed is actually staying still.

They are far enough into the countryside that the radio station starts to lose reception. As Neil turns it off, he accidentally turns the volume up. The sound of static fills the car—*krschhhhhhhhh*—before it's turned off.

"That sound . . . ," says Xavier. "That's what bubbly water feels like in my mouth."

"Now what story are we on?" asks Harriet, as though a story is a magic carpet ride. No one answers. "What story are we on now?"

Xavier chuckles. "We're driving to the orchard to pick apples."

Harriet doesn't listen to him. "Let's pretend," she says. "Let's pretend we're in a book."

Maisie thinks of *The Burrow Book* as she looks at the fields and trees as they drive. "I'm thinking of *The Burrow Book*," says Maisie. Instead of the banks, entrances, tunnels, and nests, Maisie thinks of the roots of the grass stalks and the roots of the trees, and how they are all their inverse underground. Their roots extend like tunnels and burrows, upside-down lightning bolts, or veins. Their vascular systems draw nutrients from their roots. If the burrows are like roots, simply because they look like roots, to what system are they supplying nutrients? Maisie feels the coziness of cuddling in bed. It is a nutrient beyond any nutrient that is written down.

Xavier muses out the window. "Have you ever thought about how a door looks like a book? Like you open the door like you open a book?"

"That's not the game," says Harriet. "Tell a story."

"You tell a story, Romeo," says Xavier.

Romeo grins. "Hmmm. What story do I like to tell?" He kicks the back of Maisie's seat a couple of times as he thinks about it. "A space cat . . . can't find his mom. He was mean to his sister and got put in a tower."

Harriet is impatient. "That's *Prince Bertram the Bad*," she says. "We know then a witch came flying past him and he spat a pea through a straw at her and she said she'd never help him again."

"Prince Bertram wasn't a space cat," Xavier says.

"Can I go?" asks Harriet.

Xavier says, "Go, Harriet."

She huffs. "There was a tower full of trees. It was spooky but you could walk around. Birds flew all around it, and they saw there was a little girl inside. There was lightning. She flew away because she could fly."

Harriet is quiet.

Xavier asks, "The girl? Where did she fly to?"

"She couldn't get back into the tower because the window was covered up."

"Is that the end?" asks Xavier.

"You go, Xavier," says Harriet. "You talk."

"I'm not in the mood," he says.

Harriet erupts into hysterical laughter behind them. Romeo joins her. Xavier starts laughing, too. "Look at the baby!"

"What is it?" says Maisie, a little bit worried.

Neil smiles into the rearview mirror at the laughter. Maisie turns around and can see Esme's reflection in the baby mirror across from her rear-facing infant car seat. Her little light blue pointy infant hat has slipped over her eyes and nose so only her miniature mouth is visible. Her tiny head, however, is slowly moving side to side, just as she might be looking around ordinarily, only her face is mostly covered. It is as if she is making the joke and is aware of it, as if she's pretending that she doesn't seem to notice that her hat is covering most of her face.

"That baby!" laughs Romeo.

Xavier is laughing. "Look at her, Mom!"

"I see," Maisie says, smiling and correcting the hat. When she lifts it off Esme's eyes, the baby's face starts to worry. Maisie plugs the pacifier into her mouth, and Esme's quick sucking makes the pacifier's knob quiver as her infant face relaxes. Her tiny eyes roll back in her head and close, which causes Maisie to momentarily feel the same way.

Maisie faces forward and leans her head against the window. The countryside encapsulates the minivan as they drive, and the minivan encapsulates them. Outside, the dazzling blue sky is cupped over everything. The red, orange, and yellow leaves on the trees are so vibrant that each tree looks to be vying for attention. Then, a large field, which folds into creases of countryside. The tall grass out there. They pause in traffic long enough for her to watch the grass tips wave uproariously in the wind—*Hello! The body is everywhere.* All of life calls to life, *Come back to the world.*

"Uh-oh," Neil says. They are fairly near the orchard when Maisie opens her eyes. There are houses now, tidily painted farmhouses with pumpkins and cornstalks on their porches. Cars ahead of them that are stopped. Someone has gotten out of the car ahead of them and left the door open.

"What?" asks Maisie. "What happened?"

"What happened?" the small voices ask. "What happening, Mumma?" asks Romeo.

After a moment, Neil gets out and jogs ahead. He disappears amid the cars for a few moments. Maisie turns to the faces in the back. The three of them are looking at her, *Are we scared?*

"So," she says. "Are we going to get lots of apples today? Get a couple of pumpkins?"

Romeo smiles with excitement at his mother, forgetting the concern ahead.

Harriet is wincing like she's about to be forced to eat a food that she hates. Guacamole, for instance. "Where'd Dad go?"

Xavier cranes his neck, trying to see ahead. The beginning of a disaster movie comes to Maisie's mind, as though suddenly everything is different and they are trying to flee a disaster, the traffic jam, people honking, then fighting.

"Look at me, Xavier," Maisie tells him. "Don't look up ahead. It might be fine, but it might be an accident." Her stomach feels as if someone just punched her. She imagines an accident, the real worry that a person has been hit. What if it is a child? The surge of emotion in her body causes her milk to drop. She gets out of her seat quickly and crawls into the back to shove her nipple into Esme's mouth. She wedges herself awkwardly next to the baby's car seat, lifts up her shirt, and simultaneously unplucks Esme's pacifier. She crams her nipple into Esme's mouth and her milk is met with exactly what it was looking for—the commanding suck—as her milk comes coursing out. The kids laugh when they hear Esme making little hollow glug sounds in her throat as she swallows rapidly.

"She sound like frog!" laughs Romeo. *"Urrgg Urrgg!"*

"Well, let's talk about Halloween," Maisie says.

"Me and Layla want to be a horse," says Harriet. "Me at the head, and she'd be the butt."

"I did that one year with Uncle Miles when we were little," says Maisie.

"You knew him when you little?" asks Romeo, smiling.

Xavier guffaws from the back seat. "Romeo, Uncle Miles is Mom's *brother.*"

"Uncle Miles is my brother," repeats Maisie, "just like you're Harriet's brother."

Harriet talks to him. "Romeo, what are you going to be?"

Romeo looks out the window to think about it. "Fireman robot," he says.

Everyone chuckles.

"Mom," says Harriet, "Dad says robot like ro-*butt.*"

"Does he?"

Neil slams the door. "It's a deer," he says. "A car hit a deer. Everyone's okay."

"A deer, Dad? Is the deer okay?"

"Dad," says Harriet. "Say *robot.*"

"The deer is not okay," says Neil.

Maisie watches Xavier's face change from excitement to disappointment, as if a wand was waved over his head to pull the new expression to his face.

"It's okay," Maisie says automatically, trying to comfort him.

"Not for the deer, Mom." Xavier frowns.

"Say *robot,* Dad," says Harriet.

"Robutt," he says, starting the car.

"See?" says Harriet.

"Robutt!" laughs Romeo.

"Also," continues Harriet, "when Dad has an itch in his ear? He uses his car key to itch it."

Maisie chuckles. She looks at Neil. "Did you hear that?"

"Robutt," Neil repeats, rolling the *R* with Spaniard flair.

A policeman is parked in the middle of the road. The patrol car's siren lights spin without the sound. He waves at Neil to move forward.

The deer is large, without antlers, and it looks as if it is on its knees, bowing. Its positioning makes Maisie think of a kangaroo, or a woman in labor, frozen as she waits for the pain to pass. She can see its large eye, like a skin of water on black stone. Maisie thinks of an inkwell and, for a second, imagines dipping a sharp quill into it, and the blackness that would spill out of it like yolk from an egg.

An older, tan minivan is stopped. Clearly, the minivan hit it. The woman behind the steering wheel has her head in her hands. There's a minor dent in her front hood. Through their partially opened windows, Maisie can make out profiles of children. One big sister or cousin has her arms around a littler one. Maisie sees the brief red glint of a candy apple getting hit by sunlight as they pass.

"It's a family," says Xavier.

"Just like us," says Maisie, looking over at the tan minivan. She sees the shaded movement of a ponytail, beads in hair, and a baseball hat, in the last row of seats.

"But there are more of them," says Xavier. "Over there, Mom." On the side of the road, at a slight distance in a clearing at the edge of the woods, there is a phalanx of deer standing so still that they look like lawn statues. Maisie can see antlers, white tails, long legs, smaller deer, and then her family is driving on, weaving through this county farm town toward the orchard that they visit every year. She thinks of the woman driving the car, of how frightened she must have been, how oddly she must feel to have killed such a large, living thing. She thinks of a family in a car, in a van, anywhere in the world, just like them, in a war-torn country getting blown to bits, or approaching a border that they won't be able to cross. Those were real problems, she tells herself. Terminal illnesses, tidal waves, authoritarian governments and oppressive regimes, being separated at borders, famine, diseases with no vaccine that kill children, if Neil were just home from war, his mind all rearranged with PTSD, if *she* were just home from war with PTSD, if Harriet had a congenital heart issue, if Maisie had uterine cancer, or if they were addicts, unable to stop. She recently read an article about a mother who left her twins in the back seat of her car thinking she'd dropped them at daycare, and went on with her day at work *at a hospital* only to emerge into the hot summer parking lot and the immediate nightmare that she would never wake up from.

Money was only money. A thing that stood for a certain kind of value. What was *value?* Love was the valuable thing, obviously. Her mind tells itself all of this, for perspective, and then, like a long needly pole for a pole vault, it comes bouncing back up at her face: if she is a grown-up, and she knows she is viewed as one, and if she has all these kids, which she surely does, it is her job, above everything else, to care for them so that they are safe and secure, not to be racking up debt and magically thinking she'll be making more money one day. How, as a grown-up, could she have let whatever wealth they had had to suddenly, like a slot machine when the handle gets pulled, clear itself back to almost nothing, almost zero, all because of what markets—global markets, housing markets—were doing? It was maybe as abstract as love.

Neil doesn't love his job, and, truth of the matter is, she didn't love her job either when she was working all the time. As Neil's mother says, *That's why work is called work,* and then she'd exhale her secret cigarette that she was furtively smoking near an open door or a cracked window, blowing the stream of smoke into the fresh air, *and that's why you need to find a job that makes your days feel good.*

Maisie and Neil had been lying in bed a couple of weeks ago, pre–Esme birth. The rain was lashing the house. The rain beat along the window, not soothingly, but more like an obnoxious child who wouldn't stop. Maisie couldn't see Neil in the dark, but she imagined his head shaking back and forth. "I'm a person whose job is helping people find jobs, but I need a better job."

"You work for doctors," said Maisie. "Helping them help people."

He sighed.

Maisie was deep under the covers, feeling like a child. She knew that she should also look for a job. She knew it would be mature of her to reaffirm Neil with upbeat words about how capable he is and how grateful she was for him. Instead, she slunk deeper under the covers, moved closer to him, and put her arms around his waist. She pressed her nose into the back of his neck and closed her eyes, the whole of him feeling, against her, like the softness of a pussy willow, like the smooth strength of an enormous, dignified chestnut. She wasn't good at coming up with the thing to say. She was never very good with words. Even now, here in the minivan with him right here beside her, she still doesn't know what she would have said, or could have said, or should have said. She puts her hand on his thigh and squeezes it. He smiles without looking away from the road ahead.

"Will that policeman shoot the deer?" asks Xavier. "Or will they just wait for it to die?"

"Shoot it?" Harriet sounds like she's about to cry.

"They shoot it, Harriet, so it won't suffer," Xavier explains.

"They might, Xavier," Neil tells him. "It would be the nice thing to do, wouldn't it?"

"The nice thing to do would be to save it. Her, Dad. Save *her* because it is a her."

The car is quiet.

"It looked really hurt," says Xavier, turning to the window.

Cars fly by like spaceships in the opposite lane.

"So they'll shoot it."

+>-+-

Shoot it. Maisie had seen them shoot deer when she was little. Her brother, Miles, held her hand. He'd steered her head away from it, as if he was aware that it was something that would rip into Maisie's ears and then rip through Maisie's mind, and then keep on ripping. She could feel Miles's fingers wriggle through his mittens as he gently guided her shoulders to hide her face in their father's swishy-sounding winter parka. There was the clean sound, slick into the head, and then the large animal crumpled. The sound of the shot kept going, like pain, echoing back from different corners of the woods simultaneously, mathematically. Maisie remembers thinking that if her mother were still alive, she wouldn't have let Maisie see the deer get shot. She remembers that the sounds of the echoes of gunshot were sharp, like shafts of heavy blackness, the opposite of search lights, crisscrossing each other.

→►◄←

A deadpan panic fills her, lifts her, as she watches the playful autumn leaves swish their colors above the minivan like pennants over competing swimmers. All around her is uplift; all around her is foreboding. Something terrible is happening to someone somewhere; something magnificent is happening to someone somewhere. It happens all at once: a falling from a great height, a rising from the wet ground, two winds from opposite ends colliding, then hovering for a moment, like starlings taking flight together in a lift, then a dip, then a soaring away.

Maisie takes a few slow breaths, thinks of what's ahead. The orchard. The pretty orchard with the rows of trees like people throughout history, statues of ancestors, of forefathers and foremothers, with their witchy-tipped fingers and open arms in tangled poses, all of them looking uphill, looking downhill, their roots digging as deep as their branches grow high. "Nothing prettier than an apple orchard," her father once said. Did he say that? The pretty orchard with all the different kinds of apples. Maisie likes the Macouns best. They have a dusty blue film on them, the same that is found on black plums, that when shined up against a sweater, vanishes, so that the apple is as perfect as Snow White's.

She thinks of the bees at the orchard that go haywire around the cider mill. They land on hands and faces. One year when

Xavier was small, he got stung. He went to pick up a little pumpkin on the ground, and a bee was on the handle. He'd cried, and then cried more because he was crying in a place where strangers were watching him. Neil picked him up.

"It's okay. Now you've been stung by a bee!" Neil kissed his teary cheek. "What a big boy!"

Maisie watched sidelong, maternally eagle-eyed, for any sign of an allergic reaction.

Neil pinched out the stinger. "See? It's out."

They all looked at it, the bee's left-behind body still stuck to the stinger.

Harriet, a toddler then, looked at it closely. "It look like booger," she said.

Xavier started crying again. "I didn't mean to kill the bee." His voice grew uneven with shortened breaths. "I only like to pick up the pum-pumpkin!"

＋＞＜＋

The Odyssey glides past a general store where they've gotten sandwiches before. They pass a newly painted, white clapboard church.

"Well, at least no one was hurt," says Maisie to everyone, falling back into herself, "as far as we know."

Xavier calls up to the front. "I never get that. *As far as we know* . . . As far to where? As far as what?"

"Does 'As far as I can *see*' make sense, Xavier?" Neil looks back at him in the rearview mirror.

"Yeah."

"It's the same thing," Neil tells him.

Maisie closes her eyes for a second. *As far as I can see* and she is on her bike, riding down the hill near Nana's house in the fog, riding down the hill, into the fog. To her right is the ocean, the tiny town harbor in the shape of a dog's tongue, but she can't see it because of the fog. The mist is catching on her eyebrows and eyelashes. Nana's small house whizzes past, hidden in fog but looking like Nana, roses and sweet peas knitted along her fence.

When Xavier first rode a bike, he was disbelieving of himself, even as he pedaled along, stable but squiggly. "Am I doing it? I'm not riding . . . Am I riding?"

Maisie's stomach jumps the way it would on her bike, over the swell of the bump at the bottom of the hill, Nana's house, and she imagines that she's riding through a cloud and a descent and a landing that she can't see. She thinks of her nana, and her mother, and her father: Where do the dead go?

"When I was your age," Maisie starts, "I—"

"Whose age?" asks Harriet. "My age?"

"Umm. Probably yours. Nana was driving, and it was really foggy. We hit someone's dog."

"We know," says Harriet.

"Yeah, Mom," says Xavier. "You tell us that like every single day."

"I do?"

Xavier calls from the back, "And then Nana cried in the car. It's one of the only times you've ever seen Nana cry. That time, and the Christmas after your dad died. Both times, you were scared."

Neil reaches over to pat Maisie's leg. "Gee, honey." He smirks, squeezing. "They know all your stories."

"Captive audience," says Maisie.

Neil speaks up from the front seat. "I was in a car once that hit a horse."

There's a skirmish of reactions: "A horse!" "Where?"

"I never heard this," says Maisie.

"I was in a taxi in New York City. It was dark. On Central Park South and the cab hit a horse."

Maybe she had heard this. "One of the buggy horses?" asks Maisie.

Interested voices from the back: "Did it die?" "Was someone riding the horse?"

"It was one of the carriage horses. It was tied up, so it was partly in the street. It was dark. I thought we hit a fire hydrant."

"Was it a big horse, Dad?"

"Who's *we*?"

"A horse, Dad!"

"I can't remember who I was with," he says. "The horse was okay. The owner was very mad. I got out and walked. Maybe I was alone."

"There's a horse right there!" shouts Harriet, and they all turn to see an array of horses in a beige field as the car races past.

"Aww," says Harriet, disappointed, "there were so many that I didn't see one."

"We can slow down on the way home," Maisie tells her.

"Or maybe even stop," says Neil.

The fields and the colorful trees are like calico prairie dresses, dappled and flouncy. Maisie cracks her window open, and the fresh air smells earthy, like old leaves, sunshine, and turned dirt.

As they pull into the apple orchard, Maisie orients herself.

Each year, the place is the same but her orientation feels different. The parking lot might seem smaller, or bigger, than she remembers. The barn is maybe smaller, or bigger, as well. This time, nothing surprises Maisie. The grass and dirt parking area are on a sloping hill, just as she remembers. The line of apple trees to her right looks, as it always did to her, like a line of people, holding hands, with their backs to the cars, all looking inward toward the orchard's rows. This year, though, the line of trees has the aspect of not just back-turned people, but as though the back-turned people have formed a fence, and they are both admiring and hiding something in the interior, as though the large orchard itself is in a contained pen.

The other night she came around the corner of the small TV room to turn off the TV, and on the screen was a sea lion, somewhere on the rocks of a beach in California, starting to birth a calf. She kept raising her long neck into the air, even moaning, and then out slithered a calf, covered in afterbirth. Maisie went to get Esme, who was starting to stir in a little basket on the floor, and by the time she'd changed her and settled back down on the couch in the dark TV room to nurse Esme, the show had moved on to another set of animals.

A lioness was in a rehabilitation area that looked like the savanna. Three adorable cubs romped all around her as she lay on her side, relaxed, tipped over in the sun. One of the cubs nuzzled into her belly to feed, just as Esme was nursing from Maisie in the dark TV room. The cub siblings playfully wrestled all over their lioness mother as she calmly nosed them off her head. She gave one of them a lick on the butt that lifted it off the ground. She stood up, and her babies tumbled off her like stuffed animals.

The camera followed her as she walked toward a high fence of fine wire netting. The cubs stayed near her, underfoot, swatted at her tail, and nibbled playfully at her legs as she moved. Unfazed, she stood, dignified, staring beyond the mesh of the fencing.

The camera lingered on her composed, gorgeous face. The narrator stopped talking. The wind blew across her lion ears, fuzzing her lion coat, and, out of sight, the cubs made little cat sounds as they played. Maisie came late to the program, so she had missed the reason for their containment, but she did not miss the look on the lioness's face as the lioness looked out at the world that she'd been removed from, as she looked out at the wildness within her.

For a moment, Maisie imagines the lioness inside the apple orchard, somewhere in its center. For a moment, the apple trees, orderly and lined up like the posts to a fence, seem to be the edges to a space containing a mystery, something wild and dignified. For a moment, she isn't sure whether the boundary is keeping something out, or keeping something in. She has the feeling that she is missing something, that she just had a momentary grasp of something important that so fleetingly left her that she can't trap it back—what was she not seeing? What was she not feeling? What was being kept in? What was being kept out?

"There was a lion on TV the other night," she says.

"It's not as bad as I thought," says Neil, pulling into a parking spot. "I thought it would be a mob scene."

"The tables are different," says Xavier.

The long tables with doughnuts and maple syrup are arranged differently, in a large U shape, with pumpkins scattered around the tables. There are larger pumpkins, hay bales, and cornstalks that prevent the cars from leaving the designated parking area. The barn is the same red. When she opens the car door, Maisie can smell the cider from the cider mill.

Maisie slides the side door open to get the kids. Harriet, in her booster seat, is there, glaring at Maisie like a girl in a horror movie. Her hair is parted strangely in the center, neatly and severe. Her expression is somewhat hollow; her lips are tight. "I don't want to get hit like that deer," she says.

A momentary lump rises and then falls in Maisie's throat. "Oh, honey," she says, unbuckling Harriet's seat belt. "We'll be very careful."

→-◄-

Green hills swell to the left, to the right, and bump along lumpily into the distance. The orchard's hill is studded with swooping lines of variously sized apple trees that march along the rolling pastures like weary soldiers. Farther away, distant hills puff their chests toward the blue sky. In faraway clearings on the hills, amid tidy green fields and the burnished reds and yellows of clumped trees, there are occasional brick mansions, miniature horsey-looking castles, estates as composed as fox hunts and leather saddles, that look as though they've been tacked into the rolling hills with a pushpin.

Talk about money, thinks Maisie, as a wind of affluence comes wafting over her from the landscape, as thick as the smell of the cider, lifting her hair.

Romeo stands next to the car, taking in the view as well. He sees the mansions, dotted about like castles in a fairy tale on the opposite hills. "Are those museums, Mumma?"

"Not quite, honey." Maisie glances sidelong at Neil. "You think those people commute to the city from here?"

"On their personal helicopter," he says, possibly joking. He flips open the stroller rack that Esme's car seat latches onto.

"Geez." Maisie sighs, thinking of bills, thinking of their 401(k): it has been more than halved, like someone just randomly decided to rearrange the numbers of the balance, for the fun of it.

Neil is likely thinking a similar thought because he says, "Don't go thinking that those people don't have money problems right now." He starts talking to Esme, face-to-face, in a baby voice. "Bigger money, bigger problems," he says, as he places her car seat on the stroller. He clicks it into place. Esme's face startles at the bobble and the noise.

The sunlight is warm, but the air is crisp, like biting an apple. Romeo continues to stare at the distant hills across the valley, the regal view of the manicured corrals, the toylike appearance of the trees and miniature barns. He settles his feet together and then raises his small hand to his forehead to salute the countryside, the bright blue sky, the American autumn blazing so precisely before him like a folk art painting.

"Look," says Xavier.

Two dark horses, small in the distance, like the tips of gloved fingers, are galloping steadily across one of the faraway green fields. They watch the pair disappear over the hump of a hill.

"Cool," says Xavier.

Harriet points to some plants. "This is . . . Wait. What do we call this, again?"

"Milkweed," says Neil.

Harriet quickly gets busy, hurrying toward the nearby stacks of baskets lined with clear plastic bags. "Everyone gets their own basket," she says excitedly, toppling some over. "Since it's my *birthday*."

"Okay," says Maisie.

It is not Harriet's birthday, and they all don't need their own basket. Maisie and Neil smile at each other. Harriet struggles to reach the baskets at the top of a stack. Her voice starts to grow more frantic.

"Since it's my *birthday*, we can do mostly what *I* want to do," she announces loudly, not looking at anyone. Romeo watches her with interest. She takes two, three, five baskets and quickly sets them down on the ground, spaced apart like for leapfrog.

Romeo approaches one and puts one of his feet in it.

"Romeo!" Harriet shoves him. "Get out!"

"Hey! We don't push!" says Maisie, but Harriet is lost in her chores, picking up all the baskets again, struggling to hold all of them at once.

Xavier approaches them with the hood of his sweatshirt up. "You think there's ever been a murder here?"

"Xavier," says Harriet, "you get your own basket."

"I don't want a basket," he says, hiding something.

"What are you carrying? What do you have?" Harriet scurries after him.

"Nothing . . ."

"What about me?" says Romeo. "Show me!"

Xavier opens up the palm of his hand. "Woolly woollies," he says.

In Xavier's palm, four woolly bear caterpillars are curled up into fuzzy circles. Romeo and Harriet are speechless. One of the caterpillars starts to stretch out, elongating its body with its furry copper-brown band and black stripes, its bristly fur-like coat like a bottle brush. Harriet inspects it closely.

"Wow," she whispers. Romeo looks up at his brother's face admiringly.

"Let's show Esme," says Xavier.

A woman walking by pauses to quietly tell Maisie, "There's a bee on your baby."

Esme is asleep, but a honeybee is indeed hovering near her ear. Harriet gasps. Maisie delicately shoos it. The bee zips up and down in a short longitudinal line next to Esme's head before it jets off in a long check mark toward the distant cider mill table. Did it sting the baby? Esme would have woken. Wouldn't she have woken? Maisie's chest is full of agitation and impatience. The bee would be dead if it had stung her, correct?

Xavier says this out loud, "If it stung her, it wouldn't just fly away."

Angry at the bee, Maisie watches it continue to fly like a lasso, a black speck in the distance that zags around the cider cartons, comingling with the other bees.

"They pollinate the orchard, Mom," says Xavier. "They're good guys."

Maisie takes out a wad of white mosquito netting from her diaper bag and stretches it over the infant car seat. The white netting is like a bridal veil, or a dismantled tutu. Maisie tucks it efficiently, tightly, around the seat's edges. Through the gauze screen of it, Esme looks as though she is in the tropics, a small queen protected from malaria.

"Here," says Xavier. He places the woolly bears on the netting, the reverse of the monarch butterfly setup in his classroom where the caterpillar transformative action is on the inside of the mesh. The caterpillars cling to the netting nicely.

"Good idea," says Maisie.

"I'll go get the map," Neil tells her, with a full smile that Maisie absorbs like an embrace.

The electricity of his smile wakes her up, grounds her feet to the earth, and dives playfully into the soil surrounding her. The zap in her abdomen, though, makes her feel crampy, and she wonders if the giant pad from the hospital that's wedged between her legs like a folded paper plate will be enough for today's bleeding. She smiles back at Neil, though he is walking away. Xavier follows him, and the tenderness in her son following her husband, and Esme's closed eyes when Maisie looks down at her, and the richly colored woolly bears, and Harriet, quiet now, and calm, her face with its eyelashes, its lips as she watches the fuzzy creatures on the white netting as they rear their small heads, as they wriggle along as animals do, like tiny living toys—all of it causes Maisie to swell up with something that wells up her throat, her eyes.

These postpartum surges of feeling, as sloping and as lifting as the surrounding, mounding hills, are completely nuts. She is at least familiar with them and knows that they go away. At least, for her, their topography is rounded and somewhat gentle, like the old hills surrounding her. In fact, her moods and emotions had become more like the topography of hills on a map, or like the rings in a tree trunk, starting in the center and moving out, the way everything grows, like rings that reach out around a pebble dropped in water. After she had Xavier, Maisie cried generously, without real sadness, but with deep feelings of tenderness for all that was around her, from the way the cabbie said to her, "Good luck, Mom," as she exited her first cab ride with Xavier, or her tears for the mother duck squawking madly and bravely at the passersby with her downy offspring behind her, to the way that the moon, as bright as a light bulb, came peeking around the edge of a skyscraper as if to ask carefully, "You okay?"

Her friend Joy told her that the tears were one way for her body to lose its extra water, and the feelings were obviously a way to bond with the baby, but also a way to bond with the world, now that the world was more important to keeping herself and her baby alive. "If you weren't in love with being alive before, your hormones are sure to make it so now," said Joy, "even if you find it heartbreaking." It was true that Maisie had felt a new relation with things around her after having a baby, as though she'd entered another dimension of being alive—was this true?—as though two-dimensional life didn't simply become three-dimensional, but it became strangely textured, touchable like velvet or suede, with folds and confusing buttons, surprising pockets. She felt a new yoking to nature and living, by having a child. It equalized everything, and everyone. Everyone was a mother, or a child, and in a world where she had always felt at a remove, she joined into the soup of living things, of making a living thing, and joining all the life that will die, by making something that will die.

Maisie fumbles for her sunglasses so that no one can see her crying.

"You crying?" asks Romeo, grinning. He wraps his arm around her leg as he looks up at her.

"Little bit," she says.

"Because you happy," he says, because she's explained it before.

She touches his head, and he hugs her leg so tightly that his arms and neck quiver.

An older woman in a windbreaker stops next to them. "Well, look at those little guys!" she says brightly to the woolly woollies, then to Romeo. "Do you know that they predict the winter?"

Romeo holds on to Maisie's leg. He shakes his head. Harriet moves closer. She looks at the woman skeptically.

"Oh," says Maisie, remembering, "something about the stripes?"

"If the brown band is wide, it'll be a mild winter," the woman tells them. "The more black there is, the colder the winter."

The three of them watch the caterpillars worm around. "What do you think?" asks the older woman. *She is probably a teacher,* thinks Maisie. She probably teaches preschool, or she's a retired teacher.

"They mostly brown," says Romeo.

"That one's almost all black," says Harriet.

The woman raises her eyebrows. "Maybe you need to find more today and see what they all say," she says as she moves along.

"That one dead," says Romeo. One of them is unmoving. Romeo touches it gently. It curls into a ball, like a cat, and slips from the netting.

"Nice," says Xavier as he approaches.

"It curled up and fell," says Romeo, summing it up.

"I'll find him," says Xavier, looking in the grass. He picks it up.

"Put your hand out," he tells his little brother.

Romeo puts his hand out. Xavier puts the curled-up woolly woolly in Romeo's hand. "Just keep your hand open and don't touch it, and it'll start crawling around," Xavier tells him.

"It's so fuzzy," says Maisie. "It looks like a button."

Romeo looks down at it in his hand, enchanted. "It look like fuzzy button," he says.

→>-<←

Maisie scans the place. There are many people. There are many trees. The trees are like people, and the people are like moving trees. There are many different types of winds that are blowing through the orchard to flutter the golden leaves, to bend the wheaten-colored grasses, to tousle the hair of the kids of the families, the mothers, and the fathers. The wind seems to say, *Breathe in! Wake up! It is good to be alive!*

Harriet is bobbing her head around, shaking her shoulders like she's dancing to music. She sees that her mother is watching her, so she points to a line of nearby sunflowers, their large yellow heads bobbing about like they're in a cartoon. The sunflowers are in a row, and the wind is causing them to move like tentative lanky dancers who haven't decided yet to let loose, tall women who peek out from behind one another.

"I'm dancing like they are," says Harriet, waving her head and shoulders.

Romeo sees what she means and smiles. He starts shaking his

head around like a rock drummer, overkill for one of the sun-flowers, but dancing his way.

Maisie can see Neil patiently waiting at the doughnut table. She is guessing that there were no more maps of the orchard and someone has gone to get more. They do not need a map, but kids always learn from maps. On the long wooden table underneath a white canvas tent, Maisie can see decorative corn-husks, maple syrup of varying amber to dark shades, and stick candy in mason jars, organized by color in blots of lemon yel-low, bright orange, apple green, and fire-engine red, all of them looking like coloring markers. She can imagine the red boxes of maple candy pressed into the shapes of maple leaves, acorns, and pumpkins, a candy that her mother loved and that Maisie, as a girl, would sneak pieces of even though she hated the taste, but she admired the packaging.

Small eruptions of conversations rise here and there in the same way that the sunlight falls in puddles on the ground that move with the wind. An older man's voice, passing, says kindly to someone, "It'll be okay, honey. We have all day."

Maisie watches her three kids, like bees to the cider, gravi-tate toward Neil. They touch their father like a home base, then move along to mill around the tables, investigating the dough-nuts and candy.

Maisie's stomach stirs—*money, money*—as she remembers an interaction last year with a woman behind the counter. The woman behind the cash register was striking, her face above the old wooden table, the apples in the bowl all looked to have been washed with the same wholesome rinse. On the table, bottles of maple syrup gleamed golden, miniature gourds—green, orange, yellow—looked as if they'd been shellacked, and cider doughnuts were dusted with powdered sugar. Maisie asked her, "So I pay you after we're done picking the apples, right?"

The woman nodded. Her smooth skin, clear eyes, and full mouth all possessed the familiarity that attractiveness and strength always possess.

Even though Maisie knew the answer, she asked her, "Do you take credit cards?"

"Cash or check only," the woman answered, her voice higher, softer, than Maisie had expected.

"Um," explained Maisie. "I thought I had a different checkbook with me. I have this *weird* one. Can I date the check for Tuesday? I just want to make sure there's enough in there."

The woman nodded, expressionless, but looked at Maisie more closely, presumably detecting Maisie's debt and money troubles in the same way that an X-ray detects a bone deformity. "You pay after you pick your apples," she said softly. "I will be here."

Around that same time Maisie had done the same thing, post-dated a check, to pay for Xavier's birthday party where she brought three of his friends canoeing along a canal. The canal water was black, and the leaves of the trees, the clouds in the sky, were reflected in it as clearly as a photograph. They paddled past little islands and mallard ducks in their monogamous pairs, their flipped upside-down reflections of themselves in the black water attached to them as they moved. Two herons flew overhead, their long legs tucked along their undersides.

"Like pteranodons!" exclaimed Xavier's friend Amir, pointing with his gleaming paddle.

Xavier glanced quickly at Maisie, making eye contact, full of delight.

Once, at the movie theater, her kids among other kids in the semi-dark during the previews, a preview for a Winnie the Pooh movie came on. Eeyore monotoned gloomily, "Someone has a cold"—then, his plain old sigh of defeat—"I'll probably get it," and Maisie saw Xavier snap his head toward her with a smirk, making sure that she heard.

→►◄←

Maisie sits down on a group of hay bales that are set up to serve as benches. Nearby are maps of signs and a key to the types of apples throughout the orchard. Not far from her is a sign with an illustration that explains grafting. First, there is a visual of three pictures, with minimal words. There are two sticks, branches, that look like a broken bone. The next picture is the two broken bones put together like a bone that has been set. The last picture is the bones (sticks) bandaged together. There is an illustration of a larger tree, with grafted branches, first with buds, then blooms, then fruit.

She thinks of a dream she once had where she came upon a tree that had different fruits all over it. Some of them she didn't even recognize or know their names. Some were small, like little stone fruits, shiny or fuzzy, bright pink, light orange, or citrus-skinned and yellow. Some were large, almost like a melon, but with jagged linings and circular trims, like dragon fruits, or snake-skinned looking like salaks. There were the medieval-looking ones, biblical, like pomegranates and figs. It was obvious how a life was like a tree. It was obvious how a person, a family, was like a tree, even all of humanity, but what Maisie had never thought about before was how looking at a tree, a life, considering a tree, a person, and other trees together, how they grow, how they die, was as much a part of the system of these trees as the trees themselves. *The body is everywhere, busily grafting.*

→►◄←

A man near her fusses over a little girl's shoe that the girl keeps kicking off. The little girl kicks at it, the man wrestles it on, then she kicks it off again.

"Stop it," he says calmly.

The girl giggles and kicks the shoe off again. It is a white sneaker with a pink pony on it. The pony's pink tail lights up as the man pushes it onto her foot. It lights up when it hits the ground.

Maisie looks him over. He is an older father. Is he maybe the grandfather?

"I don't want a shoe," the little girl tells him. Since the child is smiling, she is being playful. She has straw stuck to her pink sweater.

If she was sour-looking, perhaps then the man might lose his patience, as Maisie imagines she herself would. For a split second Maisie imagines gripping the small girl's leg. "Put on the *shoe,*" she might growl at her, gripping her little calf tightly, and the little girl would start to cry, and if she was another mother watching herself, she would think, *Easy, woman. Be kind.*

A few weeks ago there was a video on the local news that someone took of a mom in a parking lot somewhere wrestling her kids into the car. "Sit *down!*" the mom is yelling. She pins a little boy into his seat. His sister is crawling around the car, laughing, and the mom grabs her by the ankle to keep her from climbing into the front seat. The mom pulls her daughter by the foot, manhandles her around, and crams her into her booster seat. The girl unclips it. The mother holds her there. The boy climbs out of his seat. The mother grabs him, picks him up with her free hand, by his shirt, and pushes him back into his seat. The kids are both crying. The mom yells at them. On video, it looks terrible, but it also looks pretty ordinary. Ever since seeing the video she imagines that she's being spied on by a hidden camera—how crazy would she look? How ugly and mean? It is hard to remember, when one is an impatient mother, that a mother losing patience with a small child hardly ever looks sympathetic.

So, she imagines that she is being watched by children themselves. Which, in fact, she usually doesn't need to imagine since she almost always *is* being watched by children, she just needs to remember that they are *watching* and *listening,* which they are, all the time. They watch her from the other room, from the back of the car, through the crack in the doorway from the other room, from behind her butt, from her held hand, from the side of her bed, from the side of *their* bed, from the kitchen table, the couch in front of the TV, from their bed, from their bath, from their bike, their chair, their friend's front door, their school bus, their little backyard, their perch in the tree, their playing field, their sandbox, their dad's arms, everywhere.

She can remember sitting on her own mother's lap at dinnertime, facing out, watching her mother's hands cut the food, lift the glass, and Maisie would pretend that they were her own hands, that she was the grown-up, with the hand with the blue ring on it, placing a crumpled napkin in the middle of the plate when she finished with it. The crumpled napkin would slowly expand and grow.

Children watching. She thinks of a few weeks earlier, coming out of the grocery store into a blindingly hot day. Children were clustered around her. The parking lot was newly paved, black and sticky, aromatically hot with tar. She was engulfed in children. Esme was very large *inside* of her. Romeo was in the seat of the shopping cart, probably scanning the lot for the sight of a motorcycle. Harriet was sitting inside of the cart itself, nestled among the groceries, probably looking for the Popsicles that Maisie used as collateral in a no-whining-at-checkout-for-an-impulse-buy bargain, and Xavier and his friend Finn were walking nearby behind her, unattached from the shopping cart conglomerate, carrying a bag of potato chips that they'd opened, eating them one by one.

The grocery store was in a wealthy town. Almost inevitably, the moment Maisie drove over the town's border, an expensive car would be right on her butt, or a luxury Suburban would honk impatiently at her at a light, at a stop sign, or as she waited to merge. Pushing her kid crew through the lot, Maisie thought of how much, roughly, each parked car cost, and how much money was accumulated in a single row of the cars. One Lexus would pay off her credit card debt. Two more would pay off her mortgage. Another one would pay off loans.

Xavier came close to her and nudged her in the waist. "Mom," he said, looking ahead.

Near their minivan, there were two middle-aged women in the midst of an argument. Maisie paused the cart, as though near wild animals, wondering how to navigate her group around the disturbance to get them into the car.

Maisie could sense rabidity. One woman's expression was slick and mean. The other woman looked exasperated, her face fairly gentle, considering. She said, matter-of-factly, "Woman, if you talk like this to someone else, they might punch you in the face."

The slick woman's gold bracelets rattled in the air. She wore expensive workout gear and her body and face looked starved for something. Her giant shiny Suburban, like an army tank, was in park behind her, the driver's door ajar. It was blocking the gentler woman's way out of her spot. "I'll take my own *fucking* time to get out of your way!" yelled the woman, meanness all over her like grease. "We're in a parking lot and you *honk* at me?"

"I tapped my horn because you weren't moving," said the gentler woman. She looked at Maisie. It was clear that this was merely one time, of many, where this gentler woman had to contend with such a person. "I just want to get out of my parking spot."

"I'll show you how I tap *my* horn!" shrilled the other woman, and she climbed into her enormous car to press on the horn in loud, forceful blasts.

Maisie could feel the kids close to her. Xavier, with his friend Finn next to him, had taken her hand. Harriet was nestled up against Romeo, who had his head up against Maisie's belly, inches from Esme underneath her skin.

The slick woman slipped out of her car and looked Maisie up and down. "Who are you? The woman in the shoe?"

"I'd like to get these kids in that car," said Maisie.

"Is there a problem here?" asked a young man. He was an employee of the store wearing a reflective vest while he pushed a line of stacked shopping carts like a long caterpillar.

The slick woman looked at him sourly. She climbed back into her giant car and sped away abruptly.

The young man shrugged and continued with his carts.

"Geesh," said Maisie.

"You have no idea," the gentler woman said, shaking her head. "Story of my life right there." She shrugged and got into her car.

The kids were quiet. Maisie loaded up the back with the groceries while the AC got going and the kids got into their seats. When she got into the driver's seat, the car was whirring with the air-conditioning, and everyone, even Romeo, was buckled up. Maisie adjusted the fans so they weren't so loud.

"Was that lady poisonous?" asked Harriet.

"I think she was a witch," said Romeo, without any doubt.

Everyone laughed.

Xavier said, "Maybe she was tired. Maybe she had something really sad happen to her and that's why she was so mad."

His friend Finn said, "She shouldn't take it out on a stranger."

Maisie squirted the windshield with wiper fluid—there was a hard spot of white bird poop.

"That lady scared me," said Harriet.

"Me too," said Romeo.

"Me too," said Xavier.

Finn said, "Her lipstick looked like she drew it on with a marker."

"I feel bad for the other lady."

"Me too."

Maisie thought for a moment. There was nothing she needed to add.

She squirted the windshield again. The crusty guano was stubborn. The windshield wipers went back and forth, streaking the bird crap in white smears.

Earlier in the year, in late winter, in the same parking spot, Maisie had turned on the engine, the defrost, and the windshield wipers. It was pouring rain, cold rain that splattered down on waxy snowbanks, and the windows were fogged. The rain pelted against the roof, excitingly, soothingly. Only Romeo was behind her in his car seat, making mild sound effects of a fighter jet—*pershhh, pakoooo, ptew pew pew!*—as he slowly steered a toy fighter jet through the air in front of him.

When the foggy windshield cleared, Maisie could see a woman in the driver's seat of the car that was parked kitty-corner to hers. The woman was sobbing, great gulps of sobs, and kept collapsing her face into her hands. Her shoulders twitched as though she were trying to blow out many candles in her lap, and then she would come up from her hands, wiping her eyes with her sleeve. It was not a cathartic cry, like the crying of a woman who was releasing a lot of emotion, a lot of hormones, or built-up tension. It was not at all what one might call a "good cry."

Maisie thought of how a mother can do many things. The monster boss mother can make declaratives. *Drink the water,* she commands. *Get away from the edge,* she orders, on all sorts of figurative levels where "the edge" doesn't have to do with an actual cliff. The superwoman mother might be able to lift a car when a child is stuck underneath it, or collect her baby from a burning house, but there is nothing that the mother can do in the invisible world of a child's pain except for what the mother always does anyway: be there at the ready, on point and attentive, with care and compassion and a steady hand. Why can't a mother take a mother flame to a child's heartache to burn it up?

"Too much talking, Mumma," Xavier used to say to her when he was a toddler, as she tried to explain something to him, as she tried to correct.

It was true, thought Maisie. Words were overrated. But how was a mother to know that her child would retain what they needed and let go of the rest?

In middle school they studied the great blue whale. The largest mammal on earth relies on tiny shrimplike crustaceans, krill, as its main food source. To eat, a blue whale lunges through large swarms of krill with its giant mouth wide open. The whale's throat is pleated and expandable; it can take in a volume of water and prey that is greater than the whale's own body weight. The whale gulps in tons of water with the krill, then pushes the water back out through fringed brushes that act like a strainer called baleen plates. In class, the illustration of the baleen plates looked to Maisie like trees, spindly ones, all in a couple of rows on the edge of a woods. On her way home from school, walking along the dirt road with spindly trees all around her mixed in with the spruces, she imagined that she was walking alongside giant baleen plates. When she got older, she would remember walking home, alongside the baleen-like trees, and she would think how all of life is learning how to strain, like a sieve, for one's proper nourishment. How, as a mother, can she strain the proper things out for her children's nourishment? How could she teach them what to keep, and what to let go?

"Take what you need, and leave the rest," Nana had told her. "And that means for everything." The slogan was written on a piece of wood in Nana's bathroom, the words themselves looking like they were made to strain things.

Around that time, when she was in middle school, her brother, Miles, was reading *Death Be Not Proud*. Maisie would come across the book on the counter in the kitchen, the table in the hall, or in Miles's hands as he zipped it into his backpack. The title and the book's abstract cover made Miles look like he was carrying around a plane ticket, or some sort of pass, to a land of stoicism and maturity. When Maisie read the word on the cover—*Death*—she didn't think of horror, she thought of her mother, resting her head on a pillow, like the book was a pillow, and inside the word *death* was her mother looking peaceful, and all around that image of her mother on her bed—her quilt, the dog, her face, the bird—was always Maisie's wonder if she remembered the event like it really happened or not. Did it matter if her memory was different from what had actually occurred?

When Miles finished reading *Death Be Not Proud*, he turned to their father in the car. Maisie was in the back seat. She watched her brother's profile as he spoke to their dad.

"It's so weird when you finish a book," he said, "and you keep wondering how the people in it are doing. You, like, wonder where they are."

Their father nodded as he drove. Maisie watched from the back seat.

"They'll stay with you," their father said.

"Like a dead person," said Miles.

"Yes," said their dad.

Watching the woman sob, Maisie felt her own throat tightening. She thought of getting out of her car to knock on the woman's window. On the other hand, she felt like she should look away. The windshield wipers went back and forth, *Help her, Help her, Help her.* But what would help be?

"Less go, Mumma," said Romeo from behind, urging her on.

As Maisie put her car in reverse, she waited for a second to see if she could make eye contact with the woman.

"Mumma, let's go," said Romeo again, still playing with his airplane—*pshew pshew* . . .

The heat was on, the window was defrosted, and Maisie, in her capsule of a car, looking at the woman crying in the capsule of *her* car, thought of how this is what being a young mother was like: inside her own contained capsule, looking out at the world from her personal glassed-in car, sometimes noticing the world around her but unable to get out into the rain to really interact with it. Or maybe that was life in general, everyone in their own car, staying in their own lanes, only letting a few people in, looking ahead, anticipating trouble, keeping a safe distance, trying their best to expect the unexpected, trying not to die.

↦⤙

From her perch on the hay bale, the little girl again kicks off her light-up sneaker and it again falls to the ground. Maisie watches it fall gently into a nest of straw-like, matted grass. Its pink lights continue blinking even after it is still.

"Up to you." The older man shrugs. "Barefoot's okay. But be careful. You might step in dog doo," he tells her quietly. "Lots of dogs pooping all over the place." He looks at Maisie and smiles.

The little girl also looks at Maisie. Maisie nods. "Lots of dogs," she says quietly.

"I scared of dogs!" says the little girl, cowering.

"Can't win." The man shrugs again.

"No," laughs Maisie.

"It's a lot easier when they're your grandkids," he says, "and not your kids."

Maisie nods. "I bet." Though the idea is as abstract as becoming a mother was abstract, before it happened. She didn't know anything about it. She didn't know who these people, her children, were. She didn't even know what sort of a person she would become, and how could she have? How can anyone have any real idea of what will happen next? She doesn't know who she will be. She doesn't know that the decades, by the time she is a grandmother—if she is ever a grandmother—will have merged together like an accordion, and that they will expand like an accordion as well, with varied memories plaintively drawing out of the melancholic chords of merged time, the merged styles of the times, music of the times, and trends in clothing and colors and fads all background to her own strangely particular moments. She does not know that she will grow wiser, only by learning not to hide from pain and difficulty, and learning how to sit back, and listen. She doesn't know that even a decade later, she will still feel her milk drop when she thinks of her infants, when she hears a hungry baby cry.

She does know one thing, though, that she didn't used to know: that the special, close attention that she is learning to pay toward her children is actually toward her own heart, and her own universe. She is learning that the closer she gets to their small smells, their little humor and mischief and verve, the closer she is getting to an unfound mystery, hitting it from time to time like a vein of gold, a trickle-thin branch of a mother lode, vibrant and dazzling in dark rock.

"Do you think there's gold in this place?" asks Xavier.

Maisie is astonished. She looks at her son. "I was *just* thinking of gold."

"What were you thinking, Mom? That we could dig for gold here? That's what I was thinking, but I bet it's all just dirt."

"I don't really know what I was thinking . . . ," says Maisie. She can see Esme starting to move, slightly, in her infant seat, under the white netting.

Maisie hears an infant cry from the parking lot. It is not Esme, since Esme is sleeping right in front of her in her little stroller— but Maisie's milk drops just the same, her breasts rising.

Harriet jumps forward, singing, "We're a family, and we're a tree!" a favorite preschool anthem that inevitably made all the parents cry at the moving-up ceremony for the four-year-olds. Harriet sings it again, miming with the sign language for *family* (a circle in front of her) and *tree* (a triumphant right arm topped with a fist that pops up out of the "ground" represented by her left arm, horizontal like the earth).

"There are *Golden* apples," says Neil, "speaking of gold. And lots of *trees*, Harriet."

"Harriet," repeats Harriet, miming new actions: sweeping, and rocking, as she sings, "*Harriet clean, Harriet sweep, Harriet rock the child to sleep,*" from a Jacob Lawrence book that they read at bedtime sometimes, a poem about Harriet Tubman.

Maisie peeks in at Esme in her infant car seat, asleep under the white mosquito netting. When she sees her head start to move around, Maisie jiggles the handle of the stroller, jiggling her back to sleep.

About twenty feet away from her, Romeo inspects the parked hayride. It is empty. There is a flatbed, with wooden railing walls and hay bales for seating, hooked up to a tractor. Romeo stares at the large red tractor like it's an exotic animal that's been let loose and frozen, for him.

Maisie watches him stare at it, then tentatively walk closer to it. He looks over at her, then back at the enormous wheel. He touches it, looks back at her, and blushes.

Harriet hurries next to him. Maisie can hear her excited chatter. "Isn't it big?"

Maisie stands up. The world tips for a moment. It loses color. She steadies herself by holding on to the stroller's push handle, which is not very steady. It gives under her grip so that she almost tips it. Her vision has gone sepia, like a film negative, first silvery, then snowy. Her face feels cold on the surface, hot underneath. Her ears clog up, and for a second there is a surge in her abdomen as though her bowels might release. She sits back down. The grass at her feet looks like steel wool before regular color bleeds back into everything and her hearing whorls back to normal.

"Let's head in," Neil is saying. "The hayride's empty so let's just walk." He lifts Romeo up onto his shoulders in a pendulum swing, his strength seemingly effortless. When they were all really small, Neil would crawl on all fours, remaining silent, small children dangling off him, on his back, hooked under his arm like a football, sitting on his calf. He'd erupt slowly, raising an arm, or a leg, standing on his knees, and the little bodies would cling on, screaming with delight.

From his shoulder perch, Romeo looks longingly at the tractor with its giant wheels, as he hugs Neil's head and squeezes Neil's neck with his legs.

"I want to walk," says Xavier.

"You can push Esme," Neil tells him.

"Dad, did you see the woolly woollies? Here on the net?"

"I want to go with Mom," says Harriet.

"I'm going on the hayride," says Maisie. "I'd like to sit."

Neil looks at her. His gaze feels like he is touching the small of her back, despite being a few feet away. All of those years, before marriage, of not being touched! Of talking to people with only words and interactions! It was these years of living side by side with Neil and these growing people, skin to skin, leg to leg, cheek to cheek, body to body, lap to lap, that she felt most in her element of living. It was sometimes claustrophobic, things were clingy and irritating, but mostly it was a communication that she preferred above all of the others: touch and contact. Words could barely get there.

Neil, also a person who prefers physical contact over words, is looking at her. "Do you feel okay?" he asks her.

Maisie shrugs. "Yeah," she says. She gets a baseball hat out of the diaper bag.

From his spot on Neil's shoulders, Romeo kicks his foot out to her, pointing his toe. "Hang the hat on my foot, Mom," he tells her.

Maisie hooks the hat onto the toe of Romeo's sneaker. "Put it on your head," she tells him. Romeo kicks it off onto the grass. Without looking at it, and while balancing Romeo on his shoulders, Neil squats down to pick up the hat, curls it up, and shoves it into his front pocket.

"I want to go with you, Mumma," says Harriet, leaning into Maisie. "But I also want to go with *them*." Harriet looks back and forth between her mother and father, squinting. "I can't decide!"

Xavier starts pushing Esme. The Snap-N-Go's wheels get stymied in the thick grass, so Neil takes over. When Neil lets go of Romeo's ankles to maneuver the stroller, Romeo holds on tightly to his father's forehead, hugging it, resting his small head on top of Neil's big head, riding his father's head and shoulders like his father is an animal. He smiles at Maisie, squishing up his small face.

"Hang on tight," Maisie tells him.

Harriet takes Maisie's hand and squeezes it as she looks at the tractor, the hayride, then back at Neil and her brothers as they move away with the stroller. "I don't know, Mom," she says, her body starting to bounce with indecision. "I don't know which way to go. . . ."

"Your choice," says Maisie.

"I'll go with you," says Harriet, pained, but her siblings are walking away. "I don't know which way—" she says, and then she's running away after them. Maisie watches her until she successfully joins them. Neil looks up, waves over to Maisie, to confirm Harriet's arrival.

Maisie's arms are free. She is alone. It's as if her arms are sleeveless on a summer day. Her body feels unencumbered and free—swimming in the air of life!—like she could skate along the ground and maybe even lift off a few inches, but not fly away because there is something now tethering her, always, to the earth and the ground, to feeling slightly incomplete, not unlike when she was first falling in love with Neil and, after spending lots of time together in bed and in each other's eyes, when she went out alone, into her life and to work, it was as though part of her previous days were missing, since he was missing, but at the same time, he was with her, or at least the feeling that she had for him was with her, and she also felt unencumbered and unattached to the regular world. Instead, she felt perched, newly fresh, in a way that she felt, intuitively, that Neil would always be with her, in her body, in her mind.

How strange it was that feelings and reactions were what make up lives! How strange it was that new feelings arise in life, but get combined with everything that is remembered! Familiar things might remain familiar, but they get imbued with whatever comes before them and after them. How strange it was to eat a raspberry, in the wintertime, in a city, and to be two other places, in two other times, all at once: along the road to the dump when she was about eight years old, a late July day, reaching carefully for raspberries in thorned caverns of raspberries tangled up with rambling sea rose and hips, and then dropping the picked berries into a plastic bucket, the smell of honey, pine trees, in the sea air, but then also be transported to her nana's yellow kitchen table, raspberries piled high for making jam in a pretty green-and-white raised porcelain berry dish that had holes on its bottom so the berries wouldn't mush up, and a saucer underneath it. Maisie would fit the raspberries onto her fingertips like erasers onto pencils, then eat them one by one, like gumdrops.

Having a baby was so similar to falling in love, and so similar to grieving a death. The mundanity of time and everyday living (garbage bags, toothpaste, bills, *money*) is rendered ridiculous alongside such surreal magnificence. Maisie was so small when her mother died that she hardly remembers the woman, but instead she remembers the general feeling of her mother, the general mood of her mother that emanated from her presence, even things that had belonged to her long after she was dead (her hiking boots, the bedspread, the vase of thick glass that was more sophisticated than the others), her persona contained in something like molecules, or sunrays that beamed out of the general feeling of her mother. When Maisie's father died, even though she'd expected it, the result was more concrete. After he died, *everything* was colored with the invisible color of grief; the invisible color of the air seemed to hold not just the grief *about* her father dying, but her (invisible) father himself, slanting everything askew, as though he was in the nature of things everywhere. All the atoms, in so many places, seemed to hold some nature of her father. *All mine are yours and yours are mine, and I have been glorified in them,* someone had read those words at her father's funeral, and Maisie still returns to those words, imagining an exchange of grief, a transmutation of grief into air, from one kind of love into another kind of love, like ocean water turning to spray, or the evaporation and precipitation of rain's water cycle, and then we breathe it or drink it in.

Wasn't every person who ever lived glorified by being born? When Maisie first learned of how thousands of sperm race to penetrate one waiting egg, and how one sperm, in the end, victoriously makes it, nudging its head into the smooth egg, like they watched in the movie, she remembers looking around the science classroom at her fellow fifth graders and thinking, *We all came in first!*

Once, in church around Christmas, as the priest droned on and the start of a winter storm with dandruff-like snowflakes speckled the gray windows, Maisie was occupying herself by busily following the thread of the bay leaf garland that twirled like a candy cane, around banisters and columns, all the way to the base of the altar, when Nana bent down to tell her something.

"Listen," whispered Nana. "In all these prayers? . . . Substitute the word *Love* for any of the big words like *God, Jesus, Lord, Father, him, Holy Spirit* . . . All those, just substitute the word *Love* instead." Nana straightened up, looking ahead at the altar. "Much, much easier to understand."

Maisie tried it in her head automatically, there in the pew, as she went back to following the bay leaf garlands, twirling and draped, as though they were leading her on a gentle roller coaster of the words. "Our Love, who art in heaven / hallowed be thy name." Or "Hail Mary, full of grace, the Love is with thee. Blessed art thou among women and blessed is the fruit of thy womb, Love. Holy Mary, mother of Love, pray for us sinners, now and at the hour of our death. Amen." Once Maisie was back at home, she wrote the substituting down on paper instead of in her head. It worked. "Love, I am not worthy that you should enter under my roof but only say the word and my soul shall be healed." Or "We believe in one Love, the Love, the Almighty, Maker of heaven and earth, of all that is seen and unseen. We believe in one Love, the only Love of Love, eternally begotten of the Love, Love from Love, Light from Light, true Love from true Love; begotten not made, one in being with the Love."

Later on in life, when she told Neil of this substitution trick, he suggested, shrugging, "How about if the whole thing was female?"

Maisie had actually thought the same thing when she was making her confirmation when she was thirteen. She'd written that out, too: *We believe in one Goddess, the Mother, the Almighty, maker of heaven and earth* . . . It was funny, but also kind of sad. Maisie had wondered if women had written Scriptures, or even one single woman, what in the world would she have said?

As a kid, Neil had gone to church much more than Maisie. Once, in the early days of their house, with Xavier bumbling around and Harriet being fussy on a rainy morning, they'd inadvertently been riveted by an Easter Mass on TV.

"Well, suddenly I get it," Neil said. "It's the past being revived, with mercy, and then built upon for a better future. That's the resurrection? Not just Jesus, not just people who've died, but every single moment that passes. Every, like, thing that gets lost that we learn from. And then live better."

"Sounds hard," said Maisie, batting a spoon back and forth on the table with Harriet.

Neil shrugged. The smoke of incense looked like it was coming out of the TV. "'We look for the resurrection of the dead, and the life of the world to come.' That pretty much sums up human nature, doesn't it? Resurrecting the past so we can look ahead to progress?"

"Now you sound like a philosopher," said Maisie.

"Aren't theologians philosophers?" Neil asked.

"*Fiffoffif*fers," spat Harriet, and banged the spoon on the coffee table like a judge. She startled herself with its force, then laughed in loud spews.

"It's through processing grief that we become kinder people," said Maisie. Did she say that? She thinks it now. She thinks it later. She should have said it. *It's through successfully processing grief—the grief for every second that passes by—that we become more tolerant, more open, and more loving.* Where can she say, now, all the things that she might have said before? Where might it have import?

Neil was a question asker, even when he was making declarations, which was very much the opposite of most men that Maisie encountered who might typically talk over her sentences like car wheels backing up over the long hem of a skirt. So often a man would say something that she'd already said, only a few minutes later, and back to her, as if it was a new idea. Her brother, Miles, wasn't that way. Her father wasn't that way. "Most men are idiots," her father would say. "But a number of them are great." Neil was what Maisie's father would call great.

They were still watching the Mass on the television, the jowly priests in their pressed robes, the shiny gold goblets, the candles, and the cross. Harriet had rested her head down on a pillow on the floor and was falling asleep with her diapered butt sticking up in the air. Romeo, as always at the time, was nursing.

Neil asked, "How can a religion of love and forgiveness ever be brutal and intolerant?"

He looked at Maisie for an answer. She didn't have an answer. She thought quickly of how human beings are kind and not kind.

Neil smiled and asked, "Is there anything that love and memory can't overcome?"

Maisie smiled. "That's a nice thing to say," she said.

"You said that," Neil told her.

"I did?"

"Yes."

"Are you sure?"

"Positive."

"What did I say?"

" 'I don't think there's anything love and memory can't overcome.' It was when I was digging a hole for the cherry tree." Neil had planted a cherry tree in the patch of grass at the front of their house. It was young and tender, like a fawn. They did not know that it would grow to be glorious, enormous, and have something big to say about its place in the world every spring with its pink-white blossoms tossing in the wind.

"I wish love and memory could make us some money," said Maisie.

⇥⇤

There they went, her collection of people heading toward the apple trees, a young little family among the billions of young little families, a dad with a kid on his shoulders, a girl skipping alongside an older brother, and a new baby in her snug little car seat, wobbling up a countryside hill to go apple picking. What would they look like to her if she was someone else? Or, if she was herself, but younger? Would she recognize them as something related to her? There was a period of time in her life when she imagined that she would probably never have children. Not like it was a plan, or even a disappointment, she just imagined that it wasn't what her life would be. In fact, she even thought she would have a hard time getting pregnant, or she would have an illness, like her mother, if it ever came time for her to have a baby with a partner. Instead, it was almost a blur how it happened, and here she was, with a family that called her Mom, and another baby looking at her, puzzled, in the small hours of the morning.

As Maisie watches Neil's back move away from her, it occurs to her that this is probably the farthest away, physically, that Esme has been from Maisie's body since she was born, other than in the hospital when the nurse had taken her to the nursery for a couple of hours so Maisie could sleep.

How strange to wake up in the dark in that institutional room—a hospital!—with its cold, hard surfaces, the red EXIT sign glowing above the door, her discharged roommate's bed looking like the bed of someone who had left the world because the sheets had been stripped and the new ones were folded militarily in the corner, with her body ready to feed her baby, and then have the door almost immediately crack open, the hospital hall light gushing in at her filled with Esme's infant wheezes and rasps, silent cries, as a nurse wheeled the infant toward her in the semi-dark, a small, feisty bundle in her Lucite-looking bassinet, a small queen, her tiny countenance treasured and hallowed, being wheeled in by Rita, Maisie's favorite nurse.

"The moms always wake up just before we come in," said Rita. "The baby sends the signal through the ether."

Maisie remembers it the same, post-C-section with her other kids, waking up, breasts a-ready, and the infant coming crying from the nursery, right on time.

The ESP extends beyond nursing. One night she dreamed that Xavier had a tick on his scalp. In the morning, Xavier came down the stairs, panicked, holding the back of his neck, "There's something crawling into my head!" At the top of the nape of his neck, a tick looked like it was diving into his skin, its tiny hair legs flicking around as it tried to bore in.

Maisie sees Neil pause with the stroller. He holds on to Romeo's ankles with one hand as he bends over to peel back Esme's netting. Xavier and Harriet fuss over the woolly woollies, plucking them from the netting. Her milk drops again—pins and needles like they are filling with sugar, flexing with crystals—as she watches Neil put Romeo on the ground and take Esme out of her seat.

Maisie meets Neil halfway to take the baby from him. She has the baby harness on, always at the ready, like a cowboy has the gun holster. Neil has also brought the abbreviated diaper bag—a smaller bag that lives within the main diaper bag—that contains two diapers, a thin travel packet of wipes, a piece of waterproof fabric that Maisie had cut from a mattress cover, and

a thin muslin receiving blanket that Maisie can use as a place
to change Esme, or as a cover for nursing, or as something to
shade Esme's head and face once she's in the holster and they
are walking about.

"You good?" Neil asks her.

"Yeah," says Maisie. "You keep asking that. Do I look bad?"

"You look a little tired," Neil tells her. Neil's face reminds her
of money again, and when she looks down at Esme's miniature
face, it looks as tiny as a blossom bud that hasn't even started to
open, so tight and so small. The little hat on Esme's head cost
about ten bucks. Maisie could have gotten a cheaper one.

Maisie can smell that she needs a new diaper.

"We'll find you guys in there," Maisie tells him. "We'll probably be a while."

"We'll start along the Red Delicious, then head down that
area where it's not that busy by the Romes and Macouns."
Maisie knows what he means. Neil continues. "If we don't see
you up there, we'll see you at the playground place near the
little bridge."

"Okay," she says, glad for a plan.

Neil kisses her on the mouth, juicy enough that for a second
she feels warm desire, and she smiles. The money thought has
been smothered, made inert by the kiss, and by Esme.

The wind picks up. Sunlight trembles pockets of light through
the lifting leaves. Branches dip and sway as light spangles across
Esme's face. A cloud covers the sun for a moment, and the
shadow crosses over the grass, moving along, as though the wind
is blowing it. Esme's small body wriggles against Maisie's chest.

In the distance Maisie can see the playground place that Neil mentioned. She can picture its awkward jungle gym made of tires, its swings with the chains that pinch little hands, and its excellent slide. Next to it is a small bridge, and a river that in some years is relatively dry and some years flowing along. One year, when only Xavier and Harriet were alive, on the bank of the small river, under the little bridge, there was a water snake in the process of eating a bunny. A fairly large group of people had gathered to watch it, like they were all at a zoo. It looked as if the dead animal was stuck halfway into the snake, and halfway out, as if someone had aggressively shoved the bunny into the snake's face—*Take that!* The snake looked tired, like it had decided that actually it didn't want to eat the entire rabbit after all. But then a little bit of the bunny would slowly move into the mouth, mechanically, as if there was a glitch on the conveyor belt as the snake sucked it in. One boy who was watching kept telling the snake to hurry up. His dad answered, "It takes time to take so much in."

Maisie scans the area for an appropriate spot to change and nurse Esme. To her left, the grass is still somewhat mowed, and there is a post and beam fence. On the other side of the fence is a pasture, a meadow of high, beige grass that ripples in the wind like a water's surface. *Over there is good,* she thinks, eyeing a specific spot. She touches Esme's foot that dangles out of one of the baby carrier's holes.

An older mom smiles at Maisie, with Esme, as she passes, clearly smiling at the two of them from her own later phase of mothering: pre-grandmother but post-child. A handsome son is walking with her. Maisie guesses he's around twenty. She thinks of a morning at the library when she was helping unload and sort book donations—she had a baby in a carrier with her then as well. Was it Romeo? Harriet?—and, more than once, an adolescent boy came in carrying boxes from his mom's or dad's car. There was a variety of them, these sometimes gangly, sometimes tightly athletic, sometimes strikingly handsome guys, in all different shapes and sizes, skin colors, demeanors, smelling like baby powder, or weed, Old Spice, BO, or their dog. Every time one of them entered, helpfully carrying a heavy box and putting it down on the card table, all the moms, particularly the older ones, would practically blush, and certainly smile with a maternal, closed smile of delight and pride, as though there is nothing in the world like the appearance of an adolescent boy, breezing through a room with his awkwardness or cockiness, carrying a heavy box, to make a mother smile.

Another woman who walks along, passing, looks only at the top of Esme's head, inspecting the infant. The woman is nodding, saying "Mm-hmmm" to something that her companion is saying, sounding puzzled.

The next people who pass don't look at her.

"It's like the air is talking to me," a woman tells the man that she's with.

"Isn't it always?" answers the man.

"It's like there are messages that I know are there, but I'm not receiving them," says the woman. "It kind of feels like a nightmare."

Maisie remembers a dream she'd had that she had valuables—lots of money and jewelry and stuff—in her car and she forgot to lock it. She was too far away to lock it—she was so far away that she was in a dream! Thinking strange abstract things like how she was so pleased that her husband's kiss came from two sides, so nicely balanced, simultaneously. It was good how it did that, she thought in her sleep, but her location was north-facing, along a road in a town where she grew up, the ocean to her right.

There was a house in the town where she grew up where a father had backed his car out of his driveway and run over his two-year-old daughter and killed her. At sleepovers, she and her friends would go over it as a ghost story: baby Charlotte, forever toddling around small driveways, searching for her own body so that her spirit could join up with it and live the rest of the life that she never got to live. As Maisie grew older, as she'd bike past the house on her way to babysit a little boy named Billy, the house would emanate a dull and heavy sadness, like a melancholic smell, that came steady out of its crooked gutters, its stooping pine tree, large-shouldered and heavy with grief, that stood forsaken on the little front yard, and the upstairs windows, like downcast eyes, that seemed to be glancing sidelong at the driveway, at the place where the terrible accident must have occurred. As Maisie grew even older, became a mother, and when she had a small driveway of her own that she regularly backed out of, and her children regularly Big Wheeled around or drew in colored chalk on the macadam, she would imagine herself, or Neil, in such an unimaginable horror.

She would think of the father, and the accident itself. In one moment, the man was starting his car, thinking about wherever he was going: Was he going to meet a friend? Maybe he was going to get something like batteries at the store, going to pick up another child from school or a baseball game. He might have been in the midst of an argument with his wife, or a brother or a sister, and hurried unnecessarily into reverse. Maybe he was in a state of sweet contentment, having just made love to his wife, having just carried his young daughter downstairs for a snack. It might have been autumn, with the clean, clear air nestling into the folds of the changing leaves. He might have just thought, *I am lucky*. Or perhaps he thought nothing, or was thinking of what kind of batteries would work best in the flashlight that wasn't turning on, or trying to remember the date of a coworker's birthday, or whether or not he had inadvertently offended a friend and how he might apologize. Whatever was happening, it would have ended abruptly with a lumped lift of the car, and then a terror that must have eclipsed everything, eclipsed his entire life from himself. From that moment on, a terror must have lived all around him and his family, and then *in* him and his family, for the rest of their lives. *And here it is, living in me,* Maisie would think, though obviously not as distressingly or as painfully, but simply as an imagined occurrence of something that actually occurred.

Almost every time Maisie backs out of her driveway, she thinks of that man and that baby girl named Charlotte, and the house on Sea Street, and then she thinks of her own mother, and how nothing stays the same for very long, and how whatever happens to us stays in us, even the things that happen along our periphery, living around us and then attaching, growing in, like those grafted branches on the apple tree, the many branches of grafted pain, grafted breaking and healing, grafted love, grafted growth. *The body is everywhere. . . .* Who is saying that to her? *The body is everywhere, and everywhere is you.*

"Mumma," said Harriet, once, when she was littler, from her car seat as Maisie backed out of the driveway. "Mumma, you put the window up and it almost bit my hand."

"It can't get you, honey," Maisie told her, thinking instead of her daughter getting run over like baby Charlotte, a lump, and then a rise of the car. "If your hand's in the way, the window won't close. There's a safety mechanism."

"Meccamism," parroted Harriet. She popped her thumb into her mouth, settled into her seat, and looked skeptically at the top of the closed window.

Once, when Harriet was very small, and Maisie had said to her, "I can't do that with you right now. You are misbehaving."

"I en not Miss Bee Hiving. I am Harriet."

Maisie sees herself from the outside: a woman with an infant, probably looking out of it, moving aimlessly through the apple orchard's base in search of a suitable spot for a diaper change and a nurse. She has no idea what her face looks like—is it bloated? Worn out? Neil had said she looked tired. She hasn't looked in a mirror in days. She probably looks harried, or does she look calm? In any case, here she is with a baby again. Here she is, again, carrying a baby around like a basket. Again, a baby is with her, nonverbal and warm. In a few months, if all goes well, the baby will still be with her, getting carried around with its solid little bum hooked onto Maisie's hip, with its watchful gaze and its little countenance like the figurehead at the prow of a ship on the lookout for life, slicing through its waters, gliding along with her as she goes.

Is it from a book or a dream, or maybe a ghost story that Maisie was told, or is it simply her own mothering mind that conjures up the character of a young woman, dressed in white, carrying a solid-sized baby in her arms wherever she goes, forever and ever? This ghost baby is old enough to sit upright with perfect posture, but not old enough to walk. The ghost mother has the baby with her forever, throughout time, in whatever the ghost story is, even though all the people around her age and grow and change. For the rest of a mother's life, the mother carries the baby. The baby is as much a part of the mother's body and soul as her heart, or her head, or her cheek, or her knee. It did feel true that a child, in all its formulations of character and growth, in all its machinations, remains with their mother, their invisible weight carried around by her: the baby, the toddler, the child looking at the mother warily, the tween, the teen rolling her eyes, the baby adult with its perfect specimen body, the young adult, the grown person, the old person, et cetera. The crowd of these kids travel, like time travels (or is it how love travels?) somewhere in her body. How is it that once one cares for something so closely, not only does that thing seem related to one's body, but the rest of the world seems related to one's body as well?

Here she is again, her body and her mindset a thriving, busy industry of answering the needs of an infant, just as every single person walking around her in this orchard had someone care for them at one point. She is doing her natural part of nature, no different than the bees at the cider, and their industry, or the samaras pinwheeling from the sugar maples in twirls, or the group of silent deer on the side of the road, looking like statues as they looked back at their injured member. It was no different than the capriciousness of the weather, on its own mysterious system, or the cycle of days and nights, with the lush, deep shadows that seem to fall quietly in the corners of her body, and the bright, surface sun that shines along its skin. She wasn't making any money, though. What about *that* system?

Forget about the money; she knows the drill by now with the babies: first, they watch, and then cry, then they watch and smile and blabber their busy-making words like old cronies with no words but full of cadences and sighs, full of nonsense but all with the expert comedic timing of human expression. Here she was again, holding a small baby with its discerning eyes. She can still feel the weight of each of her previous kids—Xavier, solid and strong, sound and grounded like a dignified and handsome tree; Harriet, compact and ready, like a completed thing of such cupped potential that she might open up into a small umbrella, or a sail, to lift away; Romeo, so flexible and nimble that he was almost weightless, like a dancer, whenever she picked him up—and how each of them looked out at the world with the corresponding personality of their baby weight, and how each of them still looked out at the world in the same way: Xavier, always watching, always curious, and always ready for wonderment and to be amazed. Harriet, always watching, always alert, ready to amuse and be amused, or concerned, ready to be activated. Romeo, always watching, ready to smile, and move in to be touched, and move his body in a jump or a leap. Esme . . . what was she like? So far, she was kind of intimidating with her penetrating gaze. "Like the pretty girl at the party who won't make eye contact with you," Neil had said. What did Esme's body weight feel like? It was cliché, but she had a different little beauty than the others in the shape of her forehead and the curve of her bum, slightly mysterious and removed but also central, like a lovely tree that sits alone in a pasture, or a stone wall that snakes away down a hill, and a smoky expression that seemed to say, *I am relying on you now to do everything for me, but one day you will rely on me.* It was hard to name a baby's character before seeing it grow, but, looking back, it's clear in the moment that they first look at their mother.

Does any parent look at their newborn, that very first second, and think, *Yes, this is exactly the squished-up face that I expected to see?*

"You just wait," her older friend Sarita told her once. They were in the park while the kids climbed around on the playground equipment. "The teenage years are just nuts." Sarita had two kids in high school, and two stepkids in college. Her youngest, a boy with her second husband, was in school with Xavier.

Sarita explained, "Teenagers will test you more than you've ever tested yourself. In fact, the older my kids get, the more I realize that whatever they are driving me crazy about, whatever it is that I am worrying about over them, it's usually really a part of myself that's the issue. Not them. It's like they're showing me parts of myself. Which is I guess what the whole wide world is doing all of the time anyway, right? But anyhow, teenagers . . . And when they first become teenagers. Hard. On the one hand, the kids seem indifferent to you. But on the other hand, you are being scrutinized like you have no idea! They are like undercover spies, these kids. They *act* like they aren't paying attention, but they're watching the way you talk, the way you eat, the way you drink—and by that I mean alcohol. They watch the way you get angry, the way you interact with your spouse, the way you treat your friends, your dog, the waitress, people on the phone, the way you manage your money, the way you work, the way you relax, the way you cope, the way you *live*—it is terrifying!"

"That does sound terrifying," Maisie said.

"It's really around middle school that you start to be under the microscope. At least that's when I started paying closer attention to what I was doing, and what they were seeing. It's pretty much why Daniel and I got divorced. Neither of us wanted the kids to think that a marriage should be like ours."

Maisie didn't know what to say but wondered what kind of a marriage, exactly, Sarita had that wasn't worthy of emulating.

Sarita continued. "In fact, that's when a bunch of people I knew got divorced. When the kids were younger, I'd hear people say, 'Little people, little problems,' and 'Big people, big problems,' and all of that but no one ever told me—or at least I never heard them—that with the bigger kids you really have to tend to *yourself*, you know? To show them how an adult behaves. At least for me." She paused. "In fact, when they were heading to high school, all of them looking at me made me want to stop drinking altogether. There I was drinking a bottle of rosé practically every night. *That* wasn't something I wanted to model for them, as much as I loved drinking." Sarita stared ahead at the playground, as if the play structures were encouraging her to continue. "My own parents definitely had drinking problems, and I never even realized they had problems because I had no siblings to commiserate with." She was worked up enough that some spit droplets were visible in the air in front of her. She continued, mimicking an interior voice: "Get your shit together, woman! These young people are watching you!" Sarita shrugged. "Maybe that's the basic midlife crisis everyone talks about. But I never heard about it as a crisis being brought on by kids *watching* what you were *doing*. Wondering who the hell you think you are." Sarita looked at Maisie. "Did you?"

Maisie was speechless. She shook her head.

"Bottom line is that the forties, maybe fifties, is a big time of reevaluating, whether you like it or not. All the ways I managed to cope my whole life just didn't cut it anymore. It sounds hard, and it is, but it's also totally exciting because it's a whole new lease on life."

"Okay," said Maisie. She could understand this.

Sarita continued. " 'Midlife crisis' always sounded so self-involved and like some bald guy buying a sports car." Sarita shrugged again. "Looking at myself through my kids' eyes has made me try to be a better person. It's forced me to pay atten-tion to myself." She laughed. "But now my hang-up worry is about not working enough and how financially dependent I am on Terry. I mean, I wouldn't have a pot to piss in if Terry ever left me, or something, and what message does that send to my daughters, or my sons?" She watched a bird hop in bounces across the street. They were waiting for the school bus to arrive.

"But on the other hand," she said, "Terry and I formed a partnership. Making money wasn't the only priority."

"Yeah," agreed Maisie. "Should money be the main priority?"

Sarita shrugged. "Maybe for some people."

Since Maisie has no older sister, and no mother, she listens to older moms, follows them around, practically, to hear what they have to say. Every single one of them, it seems, has left any kind of certainty behind. They were not as righteous as the younger moms, or as meek. The ones that Maisie was drawn to would say things like, "Being a mom has completely kicked my ass," or "If anyone's spouting advice about parenting and their kid is under five, no thanks," or "I was the most self-centered person, I think, in the entire world. Becoming a mother, no question, was the great equalizer for me. Now I try my best to keep my mouth shut, and listen," or "Every kid is completely different, so . . ."

→→-←←-

Maisie steps over an apple decomposing in the grass. A young couple sits on the top rung of the fence about ten feet away from where Maisie is thinking of settling down with Esme. They are holding hands and giggling, nuzzling into each other. Maisie calculates that if she sets up a blanket, lies Esme down on it to change her and nurse her, the couple will leave. She is correct. As she approaches the area with the baby carrier contraption strapped to her body as though she's about to belay down a cliff or zip-line across a jungle, the couple takes one look at her and, in the middle of their giggling and canoodling, they move hurriedly along.

Maisie watches them walk away. The young man puts his hand on the woman's bum and squeezes it. The young woman's hair shines as she turns to kiss him. When Maisie first met Neil, there was a specific thing about his body that she couldn't identify. She still can't identify it. It is in a certain slope in the outline of his face, a specific line along his shoulder and upper arm. It's a sort of presence inside of his own presence, like a ghost inside of his eyeballs, that seems as though no one but her can see. It's almost like there is a part of something inside of him that's from another place, but that's homesick for something that's here, so it is glad to be here, looking. Sometimes it seems like Neil himself isn't even aware of it, and he's a vessel for something that only Maisie can see, as though Maisie and this strange familiar something have the real connection, a secret, unbeknownst even to Neil. When she thought of science class and the sperm race, she imagined once that it was the millions of sperm in him, deep inside, looking out at her, looking for her eggs. Or, she thought, maybe it was something more spiritual and ancient, the thing that made the connection, more like small aspects of past lives, souls, the way she'd imagine dogs and cats, birds and other animals, were really her mother or her father dropping by to give her some kind of sign.

Their first kiss felt like two things at once: a prize for finding something that no one else had found, and a return to the place where she was, that she hadn't known she'd left. They were outside on a balcony. The warm night surrounding them was vibrating. There was the sound of crickets, and a whip-poor-will. After the kissing, Neil pulled back in the semi-dark to look at her more closely. His outline was good and sumptuous. He had a half smile on his face.

"Well," he said like a statement, almost sounding like *wow*.

"Well," Maisie said back to him.

They stood smiling at each other, not touching. The night air smelled like honeysuckle.

Her arms tingle as she thinks of it, and, as she readjusts Esme, the baby's face reminds her that, for a moment while she was transported to that memory, Maisie had forgotten about her baby. She had forgotten about money and the house and the debt. She can smell the honeysuckle, as though a piece of the moment has traveled through time to reach her nose, as she rests Esme on her shoulder to spread out the receiving blanket on a clean patch of flattened grass. She can smell the honeysuckle as she places Esme down gently and the baby's face looks at her with a flat expression that says, *Now what are you going to do to me?* She can smell the honeysuckle and feel the hushed electricity in that night air when she asks her infant, "Who will you love one day?" The small face looks back at her, unchanging, as if the infant already knows the answer.

Maisie positions her own body so that her torso shades Esme's face from the autumn sun that's flickering jangly in the wind. Maisie can feel the dampness of the grass seeping in through her pants at her knees. "Who will it be?" Maisie asks her as she unsnaps the tiny onesie, as she gets out the mini packet of wipes. The yellow price tag sticker on the wipes packet injects the thought of money into Maisie's transporting moment. She'd bought the wipes at the drugstore, along with diapers, and Romeo had leaned on her leg while they waited in line at the cash register, both of them watching a woman in front of them argue with the cashier about coupons. When Maisie used the credit card, she wondered if it was at its limit, but it went through.

"That's a little one!" a woman exclaims, brightly, as she passes. "How old?"

"Two weeks," answers Maisie. She knows it is too early to be out of the house.

"Oh!" exclaims the woman, walking away into her own life, her own judgments.

Most mothers know not to make pronouncements or give directives and unsolicited advice to other mothers. When it is an older mother, Maisie usually doesn't mind, and even appreciates what they have to tell her or offer.

When Xavier was practically twenty pounds at six months old, Maisie had him in a BabyBjörn carrier whose straps crisscrossed through a plastic buckle in the middle of her back. As she waited for a light to cross a city street, she was startled by someone's touch on her back. A petite, older woman said gently, "Hold on," and slid the plastic buckle from high up on Maisie's back to her lower back. It was as if Xavier suddenly weighed five pounds less. "Better?" asked the stranger.

"Thank you!" Maisie smiled.

"Enjoy," said the small woman, and then she disappeared into the stream of the city crowd.

But there were also the nags: "That's no way to hold your baby!" from a person who perhaps has never walked and nursed their baby at the same time, or perhaps has hardly ever held a baby at all. Or "If you let your baby play with your keys like that, she will get a bacterial infection," from a young woman who presumably cannot predict the occurrence of bacterial infections. Or, a man, saying, "Don't ever let your child get so close to a dog's face," when the dog is your friend's retired service dog who has never bitten anything in its life. Or, another man, saying, "Your child is too high up on the jungle gym!" so that your nimbly climbing daughter looks down at you warily, suddenly made frightened of either the man, the height, or her own confidence, or most likely all. At the same playground, on the same morning, as another child cried as he was strapped into his stroller, a different man who was reading on a nearby bench yelled to the mother, "Can't you control your kid?" And the mother, without a second passing, replied, "Can't you control yourself?" as she smoothly moved away.

That baby should be wearing a hat. *That baby needs some* socks. *Have you thought about feeding your baby* organic *food? Have you thought about a* natural birth *instead of a C-section? Your baby looks hungry. Your baby looks full. You should supplement with* formula. *You should only breastfeed. You should* never *let your baby do that. Those are all your kids? Is your child going to apologize for walking in front of me? Your baby looks hot. Your baby looks cold. Maybe you should get that checked. He shouldn't be barefoot here. Your daughter should have a shirt on. That blanket might suffocate your baby. My family doesn't vaccinate. That necklace is a choking hazard. That baby is too big. That baby is too small. You shouldn't give in like that. If you give them what they want they'll just keep whining. Can you get these kids out of my way, please? That's the worst thing you can do. His shoes are on backward. If you carry your baby all the time they won't learn how to walk. If you pick her up when she cries, she'll learn to cry all the time. You don't need to lock that. Don't let him play in the sandbox like that. Don't push the stroller without clipping him in. Looks like I know who's the boss around here. Feed her every four hours; she'll learn! Why would you have so many kids? Give her some cough medicine and she'll go to sleep. I've never liked children. I don't envy you! You've got your hands full! Look into my advice. Do a little research, you'll see.*

She vows to never offer any unsolicited advice, ever, to

another adult, without asking first if they'd like to hear it. Pronouncements and observations about parenting were fine: *One never regrets a baby or a swim. One's got to have a sense of humor! Sometimes you just don't like other people's kids. Everyone does it differently. I have learned to have more patience with everything and everyone. It has been very humbling. We are all a work in progress. We are all in our own worlds, just doing our best. Good things do come.* Among the good things, the moment on one winter evening when the windows were pitch dark already at five, the house bright and warm: Maisie was on the floor picking up board books and miniature plastic sharks when her first baby, Xavier, toddled over to her, cupped her cheeks in his little hands, looked directly into her eyes, and with a trail of dried snot beneath his nose and his little chin jutting out like Marlon Brando in *The Godfather* said, for the first time ever, "I lub you, Mumma."

Once when she was watching the news with Harriet, an ad came on for some indistinguishable pharmaceutical product. What was the drug for? It was unclear, but in a verdant field a pretty young mother wearing a floral dress twirled her young daughter around in circles by the arms.

"Why can't you be like that mom?" asked Harriet, snuggled into Maisie's side.

Why indeed? thought Maisie. She could hardly remember the last time she put on a dress. "She's just an actor pretending to be a mom," Maisie told her.

Harriet shrugged, as if to say, *So what?*

Maisie continued. "I spun you around like that on the beach, remember? Then I dragged you while I ran, and you made those wavy lines in the sand with your feet?"

Harriet smiled. "Oh yeah." She smiled wider. "Then that lady told you that you might pull my arms out of their sockets."

→-◄-

On her knees, Maisie smooths the baby blanket over the grass. Is the spot too close to other people? No, she has moved to the side of any foot traffic, and the hayfield is to her left. An older woman and a young woman pause, however, very near her and so soon, seemingly unaware that she is with a baby on a blanket near their feet. The older woman puts her hands on the younger woman's shoulders. Maisie can hear her clearly, as though she is in the front row of a play, and they are performing.

The older woman continues. "Look, you have everything you need. Right inside *you*. You're a brave person. You're a brilliant person. Most important of all, you are a *kind* person."

"Thanks, Grandma," says the young woman.

"Your mother is not as strong as you are," the grandmother says plainly. "It's that simple, Beverly."

"Thanks, Grandma."

"Well, it's the truth. I'm only stating the plain and honest truth."

They move past, but Maisie repeats what the woman said to Esme, as she quickly changes her diaper. "You're a brave person; you're a brilliant person," says Maisie, as though she's talking to a puppy. "It's that simple, Beverly."

Esme feels more minuscule than ever, since this is the first time that Maisie has changed her diaper outside in the wide-open air. Esme's little bum is as small as a peach. The world is so large. The sky above is huge, a dome with no roof, like a pregnant

belly and they are all inside of it. The green blades of grass
tuft up around the edges of the receiving blanket like decorative fringe. Each growth of leaf is older than Esme. Each of the
many stems seems to be peering at the baby from its edge, trying
to get a good look like an interested, upright audience—*Wow!
You're little for a person!* they say, then quiver from the wind. The
area feels wide open, exhilarating and lovely, but also possibly
dangerous. Maisie has the feeling that someone, a wayward boy
trying to catch a ball, perhaps, might run near them and stomp
on Esme with a muddy sneaker. At least they were in fresh country air with the sunlight's vitamin D. The shopping mall with a
small baby was the worst with its stale air, its smell of plastics and
perfumes, the factory fabrics, the grimy flip lids of the stainless
steel trash cans, its fluorescent lighting that invariably makes the
baby's face look as though it has a deadly rash, not to mention
the coughs and sneezes and nosy looks of passersby. The mall felt
like an assault on the naturalness of the baby. The mall seemed
to release a silent, invisible residue of consumption, dirtier than
germs, that contaminated the baby's organic constitution.

Maisie glances around, protective and alert, hunched over her
baby, a lioness on the savanna, a mama chimp in her jungle,
or a mother blackbird at the edge of her nest with a wing half
raised like a shield. How strange it was to have a newborn! How
strange it was to be a person who has a miniature person who
came out of her body two weeks ago!

Maisie settles cross-legged on the blanket and begins nursing Esme. People are moving about the orchard as though they
have been told where to go and are following through with their
directions. Some seem rushed; some are slow.

Esme is fixed on Maisie's breast, and Maisie is pulled into tiredness as the nursing gets going. The animal in her—it is all animal now; everything is animal. Sometimes she surprised herself when she and Neil actually spoke in a thread of more than ten sentences, like people, like human beings who use language to converse and relate. But wasn't the body, the silences, the language of how they moved around each other and with each other, all so much truer? All so much more simple, unambiguous, and clear? Words were always stopping her up when she tried to say them. The moment she said something definitive, she often thought, *Well, that didn't capture what I meant.* Whispering *Sweet dreams* to Xavier, or Harriet, or Romeo, seemed pat. Telling Neil *I love you* fell flat of encompassing the trust, erotica, fear, and ineffable tenderness combined with impatience. It was sometimes more effective to say nothing, make love, or just lump into the moment, body against body in togetherness.

How was anyone to feel their worth? The days slide away, like thin water over a smooth stone in a stream. Where is the stream headed? She is a mother. People depend on her. She brings meaning to them. What is the meaning? Why bother at all?

Maisie opens her eyes from nursing and feels as though she is in a different reality than where she was a moment ago. The arrangement of the place feels like a different dimension—why does the barn look like it's in the same place, but like that same place is different, and its angled roof looks flat instead of 3D? The blue sky feels like a piece of simulated blue sky, the grass looks suddenly cultivated as though it is a part of an exhibit or a Disneyland experience. Is she dreaming? She hears a cackle of laughter, as though it is a clue. She looks around. On one side is the orchard into which her family has disappeared. There's the parking lot, the barn, then the other side is a meadow, a pasture used for hay, which is how it was a moment ago, yes.

A large crow swoops down and lands on the top rung of the fence, very close to Maisie, as unafraid as a pigeon. It looks at her with a tilted head, a beady black eye. It hops from the fence to the grass, closer to Maisie and Esme. Its feathers are glossy, luxuriously black. It is as big as Esme. Its head twitches, waiting for a bit of food, presumably, before it flies away. The baby suckles. A smaller bird lands where the black bird had been. Maisie's nipple is firm and at attention, as are her ears, when the small bird trills like an instrument made from metal, a bike bell on a handlebar.

"It could have been a lot worse," she hears a man say.

"Well, sure," says a woman sharply, "anything can always be worse."

Once, in their neighbor's backyard, a red-tailed hawk swooped down and picked up their miniature dachshund, then dropped the dog after about five feet. Harriet was a baby and was sleeping in a Pack 'n Play outside while Maisie had gone into the kitchen to get a glass of water. What if she had left Harriet on a blanket, out in the open? What if the hawk had picked up Harriet?

A woman yells, "Oh!"

A man calls, "Watch out!"

Maisie hunches over Esme in reflex, as though an errant, airborne soccer ball might be coming her way. The wind blows Maisie's hair across her face and into her mouth. She clears it away and looks up to see a chestnut horse galloping wildly through the dirt parking lot. Its hooves clop frantically, its feet moving as if the ground is hot. It runs forward, and then awkwardly tries to reverse out of a car-filled area. It rears slightly. Some people shriek, or laugh. People move aside collectively, as though they had previously learned the choreography. The horse turns around. It walks a few paces forward, a few paces back. Its mane floats as it moves: another thing that looks like seagrass underwater. It pauses at the edge of the parking lot. What had initially seemed like a frightened and nervous animal now seems wiser and annoyed. It quivers its whole body, as if to shake off its nervousness and discomfort like dust, revealing only head-held-high dignity.

An employee of the orchard approaches it calmly, holding a bridle. She lowers her arms, like a musical conductor, to ask for general quiet and calm from the surroundings. The horse watches her approach. It has a blaze of white down its nose.

Maisie stands up, baby Esme still plugged to her nipple, and leans against the fence. Is Esme drinking milk that is laced with guilt, with debt? And what will that substance do to her little body? Maisie is unfamiliar with horses, other than seeing them at a distance. She has never in her life ridden one, except for maybe a pony ride at a county fair. She can remember feeding one apples, carrots, and sugar cubes when she went with her friend JoJo to visit JoJo's aunt and uncle when she was a girl. It was one of the prettiest places she had ever visited: a saltwater farm on the top of a giant, sloping hill that rolled down to the ocean. An enormous bay spread out below like a giant, upturned palm that was made vaster and more breathtaking because it was speckled with islands arranged like stones that it held in its hand, or the islands looked like casserole dishes on a large blue table, or lumps of a giant submerged animal that might stand up at any moment, water trailing from its legs, to shake like a giant wet dog. The ocean was healthy and blue, a mirror for the sky, and the large wide field that dipped down the hill acted like a long green carpet, a long kind arm introducing the enormous bay, as if to say, *Take a look at this beauty!*

The horse sidesteps around the woman holding the bridle and calmly walks in Maisie's direction. A group of people move out of its way, like birds in flight together, smiling. Instinctively, with Esme still at her breast, Maisie dips through the rungs of the fence so that she's on the other side. Under the drape of the blanket, Esme still pulls on Maisie's nipple, though Maisie can feel the frequency of her little mouth's suction is starting to fade. She is almost asleep.

The horse continues in their direction. It is approaching them as though it knows them. Maisie is somewhat frightened but glad to be behind the fence. It is a large animal; its ears are pricked up straight. She doesn't know any horses. The milk in her non-nursing breast surges at the uptick in adrenaline, and Maisie smashes her palm against her nipple to quash any leakage.

When the horse stands before her, Maisie can see that one of its eyes is not an eye at all. It is a clean depression, where a large marble would fit, that's covered with the brown fur of the rest of its body. The horse shows her its real eye, glassy and brown. It looks as though it has black eyeliner on, and mascara. Its eyelashes are as sweet as a boy's. The horse takes another step closer, looking at her, but also past her. Maisie looks at the post of the fence a few feet next to her. There is an apple balanced there, as though it's ready to be shot at for aiming practice. She hadn't noticed it. It is a red apple. Maisie takes it in her hand and holds it out to the horse. The baby continues to suckle. The horse gently takes the apple from Maisie's hand, its enormous dark lips curling around the shiny fruit, and then crushes it in its mouth as it eats. Maisie can see the white insides of the apple, like ocean foam, in the deep of the horse's mouth.

The first time she ever went to a zoo, her brother, Miles, supported her arm as she held out her hand to feed an elephant. The enormous trunk, like a vacuum's tube that had become animated with life, magically reached over a small fence to delicately approach her little hand. The darkness inside its tube scared her the most, and the moist feeling of the trunk touching her palm made her drop the food in recoil. With her friend on that salt-water farm, they'd fed the horses sugar cubes and carrots. "These are their favorites," a man there had told them. Maisie could see why, the sweet twinkle of the sugar to suck on, the crispness and orangeness of the carrot. As she fed them, Maisie wanted to use the sugar cubes as miniature balls, and swat at them with the carrots like they were miniature baseball bats. She thought of this as she watched the last carrot get smashed in a horse's mouth.

The horse looks at Maisie with its one good eye as it chews. Its jaw muscle bubbles up and down like a man's bicep as it chews. Watching it eat while feeling Esme suckle, the horse feels familiar: just another soul looking for an apple or two, looking for energy to maintain its system.

"I can help," a young woman announces. "I know this horse."

She is younger than Maisie. She wears black rubber riding boots that come up to her knees. The boots are splattered with old mud that's the color of coffee ice cream. She clucks her tongue quietly as she feeds a green apple to the horse.

"It has one eye!" shouts a little boy joyfully.

Maisie steps back. She is aware that eyes are on them, as though she, the horse, and the woman in the riding boots are on a stage.

"The horse probably likes your baby," the woman with the riding boots says to her.

"Really?"

"This horse seems to like you. Probably because of your infant."

"Not because of the apples?"

The woman reaches under her shirt and, after maneuvering around as if she, too, had been nursing an infant, she pulls out an unattached lavender bra. She smiles at Maisie as she waves it in the air. "I've only had to do this once before, but it worked."

The horse is calm, eating the green apple. Like magic, the woman clips the lacy lavender bra onto the horse's nose like a bridle. The pale purple threads are vibrant against the white blaze down the horse's forehead, the deep chestnut of the horse's shiny coat, the bright green of the apple, and suddenly the horse looks like a flamenco dancer. The bra is lovely, sheer and sophisticated tulle with Swiss dots and delicate lace trims. Maisie thinks to ask the young woman where she bought it.

"Wow," says Maisie. "You know what you're doing!"

"Well, you look like you do, too," the young woman says back to her, eyeing Esme.

Maisie looks down at Esme's grapefruit-sized head nuzzled under Maisie's shirt. Esme's body is in a diagonal across Maisie's chest like a small automatic weapon wrapped in folds of fabric.

Maisie looks at the young woman with the lace bra, the brown-black horse, and imagines that this young woman might have no idea what all this baby stuff is, but for all Maisie knows, she might be a financially savvy young woman who's already socking money away, planning for her future, planning for her *retirement,* accumulating wealth. Look at her, thinks Maisie, she and the horse, both as healthy as a horse, as strong and as vibrant as the wind that blows through the horse's mane to lift the mane in pieces so that it feathers and frizzes like sea spray.

The young woman is looking plainly back at Maisie, the wind blowing her hair away from her face as though she's soaring, when she blurts, "I'm pregnant."

As if on cue, a small white-haired man approaches them busily with horse stuff in his hands. "What trouble is she up to now?" he asks. He moves like a young person, agile and quick, though he is clearly not young.

"Hi, Frank." The young woman smiles.

The horse's head moves in recognition as Frank touches her head. "A brassiere!" Frank smiles. "Aren't you clever, Amber!"

The young woman blushes.

Frank's hands are nimble but worn and stout, as he removes the lacy, delicate material from the silken horsehair. His fingers have dirt on them, but somehow still look clean. She imagines his hand touching a woman, the lace, his thick fingers against bare hips, squeezing bare thighs—Who was this man's wife? Or partner? Was it a woman? A man? Frank winks at Maisie, as though reading her mind. Maisie watches his hands put the bridle on the horse, quick with the leather straps. For a moment she imagines his hands flipping a raw chicken breast around in a bowl of flour, then nestling it among others on a sizzling pan. The bridle fits the horse perfectly.

"Well, I think lavender is your color, Esme," he says to the horse, but for a second Maisie hears it for her baby. "Very *you.* Maybe it's Amber's color as well," he says, "but that I will never know."

"Is the horse's name Esme?" asks Maisie, patting her baby's back.

Frank looks at Maisie. His eyes are lively, like the sunlight and the wind are inside of them, twinkling. How is it that some eyes are like that, and some look dead?

"Yes," he says, revving up his eye sparkle. "Esme."

"That's this baby's name! It's actually my name, too," continues Maisie, "but I go by a nickname."

"That's a small baby," says Frank. "My daughter has a baby girl a couple of months older." He adjusts the horse's bridle. "If I had my wallet, I'd show you a cute picture." He pats the horse's neck, looks into the horse's eyes, and asks the horse, "Why are you way over here?" He tells Amber, "Something spooked her. The other two were such scaredies they went right into the barn."

"She seems good now," says Amber.

"Yeah, well, she's old enough to know when to be scared and when to let it go."

"Meaning she was right to be spooked." Amber laughs. "Will I learn that when I grow up?"

"I saw two coyotes last night, but they don't scare her," he says.

"They don't scare horses?" asks Maisie. "Coyotes?"

The man shakes his head. "Nah, I've seen a coyote run through the paddock and the horses just keep eating the grass."

"What scares the horses?" asks Maisie.

"Oh, it could be anything. Our neighbor got goats a while ago, and when one got loose for the first time you'd think a spacecraft had landed the way the horses got all worked up. I have one mare who every now and then decides to be scared of her feed pan. Riles everyone up. The same mare is also scared of my dog when he has a jacket on—we only did that once—or when the dog carries around a stuffed toy cat."

Amber laughs. "Luther's scared of me when I wear a hat with a pom-pom."

"Plastic sleds. Helium balloons. A baby bunny in a stall. Scary, scary stuff." Frank pats Esme the horse's neck. The horse seems to be listening and agreeing, *What he says is true,* her expression confirms.

Maisie laughs.

"Esme doesn't usually get spooked. Instead, she acts peculiar. In fact, she's frightened *me* with the way she gets, but I've learned she's not spooked. Sometimes she just stands in the middle of the paddock like a statue"—Frank stands still to demonstrate, looking into the distance—"like this," he says, "scanning the edge of the woods." Beside him, the horse also looks off into the distance.

Maisie looks in the direction that both of them are looking.

The grass sways. They watch the trees crinkle and swish in the wind. Something seems to be hidden within them.

"The first few times she did it," says Frank, "staring out with her *one eyeball* in a trance, it kept me awake at night even as she slept in her stable. I even went to look for animal tracks, with a flashlight, yelling into the dark for some rare mountain lion." Frank shrugs. "Whatever it is, I'll probably never know. She just stares, very focused, like she's on the lookout. I've been here thirty years, and I've never seen a bear. One time, *one* time, we found scat around the trees a ways from our barn." He shrugs again. "Maybe she's just in a trance, like she's meditating."

Maisie looks at Esme the horse's face. With a name and a character for context, the horse's face now bears with it a distinguished profile, wise and discerning. Maisie imagines Esme the horse in her paddock staring at the forest's edge and imagines what that forest might look like: American beech mixed with oak and tulip trees, plenty of maples, the collected line of them maybe at the bottom of a forest-filled hill. The trees at the forest's edge might look like a line of people at the front of a large crowd. Today, the trees are certainly aflame in the blaze of autumn colors, their tips such a vibrant red, orange, and yellow against the bluebird sky that it would be hard to imagine that each tree will become brown and bare in the winter and the forest will look like a twiggy thicket of dark lines against white snow. In the spring, the same trees will become chartreuse fuzz balls, almost fluorescent green, merged together like static. In the summertime they will settle in, deep-leafed and developed, dark green and glossy, as perfect as hands.

Maisie rests Esme's little chest on her shoulder, then thumps the baby's small, warm back to burp her. As she thumps, Maisie watches Esme the horse, the long line of the horse's nose, her mascara eyelashes, and feels an affinity with the horse's long, clean profile, her lines, as though drawn, that collect and pull like reins toward a vanishing point in the distance.

Like the horse, Maisie is always looking out, at woods, at the edge of something like a body of water, out a window, down a hill, like a forest, looking out at the edge of herself, scanning its border and periphery, feeling part prey and part on-the-lookout, but also part commander in charge, the protector of all protectors, but also vulnerable and small. Caring for a baby made one languish and flourish at the same time. Time was swallowed, and simultaneously she felt full and empty. Everything was so delicate, while everything was also so strong. Why was that? Was it because that is what being alive, overall, is like, really? A series of languishments and flourishes, of withering and blooming, that work off of each other? And wasn't caring for a baby pretty much a lesson for caring for life in general? Life never cried out for help and attention; life doesn't care whether it is lived or not! But a baby will remind you that your life needs attention and affection: your life needs effort; your life needs care.

Maisie drums her infant's back, feels the wind touch her baby and her own hands and hair as though, like music, it is encouraging something to stir within her. Maisie has felt this before, for sure, this absolute mixture of vulnerability and courage, of humility and confidence that rises from the small quiet place that is the bedrock of motherhood, where her little mind feels larger, enormous, and swept clear as though a delicate wind has come in through an open window from the sea to lift a sheer curtain, lifting the soul, stirring an area in her that had no outline, no shape, but instead the fleeting touch of something correct.

Maybe Frank is right, thinks Maisie, that meditation is actually being "on the lookout." When she looked outward, wasn't what she saw really what was inside of her?

Amber says. "I very much believe animals see things that we don't see."

"Oh, I do, too," says Frank. "No doubt in my mind."

Maisie thought of her friend Stacey, and Stacey's cinnamon-colored dog who followed Stacey around devotedly, watching her every move. Before Maisie had met Stacey, Stacey's son had died of sickle cell anemia. He was six years old. His name was Brandon. One day, when Stacey and Maisie were sitting in Stacey's little backyard, chatting while holding their small babies in their laps, Stacey's dog started barking happily, wagging its tail at a completely blank space in the yard. Their babies, both with their preverbal countenance of seriousness, were not alarmed at the barking but instead looked slightly stunned and mildly interested.

"Buddy, what are you doing?" Stacey smiled.

Buddy kept barking at nothing, like a dog barks when it's happy and wants someone to throw a stick for it, or play.

"Buddy! What are you barking at?"

Buddy came over to Stacey, wagging, received a few ear scratches, and then lay down on top of Stacey's feet with a groan, his head in his paws. The dog's soft eyes looked up at Maisie.

Stacey smiled. "I'm going to sound totally nuts, but when he barks like that? Wagging his tail like that? I know it's crazy, but I think he's telling me that Brandon is here, that Brandon has just walked into the room. Or the yard."

Because she was holding a sleeping Harriet on her lap, Maisie could only reach out to Stacey with a glance, a certain look.

Stacey continued. "Poor Buddy probably wonders why I don't hug Brandon when he sees him." Stacey laughed, shrugging a little bit. She looked down at her baby daughter, Naomi, in her lap. Stacey whispered, "Sometimes I think Naomi is really Brandon reincarnated."

She looked at Maisie and they laughed.

"I have lost some of my marbles," she said.

"Maybe just the right amount," said Maisie, and then she imagined that probably there were many moments when Stacey would talk to her dog and her dead son, and her baby daughter and her dog, and her dog and her dead son and her baby girl altogether.

Stacey didn't want to stop talking about it. "Thing is," she said, "when Buddy dies, who's going to bark at Brandon to tell me he's there?"

Maisie felt her throat warm up. "Oh, Stacey," she said.

Stacey lifted her bare foot and patted Buddy with it. "I *know* Brandon is here. All the time."

Buddy tipped over to lie on his side. He let out a deep sigh, as if to say, *You can say that again.*

Stacey said, "I pretend he's here all the time. I pretend he's in another part of the house. Or I pretend he's at a friend's or something. Or I pretend he's off at school, or sleeping."

A white-throated sparrow sang its plaintive, familiar song: *Deeee deeee . . . deee de deee . . . deee de deee,* which made Maisie feel like her own dead father was nearby. An airplane droned. A dog barked down the street.

Stacey stared at the ground in a trance as she smoothed her foot over her sleeping dog's back. "Like right now I'm pretending," she said.

People see different things, too, thinks Maisie, looking at Frank and the horse. Some people see things that other people don't see. She thinks again of Stacey, and how when Stacey learned that Maisie's mom had died when Maisie was little, Stacey's shoulders relaxed and she smiled. Maisie could see the feeling because she knew the same relief: *Here is a friend who shares a sliver of a similar experience; we overlap as close relatives to a slightly similar grief. My experience will not frighten her, and her experience will not frighten me. Nay, her experience will endear me to her. Is that a sort of telepathy, like horses seeing things in the trees that we can't see?*

Neil told her once that 80 percent of women have been mothers, but only 40 percent of men have been fathers. "Throughout time?" Maisie asked him.

"Yes. In all of time. Most young men died, I guess, before having a child."

"Died?"

"I don't know." Neil shrugged. "War."

Maisie sees the hominids, the ancient peoples, of grasslands, of tropics, of jungle, of snow, of plains and soft-sloped mountains, jagged mountains, of lake and river, swamp and bog, peat and marsh, of desert and oasis, rainforests, canyon and steppe, tundra, forest, hills and sea. Islands. It was dizzying to think of the earth, and dizzying to think of the character of each of its landscapes, its oceans, its weathers, let alone the character and landscape of each individual human life—the downtrodden, the victorious, the harmonious—that has ever lived.

"The same men must have fathered a lot of babies," said Maisie.

All of those females, thought Maisie, the young and the older, the pampered and the beaten down, the beloved and the rejected, moving about the world like living ovens for a living creature to slowly come to form in a circle in the middle of their body, underneath their lungs and heart, biology transmuting the cells of a new heart, new lungs, eyeballs, the toenails and kidneys, the shreds of vein and nerves all getting knitted together into its own landscape and character before it even emerges into the air. All of those females, heavy with child, whether inside their body or at their breast, or on their back, literally and figuratively, weighed down to slowing up, trudging along, or even forgetting about an outside world entirely as they focus on the hunger, health, and comfort—both physical and emotional—of novice persons: a rashy bum, a tantrum gone haywire, a toddler drifting to sleep. No wonder the world over was mostly misogynistic. How could the men, dying, mostly, and never mothering their offspring, feel invested in much more than power? And how could females have had the time to say much at all about it except to either hitch their exposed and preoccupied wagon to a kind, strong man who would protect them, and their babies, while the lot of them, altogether, were as vulnerable as underbellies?

"Well, little Esme," says Frank. "My Esme the horse here might have come to find you. A little bird might have told her that another Esme was over in the orchard and that she should head off to meet her." He winks at Maisie. "I always envied my wife when we had a new baby. In fact, I've always been jealous that my wife is the mom."

Maisie and Amber smile. "But being a dad isn't half bad," he says. "And I get to name the horses." With the help of the fence, he mounts the horse, bareback. He tips an imaginary hat at them, and rides away.

"I'm pregnant," Amber says again as they watch him go. The first time she'd said it had become like a ghost: released into the air, but had she really said it?

"That's good news!" says Maisie, unsure if she's correct.

"I think so." The strap of Amber's lavender bra dangles out of the pocket of her pants. "I don't know why I just told you that," she says. She tucks in the strap, as though tucking in the secret. "I haven't even told my boyfriend yet."

Maisie feels the tiny flex and release of Esme's stomach when she spits up a little onto the cloth on Maisie's shoulder, and can quickly smell the sweet curdled smell, as though it is all from her own body.

Amber says, "He's actually been wanting to have a baby." She watches Maisie pat Esme's back. "I guess he'll feel happy. Is this your first baby?"

"Fourth," says Maisie. She is almost embarrassed as she says it; back again comes the money-surge worry that speaks up to her: *You have four children and you are in debt?*

"Well, you look like life is working out for you. So maybe this is a good sign for me that Esme came clopping around to you today! My boyfriend will make a great dad. I don't know if I'll be a great mom."

"No one's a great mom," says Maisie. "Just like no one's a great person."

Amber looks puzzled. "Some people are pretty great."

"You're right. Some people are great. I mean more like no one is perfect. Or, every mom is different. I don't know. Every kid needs a different mom."

Amber waits for more. Maisie doesn't know what to say. "My oldest is under ten. Meaning, I'm no mothering expert. I just tend to what needs tending, and keep track of who needs what." Maisie looks to the tractor hayride to see its status.

Amber laughs. "That's what I do with Frank's horses. Keep track of who needs what."

"Well, then you've certainly got the skills," Maisie says.

"Do you feel crazy, though, doing it all the time?"

"Taking care of little kids? You kind of have to just give up control and expectations, and then everything's fine."

"Oh," laughs Amber sarcastically, "that shouldn't be a problem for me."

"It's more like you kind of disappear," says Maisie, "but into another life, but it's like real life." Maisie is surprised that she just said such a statement. Did it make sense? Did she mean it? She's already forgotten what, exactly, she just said.

Amber says, "Riding my horse is like that for me. And when I sing. I ride my horse and sing at the same time. I've sung my whole life. And when I ride and sing at the same time, no matter what the weather is, no matter what kind of mood I was in before, there's this really clear and pretty green color of goodness that comes into my mind. It's like two clear colors, blue and yellow, and they cross over each other and are fully green. I don't know why I think of it like that. Maybe because my mom was an art teacher and she had those transparent color sheets in our house. Or it might be because of the church that I sang in when I was little. In the stained glass there was this one spot where if I turned my head right, the blue of the sky and the yellow of an angel's wing merged together and made this really pretty emerald green. I used to think I was the only person in the world who could see it."

Maisie smiles as she secures the baby carrier. "Maybe you *were* the only person who could see it," Maisie tells her.

Amber's expression is positive, as though she just found something, like car keys, in a place where they would have been difficult to find, but she'd found them before it was even an issue. "Okay," says Amber. "Thanks."

"Good luck!" says Maisie "It'll be great!"

Amber shuffles away, reminding Maisie of a small motorboat. Maisie watches her small wake as she heads off into a pregnancy, a life, the progression of weeks where the baby fills up her body and her imagination, right up to their edges until, there she will be, in a room somewhere, maybe in the hospital with the gleaming white tiles and nurse's clogs clopping in and out of the rooms, some of the nurses with gentle hands, some with no-nonsense gruffness; the female doctors are thoughtful enough to warm up stainless steel tools before poking and prodding, while the male doctor might do something like break her water with his finger without warning, but wherever Amber is, the pain will fill her body as it spasms in regulated intervals, like a timer on a machine, tightening up to be ten feet tall, ten feet wide, and ten feet deep in her hardening abdomen, her tightening pelvis. *From two floors up, two floors below is deep*—someone had written that down and left it on a scrap of paper in the library—what did it mean? When Maisie first moved to the city, her studio apartment was on the third floor, and there was a cove-like area in the air shaft. *From two floors up, two floors below is deep* . . . an apartment building she lived in. In labor, the pain went two floors up, then down to the ground.

If it's a C-section like Maisie's, Amber will see, in the reflection of the light above the table in the operating room, an entire mirror of what is happening below: innards placed to the sides, guts and intestines pooled in metal dishes like cafeteria food, clamps clamped in the midst of red guts and folded-back skin, the mother's arms held down on planks so that errant arms won't get involved, the measly blue curtain that is arranged at the mother's chest . . . What is inside comes out; what is outside comes in. There is the baby with white gunk all over it—Maisie already forgets what the white gunk is called—lanugo? No, that is the hair that some babies are born with all over their back . . . Vernix! It is called *vernix*, which to Maisie always sounded less like creamy stuff the color of partly melted butter and more like vermin mixed with a luxury sedan, or the name of a French comic book figure. Then, if Amber is not too drugged up and out of it, Amber will see her baby for the first time, it will be a boy, his eyes swollen shut like he's been through the fight of his life, the tiniest featherweight, and Amber will burst into tears of relief that the pain is over, that her baby is here, in her arms, like the weirdest of all the weirdest things, and her mind will do back somersaults of both joy and confusion, of the real feeling unreal, and those real and unreal somersaults will come and go for the rest of her life when she looks at her child, when she thinks of her child—a zing of disbelief: he came from *me*—dread and happiness, serenity and disturbance—opposites that braid together and embrace, because even though emotions are different, all of them, like siblings, come from the same wellspring. All emotions, like every human being on the earth, are cousins to the fiftieth degree. She learned that in a *National Geographic* article. All human beings are related, like family, the furthest only to the fiftieth degree. All emotions must be related as well, especially the ones with no names, holding hands underwater in the pool.

And then, after she births, into a new room of life she will find herself, where it's as though she has been placed in a new story, a new set on a new stage, where she is handed a little breathing football-of-a-thing, with its scraggly arms and itchy-looking face, and a deep and mellifluous, godlike voice will say: *Take it. Do not drop it. Do not confuse it. Give it dependable warmth and attention, which is* not *confusing, and which is love. Take care of it. Practice care. Take care.*

But what is that love? Is it holding the baby a lot?

Yes.

Is it feeding it when it needs to be fed?

Yes.

Is it giving it whatever it wants?

No.

Is it showing it that it can withstand things without getting what it wants?

Yes.

Is it always being nearby, not physically nearby, but somewhere invisibly close enough that you are within their reach within their mind?

Yes.

So you don't need to be there all of the time? Maybe it's better if you are only there in their head, not in their physical presence, especially when they are older?

Yes.

Is it true that it is best if the mother can be content whether or not the child is content?

Yes.

Because then the children will learn from their mother that it is not someone else's behavior that dictates another's contentment?

Yes.

The mother will be showing her love and respect for her children because she knows that they can be brave enough not to blame others, or rely on others, for their own contentment?

Yes.

And in this way, the kid will learn that everyone is trying the best that they can with what they've been given, and that the kid is no more special, and no less special, than every other human being in the world?

Yes.

This takes time.

Yes.

Am I hearing from you that moving through time is the loss that we all share (obviously) but it is how we move through loss that makes each of us unique?

Yes.

All of life is a reaction to loss, a reaction to what has happened.

Yes.

Loss is love turned inside out.

Yes.

But what about all the things that are beginning, the animals and people being born, the seeds being planted, things growing forth? All the beginnings are immediately endings? All the end-ings become beginnings immediately?

Yes.

Every second begins and ends simultaneously.

Yes.

If you could cut into any moment, like a biopsy, it would reveal both a beginning and an ending (and a middle) simultaneously?

Yes!

"The cookie-cutter shark, Mom . . . it takes a round bite out of its prey." Xavier showed her a picture. In the photograph in the book, a dolphin's arch, glistening as it crests out of the water, had a round red chunk the size of a cookie gouged out of its side.

"Ouch," said Maisie. "Eeew."

Xavier smiled. "It's weird, right? It looks like a machine did it."

Maisie thought of a hole puncher. "Yeah. Or like a person did it on purpose."

Xavier laughed. "Yeah. Like a core sample."

"A what?"

"You don't know what a core sample is? It's when they take like a tube of soil or ice or something out of the earth, and then see what's in it."

"Like a biopsy," said Maisie.

"What's that?"

"Doctors take a biopsy of body tissue. Like a tiny sample of skin, or part of an organ or something, to see if there's disease or not."

Xavier said, "Oh yeah, I know what that is. Like how they can look at people's bones and they can tell what people eat."

"Maybe one day you'll be a doctor," said Maisie. "Or a scientist."

Xavier shrugged and left the kitchen, leaving Maisie to look out the window at their small backyard, remembering an evening one autumn when she was out there cleaning up a dead squirrel. The lights were on inside, and she paused to watch her family in the kitchen like the window was a TV screen. Neil was smiling at the kitchen sink. Harriet was small, on Neil's hip, babbling and gripping on to Neil's shirt. Xavier was standing on a chair, also at the sink. Whatever was going on in the sink, everyone was happy about it. Maybe it was suds. They all smiled down at it in the warm lemon yellow of the kitchen's light. Maisie felt a wave come over her of contented love, an overload, at the sight of the three of them, and then there was another part of herself, out in the dark, a dead squirrel lumpy in a trash bag, a credit card at its limit somewhere out in the credit card ether, but at least they were about to refinance and pay it off.

Get your act together, she told herself, watching her family in the yellow light of the kitchen. *You must do something differently.*

+>-<+

Reader, she had that other baby. Reader, how might a person biopsy for disease in behavior rather than in bodily tissues? Where is a core sample taken to look into a family, a life, a culture? If memory acts as a core sample, does art act as a biopsy? The closer one looks at something, the more manageable and clear the world becomes. Look closely enough, and quietly enough, and that coveted thing inside of delight, inside of transcendence, that pocket of peace, that bubble of nothingness, expands into a sacred infinity. Where does money fit into *that*? For a moment Maisie imagines Amber, newly pregnant but as though she is the ingenue in a film. She imagines the montage in the movie, the slapstick trip to the hospital, the bumbling husband, the actress bearing down to push as though she's trying to lift a car, and then out will come the baby, more mature than a moment old, in a family portrait at the hospital bed. Who writes this stuff?

While pregnant, Maisie would read *What to Expect When You're Expecting* compulsively, even though she'd read it before, with each pregnancy, as if the book itself would somehow impart information on who, exactly, was growing inside of her, or what, exactly, the future held. She would read the same week-by-week descriptions of the fetus, the same percentages and likelihoods of chromosomal abnormalities, and the same concise descriptions of varying births and experiences. She could add her own birthing tales: there was the one with the ongoing five-day labor, sitting on a birthing ball in the hospital, sucking on so many lemon Popsicles that the inside of her lips were shredded and raw—what a riot it was to see Neil in scrubs!—where it seemed as though since the delivery day had come and gone, and that the contractions were continuing for so long, it was as if no baby was ever going to be born, that she'd given it a good go, and it was time to go home, contractions and all to forever be a part of her life. Or she could sum up in a few sentences the tale of her water breaking all over the grocery store floor, calmly packing for the hospital, and the astonishing labor and delivery that followed that was so violent, fast, and painful that she had—still has—traumatic flashes of recollection that summon a portion of its enormity, causing her adrenaline to prick in her armpits, and causing a small shadow of the feeling that she had at the time—she had thought, *Let me die. Let this end. Dying is only dying, after all*—to pass through her, a stark feeling where dying seemed plain and simple, as simple as just falling asleep. She could also contribute the story of her emergency C-section, where she could see, in the reflection of the overhead domed surgical light, her guts and intestines piled to the side of the operating table in what looked like metal pans and dishes. Then there was Esme, the scheduled C-section, where at one moment Maisie was walking into the room, leaving her shoes alongside the wall at the door as though she were visiting a friend, then she was sitting upright on the operating table having a shot injected into her spinal cord, warm numbness spreading from her waist down to her toes, like sand falling through water. Mere minutes later, with Kurt Cobain singing, "Memoria, memoria . . ." on a speaker somewhere, the doctors cut, tugged, and manhandled Esme out of her before searing her uterus shut and stapling her body closed.

After she'd reread all of the words in her dog-eared copy of *What to Expect When You're Expecting*, Maisie would study the drawings, much like she and her friend Gina would do when she was a girl with the drawings in Gina's mother's book about the female body. Maisie would lie in bed, perhaps in her own bed as Neil slept beside her, perhaps bring the book with her to one of the kids' beds as she waited for the child to nod off out of whatever disturbance had arose and which had summoned her, all the while with her belly sloping up like the orchard's hills, though her belly was even rounder, even more pronounced, like a clown's enormous round nose or a giant peach. Lying on her back would quickly feel uncomfortable, even make her dizzy, as the baby in utero pressed down on her spine and organs, so she'd capsize sideways, shove a pillow between her legs to even out her hips and tuck another one in the empty spaces around her belly, and then settle in to look closely at the illustrated diagrams of the way the baby was growing inside of her, like the burrows in *The Burrow Book*, the baby drawn oval like an ornament, or a certain kind of fruit on its winding stem. She would consider the illustrations of the women themselves, all of them with sensible shoes and sensible clothes. One largely pregnant woman used a low step stool to rest one foot while she peeled a carrot at the sink to take some pressure off her lower back. On another page, a different woman sat in a rocking chair, nursing a newborn, with the same low step stool as a footrest, as if the woman in the rocking chair had borrowed the step stool from the pregnant lady in the kitchen. If it were her book, Maisie would have had the two women meet each other.

It was no wonder at all that history, religion, and time immemorial was man-centric, that men were the leaders, the conquerors, the arbiters of power. As if it were a mystery why! Give time and strength to anyone and they will amass power. Women, pregnant ten times over in their weary adult lives, were too busy to *ponder and preach*. Surely they philosophized and reflected, in the small, darkened hours of caretaking, in their own moments of transcendence, but where would any of that be recorded? Who would've had a pen? What woman would've bothered to take on the big picture in any sort of a way when the big picture was hotheaded and toddling toward a body of water, or a stone staircase, or attacking a sibling, or bleeding out, or *failing to thrive*. When all was quiet, that woman, well, she had a moment to sleep, and another moment to rapture in the tiny fingers kneading her breast, as a cat pulses its paws before it beds down, in the glassy eye, as clear and clean as perfect water, that locks on her own eye during a feed. Maisie wouldn't have lived through labor in an earlier era since she'd had an emergency C-section. She'd have been long gone: one of the multitudes of short lives, hers, among the mountain ranges of maternal deaths.

"It's insanity!" Maisie's friend Nicole had told her. "If you thought a baby coming out of your body was crazy, wait until you see that little baby of yours turn into a *man*. Big arms! Big feet! They *explode* into these enormous people, with these enormously deep voices and simmering attitudes! My job, I realize, is simply to *stand by*, with pretty much minimal encouragement and meddling, with pretty much not so much to say. It's taken me twenty-five years as a mother, and fifty-five years alive as a human being, to learn to be quiet. Speaking up at important times is not the same as talking for the sake of talking. When in doubt, shut your mouth. Listen and learn. Some people speak so quickly it's as if they're about to get their throat slit and they have to get it out fast . . . who's really listening? Some people seem to think people are smart when they talk quickly and use a lot of words. I guess I'm talking too much right now, aren't I? Ha ha! So much for my big ideas!"

If Amber is lucky, her baby might be a sleeper, that rare bird who sleeps for six hours at a stretch, who has to be woken up by a maternal finger tickling the tiny cheek because the mother's breasts are so full of milk that if they aren't relieved they will become engorged and infected and the milk with harden like butter, or, worse, dry up and disappear. Her baby might be a screamer, like Xavier, wanting to nurse every two hours, but every two hours from the *start* of the previous feeding, so really every hour and a half, with intermittent crying jags that are so powerful and strong that they earned Maisie's respect—how hearty and alive this difficult baby was! So spirited and full of vitality! Screaming as though some ne'er-do-well, invisible imp from a dimension that only babies can see were repeatedly jabbing Xavier's heel with a sewing needle. Once, a terrible new mother mistake, Maisie diligently boiled Xavier's pacifier to sanitize it, then ran it quickly under cold water to cool it, then popped it into Xavier's screaming mouth only to hear silence for the split second of anticipated relief, followed by a scream of torture since Maisie stupidly didn't account for the tiny nipple hole inside of the rubber pacifier, an interior area where hot water had collected, and which Xavier had just sucked out. He was a terrible baby: adorable while sleeping and when awake and alert, but just terrible for a first-time mother whose own mother was dead, whose own mother wasn't around for feedback. He would stop crying not when she held him and patted his back (like Romeo, later), not when she hit his back firmly and rhythmically (like Harriet, later), but when she walked quickly in jerky, ungraceful lines, as though she was in a hurry and had to pee, so she was holding her legs together while trying to cut fast through an incoming crowd to get to a subway. He would continue to *not* cry only when she paused to lower him up and down in abrupt squats. Otherwise, in the evenings, crying would continue in her arms, the invisible demonic goggled elf zipping around them, repeatedly pricking the bottom of his little feet.

They didn't own a vacuum cleaner because the studio was so small but a combination of the Dustbuster whirring and the hair dryer (an item neither of them ever used to dry their hair but that they had bought so as to calm the infant) set askew, at a distance from Xavier's head, and resting on an oven glove for safety purposes, would sometimes whir him into a wild-eyed, steady frown-stare of oblivion. He didn't look calm, exactly, but he wasn't screaming his tiny head off, and instead had the look of a miniature man, wired on cocaine, who had just heard some news so devastating that he was trying to still his racing mind long enough to incorporate it into his humanity.

Sometimes, in the night, mostly because Maisie felt bad for keeping the couple next door awake—if she could hear their muffled arguments and drunken vomiting through the wall, they were sure to hear Xavier's screaming—Maisie would strap Xavier onto her chest in the baby carrier and head down the two flights of rickety stairs, past the stacked dishes that the busboys from the ground-floor restaurant and cigar bar left in the entry-way, and out into the city night. Little Italy, to the right, would be lit up with signs, but empty. Chinatown, to the left, would also be lit up and empty. Xavier would momentarily be calmed by the lights, the dark air above, the change in the air, and the silent hum of the sleeping city. *What is this place?* his shiny eyes seemed to be asking. *Where have you brought me now?*

One very early morning, still pitch black, after brusquely rounding the block as if she were trying to ditch someone—Xavier would begin to whimper and break if she dillydallied, if she lingered: *Keep moving, woman! No time for nonsense! Carry on!*—Xavier had finally fallen asleep, his little head fallen forward as if in shame that he'd given up screaming. Maisie paused on the sidewalk to adjust the receiving blankets and scarves to support Xavier's head, to zip up her jacket. Around her, snow was falling in the big white flakes that make the world, particularly Little Italy, look the most like a movie set, or a set on a stage. Here and there along the sidewalk, box trucks like worn-out elephants idled with their deliveries, waiting for their pickups, their exhaust wafting heartily into smoky clouds lit by the streetlights, the neon storefront signs, all mingling with the falling snow.

As Maisie adjusted Xavier inside her parka, swaying a bit

in front of one of the smaller pastry shops, something slipped across a portion of the dark window beside her, a pale ermine, a small mink, a rat? It was a woman's two hands, gloved in white latex, reaching into a pastry case in the window. The hands delivered a silver tray of exquisite cannoli. Then, like shuffling cards, another tray emerged, obscuring the cannoli beneath it. On the left half of the new tray were circles of rose panna cotta, of the palest pink, topped with dried rose petals. On the right half were rows of cream puffs, dusted with powdered sugar.

In the snow, in the darkness, and from under the pastry display's hushed spotlight, the assembly looked to Maisie like chess pieces, two teams, as if the panna cotta and pastry puffs were about to compete against each other. The pastry puffs embodied hardiness and authenticity, but the panna cotta were fastidious and cultivated. *Who would win?*

The woman's hands emerged again, like Mickey Mouse magic hands with no owner, to lay a white linen on the top shelf of the display case before smoothing it flat and then placing what looked like a raspberry meringue pie on top of it. It was the crown of the display case, the queen of the pastries, the top of the pyramid. Maisie was not a huge sweets person, except for Twizzlers and Swedish Fish, but the raspberries, and the whips of the meringue, the rustic-looking crust with bits of melted sugar crystallized into it so that they looked like rock salt, what was it? Why this? Why was her mother here, as blatant as a labeled notecard, in a pastry case in Little Italy? Here was her mother, behind a window as the snow falls, and then behind more clear glass, and then imbued in the pleated waves of a whipped meringue, in the luscious red of the raspberry, the big falling snowflakes, her presence as still and as quiet as moon-light, as quiet as her face had been as it rested, like a jewel on its pillow, when she was dead.

From the folds of her coat, Xavier began to coo, soft and gentle like a pigeon. Large snowflakes fell on Maisie's sleeves. Some remained; some disappeared. Xavier wriggled, and then Maisie could feel his warm body relax into sleep, into the warm darkness that babies know better than the living world.

The pastries gleamed in their glass case, some pink, some frosted, some powdered with sugar, all surrounded by the empty dark store, the snowy dark city.

Behind her, a delivery truck groaned into gear and moved away from the curb. A digger, reconfigured as a snowplow, rounded the corner in an active arc. It was lively, moved more swiftly than city vehicles usually do, more nimbly, as it knuck-led along the snow's surface with purchase, beeping as it backed up, tossing snow over its shoulder like salt, this way and that as it moved, like a young elephant giddy with its trunk, giddy with seeing snow for the first time and trying to touch it as much as it can, relishing it, tossing it all about anywhere, everywhere.

→‑◄‑

Maisie adjusts the straps of the baby carrier, shifts Esme into place—so much strapping, clipping, and securing with kids, like balloons so they don't float away.

Once, at bedtime as she put Harriet to bed, Harriet looked up at her, smiling, excited to snuggle, the wheat-colored lamplight shining against her wet, parted hair, and said, "Sometimes when you tuck me in I feel like you're buckling me up."

The orchard is lively. The red barn makes Maisie think of the Playmobil plastic farm people and farm animals that Harriet closes up inside of a plastic barn like a briefcase. Families move about. Children are laughing and whining. The white receiving blanket that's tucked around the baby carrier streams in the wind like a banner as Maisie walks across the matted grass, through pockets of conversations, toward the hayride.

Esme fusses. Maisie bounces up and down, sways a little, and walks briskly in a zigzag to zonk her out. By the time she climbs the stubby, metal, movable staircase onto the flatbed, Esme is asleep. The hayride is empty. Only another mom, with a boy sucking on a piece of green stick candy, is sitting in the rear, like in the stern of a boat, ready to head out to sea.

The hayride driver motions to them that he will be back shortly. Hay bales line the sides of the flatbed, with chicken wire and two-by-fours serving as backrests. Maisie takes a seat on the uphill side of the truck, overlooking the valley. She holds on to Esme's feet, tiny handles, where they poke out of the baby carrier's portholes. Maisie lets her head rest on the fencing behind her and takes a nice deep breath, like the wind, and exhales. The sun is warm on her face. Its energy dances in the orange brightness on the back of her closed eyelids. She's tired enough that this momentary eye-closing, this sweetness of the sun on her face, the wind tunneling around her ears, sleeping Esme like a lump of sedative on her chest, all cause her to almost immediately drift into sleep. She is on a boat, again, a sailboat this time, and it is clipping along, sliding across the water like a snake. It is sunny out, the water is sparkling, *as though diamonds have been tossed onto a tablecloth*, her nana had once said about both sunlight on the water and stars in the night sky. Over the water, distant whitecaps look like playful porpoises. She is on the windward side of the boat; the sail is large, bright and full across from her, until the boat starts to tip, heeling, more, and the sail dips into the water, then goes deeper. Maisie shakes her head to wake herself up, her belly still jumbling from the capsizing boat. She jerks awake. Esme stirs. Maisie's uterus twinges and tightens. Just below her belly button her abdomen tenses.

People have filled in the hay bale seats.

"Are you all right?" a woman asks her.

She is sitting next to Maisie. The woman is elderly, and has a kind and purposeful face. Her eyes, thinks Maisie, are of the beady sort, the kind that Maisie has a hard time interpreting. Either they are like a friendly animal, warm and dark and playful, or they are mean and cold, like pieces of plastic.

"I fell asleep for a second," says Maisie.

The woman smiles. "You jerked awake."

"Yes," says Maisie. Her incision pulls. She can imagine the muscles seared together, pulling at its seam because of the jerking awake.

"How old is your baby?"

"Two weeks."

"You are an adventurous woman!"

Maisie shrugs.

The woman continues. "Well, I'm with you. Get out into the beautiful autumn weather! An infant will sleep at home, or why not sleep on a hayride, yes?"

"The rest of my family is already in there somewhere."

"Do you have other children?"

"Three."

"You *are* an adventurous person! Is this baby a girl?"

"Yes." Maisie lifts the fabric away from Esme's head to show her sleeping face.

"Adorable," the woman says. "It's cliché, of course, but it all goes by so quickly."

"I'm finding that to be true," says Maisie.

"When you get ready to live," says the woman, "you've got to be ready to have a *lot* of joy and a *lot* of sorrow. The wonderful thing about life is that it has a way of teaching us how to live it."

"That sounds true to me," says Maisie.

The woman glances at the top of Esme's head. "It's so much easier seeing time progress through your children than through your own life, isn't it? Doesn't time fly when you watch them grow?"

"Kind of."

"One day, you have a baby in a diaper in the kitchen on the floor playing drums on upside-down pots. Another day that child is taller than you are and is getting behind the wheel of a car. Soon they fall in love and are led into the world. What *leads* them into life?" She looks at Maisie directly. She asks her, "What is it that has led you into your life?"

"Um." Maisie smiles. "I'm not really sure. . . ."

The woman continues. "I am constantly, in my head, living in the days when my children were small."

"Like, now, you mean?" asks Maisie.

The woman carries on. "I had three children, and my middle

one, a girl named Annie, choked to death on a grape when she was three years old."

"Oh no . . . ," says Maisie. Her body tingles with adrenaline.

"I was in the kitchen, and I had been listening to Annie prattle on to her dolls and her little sister in the dining room, which was about five feet away. Her little sister was in her high chair, and Annie had set up stuffed animals around the table by squishing the chairs up against them so it looked like they were sitting in the seats. Annie had made little finger food for the stuffed animals, like what her little sister was eating: Cheerios, broken-up pieces of chicken, and grapes. I had cut up the grapes, because they always, always made me nervous *as a choking hazard*. But, in the fruit bowl, on a small table, the grapes were in their regular form along with some oranges and some bananas. Green grapes. Annie had eaten them many, many times before. I was in the kitchen. I was in the kitchen cleaning up and doing dishes when it suddenly occurred to me that I had only heard the sound of my other daughter in her high chair, not Annie's prattling and busying about. My daughter in the high chair was making happy squeals. I went to the doorway, and Annie was facedown on the ground. She was wearing little yellow shorts and a white T-shirt."

"I'm so sorry," says Maisie. She imagines Harriet, smaller, facedown on the floor.

"I think about her at least every hour," says the elderly woman. "Imagine that! If I'm not wondering what I could have done differently to protect her, then I'm imagining what sort of a person she would be, and all the wonderful things about being alive that she missed. Learning to ride a bike, having a pet dog or cat, falling in love. But most of the time I wonder what it is she would say, and what it is she would see, and how she would see it, as a young girl, as a teenager, as a young woman. I imagine her presence as wise and watchful, and I feel her protection." The tractor starts to pull them up the hill. People passing pause at the edge of the apple trees, allowing the tractor a wide berth. "It has been so long," says the woman. "She would be your age by now. Probably even older than you. It has been so long, but it seems she is with me all the time. In fact, it seems she is with me even more than she possibly could be if she were actually still alive."

"My mom died when I was five."

The woman turns to look at her. "Well, look at us! Two peas in a pod!" She puts her hand on Maisie's knee and squeezes it with more strength than Maisie would have anticipated. "And has life been okay for you, after having your mom die?"

Maisie feels Esme move. "Yes," she answers.

"Children," says the woman. "All they really want to know about you is how you love. How you love other people, and how you love, or don't love, your own life."

"I worry about money," says Maisie. "A money problem."

"Problem shmoblem," says the woman. "Problems are there to be solved. You can choose whether you want to be stupid and feel sorry for yourself or you can look to find meaning." She picks up an apple from the hay bale next to her. She turns it, looks at it full circle, then throws it out of the hayride. Maisie sees it splatter apart as it hits the ground. "There are the meaning-makers, and there are the takers. The takers are the people for whom nothing will ever be enough, for whom others are always disappointing them, for whom grudges and resentment act as pillows that make them comfortable and prop them up. The meaning-makers, they look past their anger; they look around the nuisance of themselves to the fertile ground beyond, where positive energy grows." The woman looks directly at Maisie. "Isn't that what hell is? The difficulties we put ourselves through? The difficulties we put ourselves through and then wonder who to blame? Life throws enough hardships everywhere—it's a minefield!—let alone the ones we wade into ourselves and then wonder how we got there."

Maisie looks around the hayride. Does this woman possibly have a companion? As she listens, Maisie surveys the apples all over the ground like tiny dead soldiers. The woman continues, measured and consistent. "Life is here to be lived. Emotions have direct descendants, too. One can think that one is free of the difficulties of our parents and their parents and their parents and so on, but ignoring pain only begets more pain, begets more anger, and begets more resentment. Right? One good way to know if you are ignoring pain, or if you are projecting your pain, is if you are blaming other people for the way you feel. If you're at all resentful. Life has a way of teaching us everything, if one is lucky enough to stay alive long enough."

"Yes," says Maisie. She is listening. Would there ever be a time in her life when she would use the words *beget* or *for whom* in a sentence?

"Have you ever heard that saying that if you don't deal with your own pain, you will inevitably put that pain on someone else? And if you're a parent, that pain will go to your kids. A therapist told me that once. I hardly remember anything at all about that therapist but I was ready to hear that single statement." The woman smiles at all the tips of apple trees around them, like they are an audience. "Getting older is wonderful," she says. "Everything is elegant. It is simple, and astounding."

The hayride pulls them up the hill, through the orchard. Apple pickers move to the sides of the grassy road. Some wave, some look up at them curiously. The hayride is like a parade float. The woman asks Maisie, "Have you ever read Viktor Frankl's book *Man's Search for Meaning?*"

"I have, actually," Maisie answers. The hayride toots along, jostling them. Maisie thinks of what she remembers from the book, and of what she thinks of fairly often ever since she had read it in college: Viktor Frankl on a crowded train of prisoners being transported from one concentration camp to another, noting the expressions on the faces of his fellow prisoners as they watched, through tight window slats, a sunset light up the peaks of the mountains of Salzburg. Viktor Frankl, a prisoner at Auschwitz, relishing stale bread in his mouth, that he'd saved in a pocket, as comfort when a nearby companion was sobbing because his feet were too swollen to fit into decrepit boots and he would have to march barefoot through the snow, and the ice, into a day of labor. Or, Viktor Frankl, digging in a ditch, hell all around him, darkness, evil, and a light turning on in a house in the distance, and he takes it in as a light of hope. Or, again, Viktor Frankl, digging in a ditch, darkness all around him, hell, evil, but free in thought and lost in his own mind in the tender thought of his wife, her "frank and encouraging look."

Maisie had lost the book and then could never find it. It was a library book, and she had to pay the fee, but she had written down a line from the book in her notebook that she had eventually torn out, folded, and tucked into her T-shirt drawer from apartment to apartment, and then to her current house: "The salvation of man is through love and in love."

This elderly woman next to her says it out loud. "The salvation of man is through love and in love."

"I have that written on a piece of paper," says Maisie. In the baby carrier, Esme squirms against Maisie's tummy.

"Well," says the woman, "so do I. We are two related souls, Maisie."

"Did I tell you my name?"

"When I saw you I thought, *Yes, that's her.*"

"Who?" asks Maisie.

"You remind me very much of my daughter."

"Oh?"

"She would be your age. She died when she was only three months old."

"Oh," says Maisie, "you mean . . ."

"I had gone to our neighbor's. She had a little bit of a cold, so I'd put her carriage out on our back patio for some sunshine. It was January—a cold day, but very clear and very sunny. The patio was just a little square of stones, really. A tiny backyard, hardly any grass. I came back from our neighbor's through a gate in the fence. When I looked into the bassinet, Annie looked blue. I tried to perform mouth-to-mouth on her and her little face just wouldn't come back."

"You mean . . ."

"Another time, she fell out of a window. And another, she was hit by a car . . . or maybe we found her floating in a pool."

Maisie looks around. "Are you okay? Are you here with anyone?"

The elderly woman turns to look at her flatly. "Are you?"

The hayride driver shifts the engine into a louder gear. A tall skinny pipe next to his head releases dark smoke.

"Onward, Johnny Appleseed!" cries the elderly woman rousingly.

People around them on the hayride smile at her. The elderly woman says something else that Maisie can't understand.

The hayride is passing a small collection of people at a fork in the grassy road. A middle-aged woman down below looks up at them. Her face brightens. "Mom!" she cries. She waves her hands. People next to her turn to look, like owls, their heads on swivels. "She's right there! Mom!"

"Do you know that woman?" Maisie asks her.

The elderly woman looks them over. "I've never seen her before in my life."

"That's my mom!" calls the middle-aged woman. She makes eye contact with Maisie as the hayride is moving away. She points her finger as though pointing out someone next to her. "That's my mom!"

The elderly woman's look is unchanged.

"That woman is saying you're her mother," says Maisie.

"Who in the world are you?" the woman asks Maisie.

"I'm—I'm just someone you're sitting next to on a hayride, I'm—"

"Good God, woman," the elderly woman says to Maisie, sounding strangely like an elderly man. "Keep yourself to yourself!"

Esme starts to squirm. Maisie doesn't fight the jostle of the hayride. The discombobulation of the flatbed soothes the disorientation in her mind. She leans into the jerkiness, hoping to rock Esme, and looks straight ahead. She feels as though she has been scolded. Next to her, she can feel tension emanating out of the body of the elderly woman like heat. Or maybe it's not tension, but, rather, decay. Most likely it is nothing but Maisie's own tension, projected, along with concern and worry. The woman had seemed so thoughtful and with it! Maisie feels, strangely, as though perhaps they hadn't even spoken. Did they just speak? Maisie looks around. Is she perhaps not really awake and just had a dream? Of course she's awake! The woman is old, and simply not of a complete mind! Maisie glances sideways at the elderly woman. In response, the lady gives her a perfunctory, fast-and-then-gone close-mouthed smile, as if they'd never interacted before. As the tractor slows to a stop, Maisie looks down at the woman's hands. They are clasped in her lap. On her left wrist is a hospital bracelet.

The disorientation that Maisie felt earlier, when the barn had looked flat, returns. It feels as if the woman's disturbance has been passed to her, like a virus in the air, like thoughts floating through skulls into other skulls. The things surrounding Maisie don't look flat, but the feeling of life feels two dimensional for a moment. Is she herself? Where is she? She herself is a person whose name she does not know. Sense has slipped aside, and she looks about the scatter of her mind for a keyhole of reason to catch and hold on to, to hopefully pry into and spread out into sense. She looks down at her own knees and there is a large contraption in front of her, a blanket covering something that's pulling on her shoulders with straps that—Esme! It is her baby! She is *Maisie Moore*. This is the apple orchard. She knows this place! Neil is out there in the trees somewhere. So is Xavier, and Harriet, and Romeo. She starts to cry. She bows her head down as one might in a serious situation during a laugh attack. Her forehead is resting on her infant's head. Why is she crying? Oh, she should have stayed at home. But it is only hormones. It is only life. The crying feels fine; she could cry, happily, for a long time. She should have stayed at home. Oh, but home, her cozy home, the bed, the bassinet, the money owed, the light coming in through the windows, the letter from the mortgage company in the drawer of her dresser . . . Where was her family? Where did they go?

From her seat, Maisie watches the elderly woman march right off the hayride. A small group of people are there to meet her as she gets off. They are relieved to have found her. The woman who had called after them as they passed is there. She hooks her arm around the elderly woman's arm proprietarily. "I'll go on the tractor back down with her," she says. "She can get back in her chair."

"Are you sure you're looking for me?" the elderly woman asks politely.

"Yes, Mom. And we're so glad that we found you."

"I'm afraid that I'm not your mother, dear. You see, I have no children."

"We can talk all about it."

The hay bale seats are all empty. For a moment Maisie imagines the backs of the heads of her mother and her father, silhouetted by the sunlight. They are both turning to help her off the flatbed. She is small. She must be five. They each put their hands out, one to take her left hand, the other to take her right. She can feel their hands in her hands. She can feel how they lift her up off of the ground to swing her safely, playfully, down to the grass.

The grass. The autumn trees. Her family. Heaven is all of the ordinary: waiting in the car to pick someone up, the petty squabbling and prickly bickering, getting milk from the cooler at the store, the annoyance of taking out the trash in the rain, the lavishness of impatience, the hot water running out in the shower, the plant not growing well and dying, the dirty floor in the kitchen, the empty bank account, the discomfort in the belly, the paradise that is confusing thoughts, the worry and tenderness and sick-heavy love that holds on to her heart, all of it saying, *life, life, life.* Raising her family was busting herself open, and loving her children was leading her into life so differently than before. Where could she harness whatever power was within it? Where does one put all of that? Into more power, more grace, more growth?

If she were a prisoner of war, dying in a hospital bed, in the midst of a massive fire, or war, tyranny, killer armies roaming the streets, or sinking in a crowded boat full of refugees with water slipping in over the rubber sides, or in a refugee camp rife with dysentery, cholera, or if she were terminally ill, or if one of her children were terminally ill, severely mentally ill, lost or addicted, there was no doubt that it would be her daily life—some days drudgery, some days with dips into transcendence like a dip into a pool, the mind as naked as a body—it would be daily life that she would long for, not some perfect constant paradise, some heaven of plush comfort and eternal peace. Peace isn't anything without disturbance, and love isn't love without any of its opposites trying to foil it up.

The first time they'd come to the orchard, there was a child with a Swiss Army knife. Neil took it away from him. "I'm sick of picking apples," the boy had said. His face was severe. He was holding a Swiss Army knife, open, in his hand. He was near Xavier, who, a toddler at the time, was tossing rotten apples in the other direction.

"Where's your mom?" asked Neil, as he nonchalantly took the knife out of the boy's hand.

"I don't have a mom," he said.

"Who are you here with?" Maisie asked.

A woman emerged from the line of trees and took hold of the boy's elbow. "Fuckin' a, Trevor," she spat, then, seeing Neil and Maisie, smiled perfunctorily at them. Later, when they were home, Neil realized he still had the red knife. It felt sullied, like Neil had stolen it, and every time Maisie looked at the knife, it seemed to say, "Fuckin' a, Trevor."

Maisie wanders down a Winesap aisle because it is empty. It joins up with the Romes. Braeburns are to the left, Galas are to the right, and she knows that Macouns, dustily blue on their red skins, are behind her.

Last year, along the same aisle that she's walking, Xavier reached into the grass and then held up a smooth green snake.

"It's a baby, Mom," he said, as it wrapped around his wrist like a bracelet. Its tail curled like a question mark.

He carried the little snake with him for a while, then let it slither around the apples in their basket. It paused on a shiny red apple on the top, and Maisie and Xavier watched it, its bright green body against the apple's luscious red shine. It seemed to look up at them, like a pet, or a baby. Its miniature head was yellow under its chin, like a buttercup was there. Its round eyes looked friendly, and the broad arc line of its mouth made it look like it was smiling. Its scales were immaculate, and made Maisie think of tight pine cones and a grass green glaze of pottery. As the little snake hovered on the apple, Maisie thought of a sperm with its mighty, snaky head, the acrosome, nearing an ovum, with its plumpness of a fruit. The darkness in there—the feisty little shark head with that weird wiry rattail, the little head—is it eager? is it angry? It is competitive!—the little axle head pricking into that rich, tiny, clean egg—all so dark—and then the multiplying begins, cells multiplying, and possibilities.

"I don't know how to tell if it's a girl or a boy," said Xavier. "It's cute. I'd like to take it home, but I don't want to take it out of its habitat."

"Good thinking," said Maisie.

"Its family is around here somewhere," said Xavier, looking.

It was when Xavier picked the snake back up to put it down into the grass that an older man, helping his older wife, came around the low apple trees. Neil was with them; Romeo and Harriet hurried excitedly toward Maisie. "She twisted her ankle, Mom."

"Let's sit you down on this stump here," said the older man.

"This must be your lovely wife," said the woman. "Oh, I am a *bother*," she said, as the men placed her gingerly on the stump.

Maisie thought of her nana, also an older woman who had used the word *bother* in the same way—*I am a bother*, or *Oh, bother!*—like Winnie the Pooh, which made Maisie think of sleepy bees and honey jars.

Neil introduced her. "Maisie, my wife, Jack . . . Grace."

"Oh no," said Maisie. "Do you think it's broken?"

"Goodness, I hope not!" answered Grace.

The older gentleman, Jack, handed her two large sticks that looked like driftwood for her to use to support herself and sit up straighter. "Oh—like hiking poles!"

Neil suggested they put the apple basket upside down on the ground so Grace could use it as a footrest to elevate the ankle. She propped her foot up on the overturned basket. Grace's hiking boots were a lot like a pair that Maisie's mother had worn and that stayed in a closet for years in their house like a hushed animal. The boots in the closet, hushed and tucked in the closet, were full of quiet character with no feet.

"I'll get some ice and a golf cart," said Neil.

"I'll come with you," said Jack. "Or maybe I should stay . . . Grace?"

"Oh, I don't care, Jack," Grace told him. "I'll be just fine. This poor young mother is trying to enjoy apple picking and here we are bringing catastrophe to her afternoon."

"Oh, not at all," said Maisie. "How can I help you?"

"Want to see my snake?" Xavier asked.

Romeo's and Harriet's heads snapped toward their brother. The green snake twirled in his hand like magic.

"Well, isn't that a pretty color!" said Grace. "It looks like pirate jewelry!"

Xavier smiled at it in his hand. Harriet and Romeo hurried to his side.

Grace kept talking. "My mother had a bracelet like that. I thought it was the most exotic thing in the world."

Harriet looked quickly at Grace. "Was your mother a witch?"

"My mother was a good witch. Yes. She also had a pin that she wore sometimes that was a jeweled bumblebee, and blue earrings that looked like beetles."

"She liked bugs," said Harriet.

"She loved nature," said Grace. "But who doesn't?"

"I love nature, too," said Xavier, holding the snake.

"Me too," said Romeo.

"Me three," said Harriet.

"Well, aren't I lucky to be among such nature lovers!" said Grace. She smiled at Maisie.

Maisie laughed. Grace used the sticks that her husband had left her to prop herself up better. As she did so, the pant hem of her uninjured ankle lifted to reveal a prosthetic leg. The kids all looked at it. The way they looked made Maisie say, "I'm sorry, they—"

Grace gently shushed her. "Look," she said to them. She lifted her pant leg up a little bit more.

"Wow," said Romeo. It looked mechanical and robotic.

"Does it hurt?" Harriet asked her.

"No," said Grace. "It doesn't hurt. But right now my other ankle does!" She laughed. "But I'm okay, I'm okay."

Maisie wondered what Xavier might say. He said nothing. He looked up at Grace's face and smiled at her with a soft, maybe embarrassed smile of acknowledgment that seemed to say, *Something very difficult happened to you, and you have been brave because you are right here.* Grace nodded at him, maybe even winked.

The three kids were in front of her in a semicircle, like ring-around-the-rosy or a daisy chain.

"I used to have both of my legs, just like you."

Harriet was staring at the prosthetic ankle. "What happened?" said Harriet flatly, without looking up.

"I was in a car accident."

"A cwash," whispered Romeo.

"Yes. The bottom of my leg got badly crushed."

Harriet's posture went slack. "Were you little?" asked Harriet.

Romeo, focused on Grace, picked his nose.

Romeo asked, "Do you like pizza?"

"I love pizza," said Grace. "I make pizza with my grandchildren almost every weekend. Some of them were going to come here with us today, but they all have strep throat."

"Oh, yes, that happens in our house," said Maisie.

"Then we take the pink stuff," said Harriet. "No one likes it."

Romeo stared at the exposed part of Grace's prosthesis. "Where's the real leg?" he asked softly.

Xavier whispered at him forcefully, "She just said she was in an accident."

"I'll tell you where my leg is. It's buried under an old apple tree. We have a little apple tree in our side yard that I can see from my bedroom window. It was Jack's idea, and it was a good idea. It was a little gruesome, though, to have the bottom of my leg in a cooler like a big piece of fish or a leg of lamb. The hospital put it in a cardboard box, and before we buried it, Jack swaddled it up in a blanket that we'd all used for years while we watched TV. It was a day like this, autumn and lovely."

"We buried a guinea pig," said Harriet huskily. It was at preschool, and there had been lots of talk about how *long* life was for a person and how short life was for a guinea pig. Their teacher, Judy, had representational visuals all around the room. On a horizontal white poster board on the wall, a blue line representing a human's life span was about three feet. Underneath it in red was the guinea pig's life span line, about three inches. Two wool strings were tied to tacks on the bulletin board for comparison: the human blue string, when lifted, reached about twenty feet out into the room. The red guinea pig's string was short, only about a foot and a half. On one of the activities tables, there was a guinea pig penny jar with about a half inch of pennies in it, and a person penny jar that was filled to the brim.

"Well, then, you know what it's like to bury something that has died," said Grace.

"It's like planting something," said Xavier.

Grace nodded. "You know what I think the most important thing is when you plant something?"

Harriet raised her hand like she was in school. "Water," said Harriet.

"Yes. You have to take care of it. Have you ever watered a plant too much?"

"The plant in my classroom rotted. Everyone kept watering it instead of taking turns," said Xavier.

"You plant a leg?" asked Romeo. Everyone chuckled. It sounded like *egg*.

"Imagine if up came a tree of legs!" said Grace. They laughed. Grace asked, "Do you think that the tree looks any different now that my leg is under it?"

The kids were quiet. A wind blew across their faces. Then Xavier said, "It looks the same, but when you look at the tree you think about your leg."

Maisie's eyes filled with tears.

"And maybe the car crash."

Grace smiled at him and touched her finger to her nose. "It's like you read my mind, young man."

→►◄←

Maisie adjusts Esme on her chest, sound asleep in the baby carrier, and sits down on the same stump where Grace had sat the year before. She looks at the place where Xavier had let the green snake go and it had poured like bright green water out of his hands and into the grass. She looks at the spot where Neil and Grace's husband, Jack, had pulled up in an ATV driven by an employee of the orchard, and where she and Neil had helped Grace into the back seat before she and Jack drove off.

Maisie sniffs at Esme's small, soft head. It smells the same as what Maisie is looking at: sunlight and dappled shadows on the dog-eared grass. Her pelvis aches, and she thinks about her uterus, empty after so much action for those previous forty weeks, now slowly getting itself back to its original shape like some sea creature pulsing through the ocean.

The warm lump on her chest is a miniature female, Esme, miniature lungs, miniature heart, miniature bones, miniature brain with its still-closing soft skull, which makes Maisie think of lobster shedders, when their shells are soft. She thinks of Esme's own tiny infant uterus, and the two million eggs that a girl is born with. *Egg* was for chickens, for hens—*ovum* was better, but so stern and clinical, while *ova* didn't even sound like a word at all, but more like an inconsequential huff out of one's mouth. Esme was a generator, with her own tiny breath, her brand-new eyeballs under those closed eyes, her optic nerves—organs that *see!*—nerves wrangled around muscles, muscles winding around bones, and pliant bones that bend like green branches, all of it a production of all the processes toward wonder, in high production, fusing, grafting, learning, developing. What magic!—though *magic* isn't even a good enough word—what a panoply of kingdoms were in a body! That a body can hear, and see, and move, was as miraculous as the taste of sugar on a tongue.

In her doctor's office, while she was waiting, Maisie had read that a neonatal uterus is actually bigger than a young girl's because of the influence of the mom's hormones in utero. She thinks of Harriet, of Harriet's little womb. It is probably the size of a fig, thinks Maisie, but she has no idea what it would look like inside of a child. She did know, when she looked at the uterus diagram on the wall at her doctor's office, that it looked like a few things: a pear-shaped urn with lovely handles, a penis with the balls lifted way up high, like balloons, or a cartoon alien head with large ears . . . but mostly what it looked like, with the ovaries and the fallopian tubes joined in their hooks and loops, their sideways figure eight, was infinity.

Harriet is somewhere, likely running slalom through the trees, laughing. Where was her family? She listens to voices around her, gentle among the trees. None of them are her family's voices, but they are familiar nonetheless.

"I don't *want* to!" a little boy says loudly.

"I don't *like* you!" he whines, and, through the line of trees, Maisie sees a man tenderly pick up the boy.

In the aisle to Maisie's right, a woman says, "You always have the perfect word for things, do you know that?" in a tone that Maisie can tell is toward a child. "I bet your mother taught you a word like that."

Maisie can see a smaller person move behind the latticework of leaves. "It's my teacher," a girl's voice says. "She told us if we use a vocabulary word three times, then we'll know the word forever."

"That's very clever."

The girl asks, "Is there a word for 'unripe'? Because these apples . . . they don't look ready yet . . ."

"Hmmm. I can't think of one. Green?"

"Because some of these aren't ripe yet. I can tell." The voices fade as they walk away.

Maisie thinks of Grace last year, sitting on the same stump. Was it the same stump? She wonders if Grace is still alive. Maisie will never know. She will always know about the woman in the cart—the grape, the window—but she will never know what really happened to her. Whether what she said was true or not, it did not matter. What mattered was what Maisie heard. *What we see is who we are, and how we see it is who we become.* Maisie thinks of the tree with different fruits that she dreamed about, all of the things that are shown to her, that she thinks about, the things that are teaching her, like fruits on a tree. *The closer I look, the more I see,* thinks Maisie, *and the more I see, the more I care.*

She thinks about how some people, like Maisie's own mother, know they are dying, but then most people die *out of the blue.* *Every day,* most of the thousands of people who die are not expecting it. But everyone knows they are dying. So what if the difference is a day, three weeks, five years, fifty? What is it that emerges out of life, like a figure out of a rock? *Life.* Life is what emerges out of life.

→►◄←

Maisie wipes her cheeks with her sleeve. Tears. Hormones, she knows, are a part of it. She is probably hungry. She grabs an apple from a nearby tree and has to pull the branch, bending like a long leafy slingshot, before the apple twists off and the branch rustles free to whip back to its place. She takes a bite of it, as crisp and as sweet as autumn. Esme makes a sighing sound in the baby carrier on Maisie's chest, as if she also had a bite of the apple. The area inside of Maisie's loose pants, between her legs, feels damp and slick, like the wet tears on her cheeks, but between her legs.

There are apples on the ground. Some are shiny and recently

fell from the tree. Others are deflated, edged in brown, some-what rotten and half-submerged in the undergrowth or loamy earth. Looking at the firm, round apples, gleaming like red bil-liard balls, nestled in the green grass, Maisie imagines them like infants' heads, newborns coming out of a mother, up out of the earth, and wonders how many would fit in her own vagina, like large Ping-Pong balls lined up in a lottery popper. How many could she collect into herself, and hold there? Oh, her head feels light; her womb feels heavy, like a too-full burrow. Is a woman a burrow? Is a woman a tree? When she dreamed of that tree with different fruits all over it, some were fruits she had never seen before. Who had put those fruits, which she didn't even know, and had never even seen before, into her head to go into that dream?

She wants to lie down. The leaves on the ground look soft. She adjusts Esme and slides comfortably off the stump, resting on her back for a moment. Just a moment to close her eyes. She feels drained and light-headed, but nursing will do that.

Apples, berries . . . First the blackberry's buds are hairy, then they are small white flowers, then come the tight green hard berries followed by the black glossy ones, their drupelets each looking like the parts of an ant—the thorax and the abdomen, the mesosoma and metasoma—so shiny, so plump, so juicy and sweet . . . What did any of that have to do with money?

→>◃‹

She relaxes her body. She is along a riverbed, and they are all laughing along a trickling stream. *Keep loving patiently, like me,* says the river. *Sometimes the rain swells me up, and sometimes there is no rain and I run dry and thin, but always I move with my same patience.*

Along the little river she runs. The children run after her. "I might jump into the water!" she yells.

"Do it, Mumma!" yells Romeo.

"There's not enough water!" Xavier laughs.

"Just run in!" calls Harriet.

There are silver grooves of light, like sparks, on the water's surface. Underneath are rocks, brown flattened sticks and magnified leaves.

Maisie splashes into it and falls backward into the water. It whooshes around her ears, muffling the world.

Her family is looking down at her, radiating light, all of them with light around their heads that exceed halos. They are the delicate, heavenly crowns that are in Renaissance paintings, spindly as spun sugar, reaching in spindles of light like the long-armed parts of a king crab. *It's the people we love who teach us the most.* Nothing stays in any one place except for the thing that no one can ever put a finger on.

Xavier is standing above her, blocking the sun. "Mom?"

"Mumma!" cries Harriet, excited to find her. With the bright sun in her eyes, her kids are silhouettes dashing above her, large like herons or giant egrets.

Romeo starts to cry. Maisie can feel the baby suckling furiously. Or, no, Esme is starting to cry.

Neil says something, with authority, like a bark. She feels a small hand curl into her hand. "Can you hear me?" Neil asks her into her ear like he's blowing into a shell. The wind around her head feels coastal, near waves exploding jubilant against rocks.

"I lay down in the water," Maisie says.

"Maze," Neil says, getting his body close to hers. "You might be bleeding a lot."

It sounds like he is joking. She is fine. Stars and the galaxies, nebulae, they all look like glowing tissues floating in fluid. It is all the same.

Outside the light is wintery, silvery though there is no snow. Each thing—the tree bark, the grass, the shingles on the house next door, the straggled climbing roses, all thorns and branch with no flower, that reach along the wall toward the roof of the garage—all of them possess whatever will come after it. A plane heads diagonally across the blue sky. A child in a red jacket runs across the neighbor's tan, scrubby lawn. If everything burned tomorrow, thinks Maisie, it is still all a *thing*, lumped and smoking. If her own head was smashed rotten to the ground, each person still alive would still be longing for something beautiful, for something fleeting and good. Still, there would be color, there would be sound, there would be light and dark, smells trailing through the air, wind tunneling in, tunneling out, lifting up, lifting down, even if the sun stops coming up, even if the moon retreats into the deep of the universe, into the hull of darkness that cradles the earth, even if nothing remains.

The heart. This heart, her heart, their heart, his . . . The heart—does it ever stop beating? No. Nothing ever ends.

ACKNOWLEDGMENTS

Thank you, Jordan Pavlin and Melanie Jackson, for your patience and encouragement. I am the luckiest writer in the universe to have in my corner your kindness, intelligence, and expertise.

Jordan, thank you for getting right to the heart of it all with astounding efficiency and grace.

Thank you to the entire team at Knopf!

Thank you, Jayne Anne Phillips and the Rutgers University–Newark MFA program for my Presidential Fellowship and teaching assistantship, which allowed me to study with an amazing cohort under remarkable instructors: Alice Elliott Dark, John Keene, Kamilah Aisha Moon, Rachel Hadas, Fran Bartkowski, James Goodman, and Matt Thomas. I didn't write much of this book while at Rutgers, but all reading and writing begets new writing, and I'm super grateful for having the time and focus that the program provided after some fallow years.

ACKNOWLEDGMENTS

Thank you for enthusiastic responses to reading this book after I'd turned in the manuscript: Carrie and George Bell, Susan Minot, Alice Elliott Dark, Liz Perlman, and George Minot.

Thank you, Tara and our pack (Buddy, Frankie, Red), for providing security, warmth, humor, and sanity along the trails, particularly through a couple of very strange years.

Thank you most of all Eric, Roan, Lila, Tess, and Finn—my hearts of all hearts—for leading me into all sorts of unimaginable, gorgeous orchards.

A NOTE ABOUT THE AUTHOR

Eliza Minot is the author of the critically acclaimed novels *The Tiny One* and *The Brambles*. She grew up the youngest of seven children in Manchester-by-the-Sea, Massachusetts. She lives in Maplewood, New Jersey, with her family and two dogs.